ONE

TRUE

LOVES

Also by Elise Bryant

Happily Ever Afters

ONE TRUE LOVES

ELISE BRYANT

BALZER + BRAY

An Imprint of HarperCollins*Publishers*

Balzer + Bray is an imprint of HarperCollins Publishers.

One True Loves

Library of Congress Control Number: 2021943920
ISBN 978-0-06-298286-5 — ISBN 978-0-06-323390-4 (intl ed)

Typography by Jessie Gang
21 22 23 24 25   PC/LSCH   10 9 8 7 6 5 4 3 2 1

First Edition

For Mom and Dad—
thank you for working so hard to make my
path easy. And for loving me unconditionally
when I took the long way instead.

CHAPTER ONE

My life is not a romance novel.

That's what I'm trying to explain to my best friend, Tessa, as she's going all heart-eyed and swoony over my summer vacation plans. But the girl is having none of it.

"Lenore, you don't understand," she says, throwing herself on her bed like it's a goddamn fainting couch. "I literally begged my parents for this scenario for years. Years! Or it was *at least* in the top five."

I arch my eyebrow at her in the mirror as I add another layer of mascara. I want my eyelashes to be thick and spidery, like Diana Ross's in the seventies. "Top five? That sounds very official. Was it, like, written down?"

"Yes, in fact, but I can recite it from memory." She nods her head all serious and straightens her spine, oblivious that I'm messing with her. "Number one"—she starts pressing a pink-manicured finger into her palm—"summer camp that's conveniently popular with boy band members just trying to live a normal life. Number two, small town that's inexplicably having a monthlong Christmas festival. Number three—"

I throw my hands up. "Okay, I got it, sis. You really don't have to continue—"

"Number three," she cuts me off, narrowing her big brown eyes at me. "European vacation. And on a cruise ship too! The Mediterranean! The summer after graduation! It's like you've hit the romance jackpot! Except instead of money pouring out of the slot machine, it's hearts and cute boys and sunshine and gelato and romantic historic buildings, and, I don't know, maybe even condoms."

A mischievous smile spreads across her face, and I think back to the Tessa I first met last year—mousy and anxious and likely to fall into a conniption if anyone even spoke the word "condom" in her presence. I know this is positive growth or whatever, but man, she can be irritating.

I turn around, rolling my eyes at her. "You've conveniently left out my parents and my sister and my brother, who, oh yeah, I'm sharing a tiny little room with. Ain't no condoms happening anywhere near me this summer."

"Not with that attitude," she snorts. She holds her hands out wide, and her eyes go all unfocused, like my grandma Lenore (yes, we have the same name) when she's talking about what she got on a T.J. Maxx run. "I can see it now. You're in a floppy striped hat and that red high-waisted bathing suit you bought at Target last week—"

"How do you remember that? You weren't even with—"

"Lying outstretched on the pool deck, your skin glowing in the sun. And a handsome stranger with a, like, ten-pack walks by, and is mesmerized by your beauty, and notices you're having trouble reaching the very middle of your back with your sunscreen . . . well, maybe not sunscreen because we don't wear that—"

"Hold up," I say, and she's jerked out of her heart-eyed daze. "What you mean, we don't wear that?"

"I mean, we don't need to wear sunscreen. You know"— she waves vaguely—"melanin."

I blink at her, but no *I'm just fucking with you* smile appears. This girl is for real. "Of course we need to wear sunscreen! Tessa, are you really out here just walking around in the sun unprotected?"

She shrugs and heads for her bookshelf. "Anyway, that's not important right now."

"Uh, skin cancer is important."

"This is a love emergency, Lenore! *Love* is important. Honestly, you need to take this seriously," she scoffs, and now I don't know if she's messing with me. *Love emergency?* Ma'am, I'm going on a family vacation.

"We really don't need to be doing this right now," I say, but she's ignoring me, hands on her hips as she stands in front of her huge bookshelf with the spines arranged in a perfect rainbow. "Research," she mutters to herself, tapping her chin. "She needs to do research."

I shake my head and return my attention to the mirror,

putting on a coat of bright coral lipstick that pops against my skin. Mom braided my locs into an intricate updo earlier today, and I tuck a few wayward strands in.

This is how Tessa is. Well, it's a little extra, even for her. Probably just nerves for tonight. And lord knows I've got them too. Jay still hasn't texted. Maybe I should check one more time. Tessa's too busy to notice and try to stop me, after all . . .

A loud crash stops me from grabbing my phone that I *definitely should not* check one more time. Tessa was, judging by the chaos of fallen books around her, standing on something to reach a book on the top shelf. That wouldn't be too difficult normally, except it is right now, considering she's wearing a fluffy, pale pink tulle ball gown. Because, oh yeah, back up: we are about to leave for prom. Which means we actually really, *really* don't need to be doing this right now.

"Are you okay?!" I jump up, gathering the skirt of my teal lace mermaid dress, and rush to where she's flat on her back, lost in her fluttery confection of an outfit. The only body part I can find is an arm outstretched in the air, holding tight to a paperback book.

"I'm fine!" she insists, batting away fabric so I can see her face. "Fine, fine! This is what I was looking for!"

She smiles slowly, and then presents the book to me, cradling it like it's some sort of holy text. *Anna and the French Kiss.* It's hot pink with a heart and a picture of the Eiffel Tower, i.e., something I wouldn't read if you paid me. Well, okay, maybe if you paid me. But it would have to be enough to buy a Pyer

Moss dress straight off the runway or something, and I know that's not what's happening here.

"I need you to read this before you leave, and then"—she chuckles with a knowing smirk—"and then, well, you'll see."

I shake my head. "Get out of here with that. You know I don't have time to read this. What with finals and grad night and graduation. And the kinda big thing happening in, uh"—I check my phone for the time, and also to see if Jay has texted (he hasn't)—"two hours! Here, let me fix your hair. The back is flat now." I gently put the book that I'm no-way-in-hell reading on her nightstand and grab a pick to fluff up her curls. But her arms are crossed and I can feel the scheming energy just wafting off her. "Plus," I add, hoping it'll get her to let that book go, "I'm not even going to Paris."

She dives for her desk, almost losing a fistful of curls in the process, and picks up a piece of paper. "Oh yeah, you're right. This says Marseille. But they're both in France, so how different can they be?"

Is that . . . ? I move in for a closer look. *It is.* Our cruise's itinerary. I don't remember giving her that, but okay.

"It's online," she says, reading my mind. "Public knowledge. Anyone could find it. Not weird at all. Here, let me send you something . . . it's gonna take me a minute to find it though."

Her eyebrows press together as she types and scrolls on her phone, and I use this break in the nonsense to gather the rest of my outfit: gold starburst earrings, metallic pumps with embroidered block heels, a beaded purse that I picked up at an estate sale last week, and my leather jacket draped over my arm in case it gets cold later. I take it all in through Tessa's mirror, confirming what I already know: this look is guh-ood. Two syllables good. I hope it goes well with whatever Jay picked out. We didn't coordinate or anything because it's not like that. Like, not at all. But it would be cool if it worked out anyway.

My phone pings, and I feel this irritating flutter in my chest. Is that him finally? But Tessa chases that stupid thought away.

"Okay, I'm going to preface this by saying this is really old and way cheesy, but if you don't have time to read a book—" She pauses to give me a look that makes it clear what she thinks of my excuse. "—this is the next best thing. It's the first thing I thought of, honestly."

I open up her message to see a YouTube link. The preview shows a movie poster with a blond girl holding a suitcase and standing on her tiptoes for no damn reason.

"What is this? Did it come out before we were born?"

"Yeah, but it's still good. See, this girl goes on a class trip to Rome—which *is* on your itinerary—and there's this pop star who looks just like her, but she's missing—"

"Was she murdered?"

"No, it's not that type of movie. But then she meets this guy named Paolo—"

"Did he murder her?"

"No . . . you know, actually, now that I'm remembering it, she doesn't end up with the Italian guy in the end because he's evil or something. Here, wait, let me send you something else."

My phone pings a few seconds later, with a link to another old-ass movie. A badly photoshopped picture of two more blond girls posing in front of the Italian flag.

"See, this is some white girl shit," I say, before Tessa can even tell me the ridiculous plot of this one. I take a deep breath and toss my phone on the bed. "Nobody's gonna be checking for me when I'm on some boring tour with my family. No European boy is gonna go all ooh-la-la and drive me away on his moped to get baguettes and gelato. Not everyone gets some happy ending all wrapped up in a bow. That stuff is for your movies and your books, but not for real life, Tessa. At least not for me."

All I get is secret prom dates and unanswered texts, I add to myself, swallowing down something tight and sharp in my throat.

Tessa maneuvers around the piles of books, her dress *swish-swish*ing. Her eyebrows press together, and she grabs both of my hands in hers. "That's not true. *Everyone* deserves a happy ending. Especially you, Lenore. You are the kindest, coolest person I know, and the right guy is gonna be drawn to that like a magnet."

This type of Hallmark-movie speak is Tessa's brand. She's earnest. I'm talking Taylor Swift before she discovered snakes earnest. Like, two a.m., kissing in the rain, allllllll that shit. But she actually *believes* what she's saying, so you can't even hate her for it. And at least she usually uses it for good: these beautiful love stories starring Black girls like us that have earned her a fairly large fan base online—oh, and admission into UCI's creative writing program this fall.

"Whoa, what is going on here?" Our friend Theo is standing in the doorway, an expression of concern on his face as he surveys the mess. His black hair is slicked back, and he looks all debonair in a pinstripe suit, baby-blue button-up, and floral bow tie. "Did you finally snap, Tessa?"

"No, we're planning how Lenore's going to have an epic love affair with an Italian boy named something sexy like Enzo on her cruise this summer," she says matter-of-factly.

Theo looks me up and down, barely holding in his smirk. "Love that for you."

"See?" she says, widening her eyes in her signature *I told you so* face. "Now, can you stop being difficult and just agree to watch this stuff? We need to get ready!"

As if I'm the one who's been holding us up. Honestly, I'd want to punch her if I didn't love her so much.

I shake my head. "Yeah, whatever."

I want life to be the way Tessa sees it. Really, I do. I want an epic kiss while the credits roll, happily ever after. And having that happen in Italy or Greece or France or Spain—all the stops on this cruise my parents planned—would be magical. I'm not too jaded to imagine myself sipping espresso at a café with a handsome boy. Or long walks hand in hand through mazes of blindingly white buildings, while the sun goes down over the bright blue sea. I mean, come on. My heart isn't completely shriveled up.

But also, what if I don't need all that? What if I've already found my love story, and it just doesn't look all mushy gushy like the stuff of Tessa's love stories? That doesn't mean it's wrong.

I can't say this out loud to her, of course. I can already see their reactions now, the usual ones when I bring up Jay. Tessa's judge-y look, masquerading as concern, and Theo raising his top lip like he's smelled something funky. I don't want to deal with all that right now. And anyway, Theo has moved on from my love woes to his own.

"—and I wasn't sure if I should buy it because the rules are unclear, you know? Who buys the boutonnieres? If both of us do, they might not match. And that could be interesting . . . but then what if he'd rather have a corsage?"

It's weird seeing him like this. Usually he talks like a cross between a robot and a butler from a PBS show, all proper and shit. But right now his tan skin is turning pink, and he's all twitchy and nervous. It's really cute, but he would totally roll his eyes if I said that out loud.

"Why didn't you ask him what he wanted?" Tessa asked, switching her laser focus to him. This kinda stuff is her jam, and I'm glad Theo is taking the spotlight off me.

"Because I didn't want to stress him out about it," Theo says, adjusting his bow tie for the tenth time. "With . . . everything already going on with his parents? I just want it to be a good night for him. A happy memory."

I feel a pang in my chest, seeing the hurt on Theo's face. Theo's been out to his parents since middle school, and they're all about it. Like, marching in the Pride parade downtown in matching rainbow tutus all about it. But Lavon, his boyfriend, just came out to his parents this year, and it didn't go well. They've pretty much pretended that it didn't happen at all. And when he told them he was going to prom with his serious, long-term boyfriend, they told him he could do what he liked, but they didn't want to hear about it any further.

"Oh, Theo, it will be," I say, pulling him into a tight hug. "Because he'll be with you."

"Theodore," he growls, but he lets me hug him.

"It's almost graduation," I coo as I pat his head. "I think it's about time for you to give that up and accept my nickname, love."

"Never."

The door squeaks, and I look up to see Miles, Tessa's brother, standing there, a lopsided smile taking up his whole face.

"Group hug!" he shouts, crashing into us, as his infectious laugh makes his whole body shake.

"Yes, group hug," Tessa says, and I can hear her sniffling. "I love you all."

"You better suck those tears back in!" I say, pulling her in close. "We got pictures to take."

"Yeah, right now! Mom sent me in here to get you because everyone's here," Miles says, jerking back. "Tessa, you better fix your hair because it's so flat and you don't want to look like a flat head in all these pictures because then Sam might dump you. He's outside, and he told me he's looking for a new girlfriend anyway!"

"These are valid concerns, Miles," I add with a snort. "I was just telling her the same thing about her flat head."

"You jerks!" Tessa says, pushing out of the hug and smacking Miles's shoulder. He runs out of the room in a burst of giggles, and she *swish-swish*es after him, stopping in front of the mirror to fluff up the back of her fro.

Before she makes it outside, though, she collides with Sam, her cinnamon roll of a boyfriend. His blond hair is freshly cut, and he's wearing a black suit and a tie that perfectly matches the blush pink of her dress—a step up from his typical uniform of Hawaiian shirts.

He cradles her cheek, pulls her in close at the waist, and stares at her all wide-eyed and reverently, like she's a treasure.

"You look . . . beautiful," he whispers. "I mean. Wow. Just . . . wow."

Her eyes sparkle and a smile stretches across her face as she moves in for a deep kiss.

Of course she sees the world the way she does. I might believe this one true love, happily ever after bullshit, too, if some guy looked at me like that.

Jay doesn't. But maybe he will? Maybe tonight.

"God, get a room," I say, sounding a little more harsh than I intend.

"No one better be getting any rooms!" Tessa's dad booms, appearing out of nowhere. Sam's cheeks flame and he takes two giant steps back. "Now come on, y'all," he continues. "Carol is about to have a fit if she doesn't get some pictures for her

Facebook soon. I'm warning you, she's got poses planned and everything."

When we get outside, all the families are standing there like some sort of paparazzi line. Miles, Mr. and Mrs. Johnson (I can never call them Carol and James no matter how much they insist I do that casual shit), Mr. and Mrs. Lim (they prefer those names like normal parents). And then Mom, Dad, and my little sister, Etta, who begged Mom and Dad to come but is sitting on Tessa's porch now with her nose buried in a textbook like the freaky prodigy kid she is.

"That's good, now get together," Mrs. Johnson calls, crouching down low for some reason, getting a good shot of our nostrils. "Do you guys know the Charlie's Angels? That could be fun!"

It goes by in a blur, my brain rushing to catch up with the fact that this big high school tradition is actually happening, right now. I've been feeling this a lot lately, with every simultaneous first and last that pops up with more frequency as graduation day looms closer. You look forward to and dream about all the moments and then, hey, it's here, it's happening, and then, bam, it's over and it will never happen again. The end.

It makes me want to be present and intentional, to reach out and capture these moments so I can store them and save them for later. For when we're all spread out at different colleges and everything I know and love is never the way it is again, just right now.

For about a year when I was little, I used to carry around

a gigantic pink Polaroid camera, and whenever I saw anything interesting—a family of ants, a lunch box abandoned on the school lawn, skies that looked like watercolor—I would disappear behind it and *click*. I went through so much film, basically wallpapering my room with the photos, that my mom put me on a weekly limit. Like some old man with a cigarette habit.

"Why do you take so many pictures?" I remember my older brother, Wally, asking me. "They're not even good."

"I'm just memorizing," I said, and he rolled his eyes at me. But really, I still think that's the best word for what I was doing. How else can you make sure the little moments aren't forgotten?

I don't know what happened to that pink camera, and I don't have my own camera now. Only my phone, and it won't do any of this justice.

So, I use my mind to memorize how Theo throws his arms around me and hugs me tighter than he ever has in the four years I've known him. I memorize my mom stepping in for Lavon and straightening out his bow tie, the same way she did when my brother went to his first dance with his boyfriend. I memorize Sam pulling Miles into his picture with Tessa, right in the middle, like it's no big deal. I memorize Dad's sparkling white smile, so big you can see the pink of his gums.

I wish I could know for sure that I've gotten all of it, that I would never forget. I wish I could guarantee that this was not the end of the good, that I could ensure that there's just as much good waiting for me at NYU next year.

And I wish . . . I wish Jay was here for it all. I finally let myself admit it. In my head, of course, because there's no need to bring drama to the buzzy, giddy vibes in the limo when we're finally on our way. I know he's being irritating and not texting me back right now, but that doesn't erase the fluttery feeling I get in my chest when he whispers "Hey, lady" late at night on the phone or the ache in my stomach when we sneak away to the fourth-floor stairwell during conservatory.

I wish Jay was here to hold my hand and let my head rest on his shoulder, like my friends are all doing with their people right now.

But of course, he can't be.

CHAPTER TWO

Jay Parikh and I started talking in October. And by talking I don't mean just saying what's up in the stairwells at Chrysalis Academy, the arts high school we all attend. I mean, like, seeing each other. Not only each other, but, like, not seeing anyone else? It's casual.

It's *not* dating. Because as Jay told me after we first hooked up at Brett Kwan's Halloween party (he was Waldo from *Where's Waldo?*, I was Eartha Kitt as Catwoman), he doesn't do dating. Not because he doesn't *want* to. But because of his parents. They want him to focus on school and not get distracted by girls. That's the reason we have to sneak around a little bit— making out in the back of my mom's minivan in the library parking lot and stealing away at parties and group hangs, instead of having, like, proper dates. We've never been on a proper date, I guess. Like in the movies, when the twenty-eight-year-old-looking teenager takes his girlfriend to some fancy Italian place that's not the Olive Garden and pulls out the chair and opens the door and for some reason drives a brand-new Audi. But who *really* goes on dates like that anyway? And yeah, the sneakiness can get annoying sometimes. He sometimes takes hours to respond to my texts (if he even does at all), and then there was that one time I had to hide in his closet for a full-on hour when his mom unexpectedly stopped at home for some tea before her podiatrist appointment. But I go along with it because I want Jay.

I knew I wanted Jay from the minute I first saw him.

It was the first Thursday of this school year, in an advanced painting class. I've been conservatory-hopping since I first started Chrysalis freshman year—not because I'm unfocused, like Ms. Ramiro, the guidance counselor, tried to say. Nah, because I'm just really fucking talented in a lot of areas. But it being senior year and all, Ms. Ramiro said I could only take classes in my actual conservatory, visual arts. Minimum requirements for graduation or whatever. So that's how I ended up at an easel next to the most gorgeous boy I've ever seen in my life.

Brown skin with floppy black hair. But not, like, annoying bro floppy—cool intentional floppy. A Low End Theory shirt, ripped black jeans, and Off-White Chicago Jordans. *Style.* A half smirk and dark brown eyes that were alert, assessing. And just the *vibe* coming off him. Normally I don't care what people think of me, but with Jay, I had this immediate and overwhelming urge to get his approval. To do a little dance to get his attention. To throw myself across his workstation and demand that he draw me like one of his French girls.

And then he talked to me.

"Hey, lady."

Believe me, I know that should be corny as hell. And I probably would have laughed and kept right on moving if it was anyone else. But for some reason those words spun around in my head, did fluttery figure eights around my heart like fucking butterflies, and then hit my stomach like a lightning bolt and made me ache down to my toes. It was stupid.

It was *everything*.

I want Jay. And this sneaking around, together-but-not-really-together setup is the only way I get to have him for now. So I go with it. How can I not?

Prom is at the Aquarium of the Pacific in downtown Long Beach, which I thought would feel like we're going on a fifth-grade field trip or whatever. But I was wrong. The tanks line the walls from floor to ceiling, casting the main room in a romantic blue glow, with the fish projecting soft shadows across the bodies moving on the dance floor. And there's twinkly lights hanging from the ceilings, which seem to give everything an extra otherworldly sparkle. The only thing taking away from the magic is the old-ass Bruno Mars song blasting from the speakers, like someone's parents were in charge of this playlist, but that's temporary.

"Oh my god," Tessa exhales as we walk under the life-sized model of the giant blue whale hanging in the lobby. I can almost hear the words starting to form in her head, her hands itching to type this setting down. "How is this so perfect?"

"Are you happy?" Sam asks. His arm hooks around her hips, and he leans in his chin to rest on her shoulder.

"Yes," she says, all cute and quiet. "I love you."

"I love you too." And then they kiss, and I realize I need to stop staring because they're having a *moment* and I'm being a creeper.

"Where do y'all want to go first?" I say, turning to Theo and Lavon. "You think the moon jelly touch tank is open?"

Lavon laughs, but Theo's attention is somewhere else. I follow his gaze to the photo booth that's set up. Grayson and Poppy, two kids Tessa used to chill with junior year before she got her head on straight, are wrapped up in each other and doing the most with sharp poses and puckered lips. Which, *okay*. They ain't Gigi Hadid.

"You want some glamour shots?" I say, elbowing Theo.

"It might be entertaining, right?" He shrugs, looking much less composed than I'm used to seeing him. "But, you know, in an ironic way."

Tessa laughs, out of her Sam spell. "Yeah! We have to. We can pose like this!" She stands behind Sam and wraps her arms around his belly. Her head cocks to the side at an unnatural angle and a plastic smile stretches across her face.

"Perfect!" I shout, jumping behind her and joining in. "We gotta embrace the cheese."

Theo lets out a quiet laugh. "Yes, I know it's a bit silly. . . ."

Lavon moves in closer to him, putting his hand on the small of his back. "It's not silly if it makes you happy, babe." Theo smiles for real, the kind of smile that reaches his eyes, and then they lean in for a small, sweet kiss.

"Okay, pictures it is!" I shout, springing back from Tessa and Sam, who have that whole starry-eyed thing going again now, too. "But first, let's grab a table before all the good ones are gone. You know the early birds already grabbed the tables by those Nemo-and-Dory-looking fish, but maybe if we hurry up we can sit by the rays. They have such cute little faces."

What am I even talking about? I have no idea, but I make my way through the crowd, and the two happy couples follow.

The next hour passes by in a blur. Luckily, the music shifts from parent playlist to older sibling who's only a little bit out of touch, so there's some bops in there. I even get Tessa up to dance, and she *never* dances. Like, ever. I find myself taking out my internal camera again, trying to memorize these moments that I know are fleeting: Screaming along Beyoncé lyrics with Tessa. Sam doing some corny-ass boy-band-looking moves with so much confidence that people stop to look. The widest smile I've ever seen on Theo's face as he and Lavon move in tandem. When they play some whiny slow-dance ballads and my friends move together like magnets and I'm left alone, the fifth wheel, I just go to the bathroom. I have no interest in memorizing that.

The whole time my neck is twisting around, hoping to catch sight of Jay. I keep it on the down low, though, because

I'm not trying to get a lecture from Tessa or Theo tonight.

He still hasn't answered my texts. I hope his parents didn't make him skip the dance altogether. That would really suck, but maybe I could drive over to his place after the limo drops us off? Or I could even sneak away now, take a Lyft . . . it's not like the happy couples would miss me too much. Jay's room is on the first floor, and the screen punches out pretty easily. We've done it before. If only he would answer my texts . . .

"You're looking for him, aren't you?" Tessa asks when we're sitting at the table, taking a breather.

I guess I wasn't being as subtle as I thought. I don't answer her, but my guilty face must give me away.

"I thought you were done with him," she says sharply, which makes Sam, Theo, and Lavon drop their convo about unicorn fish and zero in on us.

"I didn't say I was done, just that I was taking a step back." Even as I'm saying it, I can hear how empty it sounds. I wasn't taking a step back from Jay; I was taking a step back from bringing him up to my friends. "Listen, he's not as bad as you guys think he is. He's really sweet when it's just us, you know?"

"Lenore, he refused to introduce you to his parents," Theo says, his voice stern.

"Well, I've told you how strict they are. That's not his fault, and he wishes it was different. It's only a couple more months before he moves out, and—"

"Even as a friend," Theo cuts me off. "He wouldn't even introduce you as a friend. These excuses you've created for him don't hold up, and I know you're aware of that, Lenore."

"And!" Tessa adds. "*And* why did he go with Rachel Chan to the winter gala then, huh? That sure looked like a date, and his parents definitely saw them there!"

I feel a flash of annoyance that she's bringing this up because we've already talked it over to death, and she knows how I feel.

"That wasn't a date," I reiterate. My body feels pulled tight like a stretched canvas. "It was a friend thing."

Tessa and Theo both raise their eyebrows, perfectly in sync. Sam looks away.

"It's complicated. Just—like it's easier with Rachel. His parents know her parents. They approve of her . . . as a friend, I mean."

"And what's not to approve of about you?" Tessa asks quietly. She grabs my hands and squeezes them. She knows the answer to this question, and I can see her expression harden.

Jay's never come outright and said it, but I know the reason he hasn't introduced me to his parents, even as a friend. I can see the real reason, the ugly reason, in the girls he does bring around his parents—Rachel Chan, Kayla Miller, Aesha Seth. I know they've been to his house for study sessions and even to hang out. I know they've been invited to stay for dinner.

And I know those girls aren't Black like me.

But he can't help his parents. And he doesn't have what we have with those girls. They're just friends. We're something more. I know it.

"We're keeping it casual until he's out of the house," I

say. It's what I tell myself for comfort, when I see IG stories of him hanging out with other girls at his house, when I saw him walking with Rachel at the winter gala, his arm on the small of her back. "There's no need for some big blowout when he's so close to being on his own, you know? He's not eighteen until the end of this month, and his parents are taking full advantage of grounding rights until then."

"If he liked you, he would fight for you," Tessa says, as if it's that simple. As if things are that easy.

I pull my hands away from hers. "That's not how real life works," I say.

"Well, it should."

"Can you just *not* right now?" The words come out colder than I intend, but I can't help it. She's always acting like life has some predetermined story arc. Like we're all going to go from once upon a time to happily ever after, and we just *don't*.

I drag a finger under my eye before anything embarrassing can slide out. But I guess I'm not being slick enough because Tessa jumps up and throws her arms around me, pulling me in so tight that my nose is filled with the scent of her rose leave-in conditioner.

"I'm sorry. I'll shut up. I just . . . I love you."

"I love you too," I tell her, putting my head against hers.

"We should leave," she says with conviction. "We should leave and drive-through In-N-Out and take it to the beach. I feel like we've gotten the full prom experience, don't you?"

"After photos," Lavon reminds us, and Theo beams.

"After photos," Tessa agrees. "But then we should go. It'll be fun. A last hurrah, all five of us."

I know what she's trying to do. Make me feel included by getting me out of this environment that *painfully* highlights how I'm the fifth wheel, the permanent sidekick. But then there's the fact that I'm the only reason we need a last hurrah in the first place. They're all staying local next year. Theo and Lavon will be at CalArts, Tessa is going to UCI, and Sam is going to some prestigious culinary institute in LA while he interns at Food Network. I'm the only one who won't be around for late night Double-Doubles and secret menu Neapolitan shakes. I'm the one who's going to be a million miles away at NYU.

I rub my fingers under my eyes again, harder this time. I need to get it together. I can't be all in my feelings like this tonight or I'm going to ruin these last moments for everyone.

"And waste these outfits?" I say, putting on the cool Lenore front that they expect from me. "Nah, girl, we need to stay until they kick us out. Plus, that limo won't fit in the drive-through!"

"In-N-Out is never a waste," Tessa says, giving me a squeeze. "But I'm down to do whatever you want to—*oh*."

I see Jay on all their faces before I actually see him. They're all silent at first, with wide eyes that shift to a spectrum of uncomfortable and mad.

Finally: "Fuuuuuuuuuck." Lavon lets it out in one long breath.

I follow their stares to see Jay standing in front of a wall of floating, glowing jellyfish.

The first thing I notice is how good he looks. A navy tux with shiny black lapels and stripes down the sides over a black turtleneck, finished off with blinding white sneakers. His hair is slicked back all suave, and the confidence that I can't get enough of just oozes off him. Like I said, *style*.

The second thing I notice, though, is Rachel. Standing close. Standing real close, closer than any friends I've seen before. And then she's leaning in closer. His hand that was, I realize, on her waist slides down to her ass, and then she's reaching up to grab his neck and their lips lock together like magnets. They don't kiss like two people doing this for the first time. They kiss like two people who have been doing this for a while. Two people who have *practice*.

"Lenore, wait," Tessa says, because apparently I'm standing up. Apparently I'm walking over to Jay and Rachel, who are apparently comfortable enough to make out in public.

I don't even say anything when I get there. I don't know what to say. But Tessa, who's right behind me, takes care of that.

"What. The. Fuck. What the fuck?!" It's probably the loudest I've ever heard her be. Jay and Rachel spring apart.

I expect him to start apologizing and explaining. He has to have an explanation, right? Not that I'm going to just accept it or whatever, but, like, I'll listen. I'm already thinking about all the ways he's going to have to make this up to me. I mean, it's going to be a long road, but maybe we can get there?

The apologies don't come though. No explanations. He

doesn't even look embarrassed. In fact, I can't read his face at all. The face I can read, though, is Rachel's. It's easy to interpret. She looks pissed.

"Uh, hi?" she says. "Do you need something?"

"Jay?" I sound so small and weak. I hate it.

"Hey, Tessa." He nods at her. "Hey, Lenore."

Lenore. He never calls me Lenore. *Hey, lady.* That's been our thing since the very first day in advanced painting. It's what he called me during our library parking lot hookups, during our fourth-floor stairwell meetings. That one night I snuck him into my bedroom and then out before five a.m., even though my dad would have murdered us if he ever found out. Never just Lenore.

What's going on? Is he . . . here with Rachel? Is he cheating on me with Rachel?

"I, um, like—" I can't form a complete thought, and I can feel my mouth hanging open and my brain tries to interpret all the information in front of me, to put everything together in a way that comes to some other, perfectly reasonable explanation.

Rachel looks between us slowly, and then turns toward Jay. "What's going on, babe?"

And that's when it all clicks into place. Jay isn't cheating on me. He's cheating *with* me.

"Jay?" I say again, my voice stronger this time. "What is she talking about?"

He winces and looks uncomfortable. But I realize, with horror, that he looks uncomfortable *for me*. Like I'm the one doing something cringe-y here. He holds his hand out like he's holding me back. "Lenore, it's just—you know I'm with Rachel. Don't make this weird."

"Weird? Weird?" I'm reduced to a single word. "WEIRD?!"

Rachel's eyes are flicking between us faster now, and I can see her putting it together. Jay's cool facade starts to break a little.

"Can we talk later, Lenore?" he says, using the name that sounds so foreign coming out of his mouth. "After you get back from that cruise."

I can feel my nose scrunch up as I flash back to the joke he made when I first told him about it. We were at the beach together in the back of his car, watching the waves while we cuddled close in a blanket. "Is a cruise a good idea considering you can't swim?" he'd joked, wrapping his legs around mine. Which, whatever, I can't swim, but I hadn't told him that. Why did I let that ignorant shit go so easy then? Why did I laugh and even imagine us on the cruise together, one of Tessa's stupid fantasies come to life?

I was so stupid. I thought I was chosen. Treasured. But I was just his chick on the side while he gets serious with Rachel Chan—someone he doesn't have to hide from his parents.

But fuck it. I don't need him. I've never needed any boy, and I'm not about to start now. I'm mad at him, yeah, but even more so I'm mad at myself for how little I was willing to accept from someone.

"Jay, we are never speaking again."

Inside I'm doing a stank-face, booger-nose goodbye power ballad like Jennifer Hudson in *Dreamgirls*, or when she was the freaky CGI cat thing. But on the outside I'm stone. He doesn't get to see me cry.

"Lenore—"

I turn around and leave before he can finish that thought. Tessa follows after me. "Come on, we're leaving," she says to Sam, Theo, and Lavon when we reach the table.

"Lenore, I'm so sorry," Theo says.

"It's fine," I say. "It's nothing." And it really was nothing, apparently. Jay doesn't chase after me. "And hey, you need to take your pictures on the way out."

"Are you . . . are you sure?" he asks. I know he wasn't going to push it, but I also saw him pining for those cheesy photos on the way in. He shouldn't miss out just because his best friend is a disaster. Because I'm doomed to only attract fuckboys and assholes, because my judgment is a complete joke.

"Lenore, we really don't need to do that," Tessa cuts in. "We're going to get you a Double-Double, two orders of fries, and a Neapolitan shake, and we're going to listen to SZA really loud and then we're going to, like, scream into the ocean."

"No, I want Theo to get his pictures," I say, trying to control the croak of my voice. I rub under my eyes again. "You and Sam too, Tessa. I'll hold your purse."

"We can't do that . . ." Sam starts.

"Really, I insist, you guys," I say. "Don't—" My voice catches. I try again. "Don't change your plans because of this.

It's only going to make me feel worse. I can't let him ruin every-one's night . . . I can't let him affect me at all."

"Oh-kay," Theo says slowly. "But can we just take one of all of us? That's what I would like to remember . . . all of us together." He squeezes Lavon's hand, but then comes and gives me a hug, wiping something off my cheek. "I love you, Lenore. He didn't deserve you."

I take a deep breath and find the Lenore who's always there, the one they're used to. Cool, calm, confident. "No one does. Now let's go take some photos that we can look at when we're old and crusty, so we can remember how beautiful we were at this very moment."

So, that's how I end up with pictures of me in a pink boa, with smudged mascara and the fakest smile there ever was. My two best friends, their one true loves, and me.

Alone.

CHAPTER THREE

If this were a Marvel movie, this would be my villain origin story. I would devote the rest of my life to rooting out fuckboys, exposing their crimes against womankind, and then like murdering them or whatever, until some guy in spandex knocks a building on me.

But it's not.

So, instead, I move on with my normal, non-murder-y life.

And my friends make it easy. Theo and Lavon take me out for French toast at Starling Diner the next morning, and Tessa calls me five times just to check in. I even talk about my feelings during the last call, against my better judgment. But by Monday morning, I'm back to the Lenore they expect. The one they need. Tough, resilient, funny as hell, perfect eyeliner. "I don't care," I insist when Tessa tries to wrap me in her arms and escort me to class like I'm some trauma victim. Because I don't care! Really.

And I shouldn't have even been surprised anyway. What Jay did . . . or I guess, what he had been doing . . . since October . . .

Well, it's not like it's an outlying incident. It's evidence that confirms my view of love, which is that it's not going to happen for me.

Jay isn't the first to decide he'd rather be with someone other than me. And he won't be the last. I'll protect myself better next time. No getting caught up in someone's style or the way they make my body feel, and then putting blinders on to the trunk full of red flags. I'm going to live in the real world with my guard up and my heart on lockdown. I don't have time to be catching feelings and investing in someone who's just hooking up with me until he finds someone more appropriate. If there even is a next time!

Which, whatever, because I DON'T CARE.

I don't.

Graduation is the week after prom, and it comes fast. Another one of those big moments that I've imagined forever, and I'm freaking out about it finally happening. And then right when I begin to chill, it's over.

I focus on the moments again, memorizing them and adding them to my mental stash. Tessa nervously adjusting her grad cap over her fro. Grandma Lenore sounding her airhorn for not just me but every Black person who walks across the stage. My whole family (even Wally) jumping and shouting like they're in church when my name is called. Wally tried to stay home, saying he was busy with law school prep, which is irritating because I didn't even think about missing his college graduation last month. But Dad gave him one of those signature *Boy, you better watch yourself* looks and that was that; he showed up.

I don't memorize Jay with his arm wrapped around Rachel as their parents take pictures. That moment can go drown in the ocean.

After the ceremony, we head over to Grandma Lenore's house in Artesia, for a graduation party to celebrate both me and Wally. Grandma Lenore has the smallest house out of everyone, but it's the center of the family. We've celebrated every holiday, birthday, and good report card in her cozy Spanish-style house on Lilac Lane. It's orange with a terra-cotta roof, and two giant palm trees framing the door. Wally convinced me that he could climb those trees when we were little, showing off the bananas that he supposedly picked from the top. And now I know that's ridiculous, but I tried and tried until my legs were all scratched up and I went inside and told Grandma Lenore on him. She came outside waving her dish towel around and threatened to whoop his behind "since your mama won't!" Grandma Lenore has always been my fiercest protector. I wish I could send her after Jay for me.

When we walk up the steps, she's standing there at the door. She probably just got here a little before us, but I'm sure Auntie Stacy and my cousin Jerry are in the kitchen holding things down.

"Oh, my babies! Look at my educated, degree-having

babies!" she says with her arms outstretched. She's wearing a giant pink leopard-print muumuu that makes her look like a high priestess of Lisa Frank.

"They haven't given it to me yet," I say, giving her a tight hug. "That little folder thingy was empty. Can you believe that?"

"Well, speak for yourself. I have mine already," Wally says with a smirk. "Maybe they'll come to their senses and never send yours."

"I could have my high school diploma already if Mom and Dad didn't make me stay back," Etta says with her nose up, and I roll my eyes because it's true, but she doesn't have to do me like that. Even though she's only ten, she's taking online college classes.

"Your big heads need to shut up and let me have my moment!" I say, slapping Wally on the shoulder. He tries to get me back, but I duck behind Grandma Lenore, protecting myself.

"Marla, come get your children," she says to my mom with a side-eye.

"What children? These children aren't mine," Mom laughs, shaking her head. She bends down to kiss Grandma Lenore on the cheek, and Dad follows.

"Mmm-hmmm."

Grandma Lenore and Mom look nothing alike, except for their coppery skin. Otherwise you wouldn't even know they were related because Grandma Lenore is short and plump, while Mom is slim and stretched out, over six feet, just like Dad. And Mom usually wears her hair natural, in a low bun, but Grandma Lenore always has a different wig for every mood. Today it's blond and spiky in the back, with a perfectly layered bang over her right eye.

Mom, Dad, and Etta go inside, and Grandma Lenore pulls me in close. She smells like coconut oil and her lavender laundry detergent.

"Hey, pretty girl," she says. Her nickname for me since I was a baby. "I'm really proud of you. Could you hear me up there on the stage?"

"Yes, I think all of Long Beach could hear you, Grandma." That makes her eyes light up, and she squeezes me tighter. She barely comes up to my shoulder, so I rest my head on top of hers.

"Now what is this you got on?" she says, eyeing me up and down. I'm wearing a hot-pink jumpsuit with ruffly cap sleeves and bright gold buttons I sewed on myself.

"Another one of her extra outfits," Wally scoffs. Grandma's kitchen towel appears out of nowhere and swats Wally across the legs.

"You better hush now, Wallace," Grandma Lenore says, calling Wally by his full name. He scampers inside the house, laughing. "I like it, pretty girl. Get me one in my size."

She leads me inside, and it's warm. Warm because she doesn't have AC and refuses to let my parents pay for it. And also warm because it's full to the brim with people I love. I can hear Auntie Stacy and my godmama Arlene singing Whitney Houston together over a pot of something delicious in the kitchen, Auntie Mae's car-that-won't-start laugh floating in from the back patio (she's not allowed to cook after the potato salad incident), the sound of lightsabers coming from a PlayStation that one of the little cousins set up in the living room, and my uncles arguing and slapping down dominoes on a card table in the garage.

"Hey, little cuz!" I look up to see my cousin Jerry walking down the hallway, a dirty apron tied around his waist. Most of the people in my family are Grandma Lenore's size, but Jerry is tall, even taller than my dad. His hair is in a bald fade that he gets shaped up every two weeks, and he has a permanent smile stretched across his face from one ear to the other. "Congratulations! We all knew you would make it somehow."

"You need to leave my baby alone," Grandma Lenore grumbles as she swishes past us into the kitchen.

"Why is everyone coming at me like this?" I shout. This just makes Jerry laugh and nudge me with his elbow. "I took honors and AP classes! I had a 4.2 GPA!"

"Ah, but that don't mean nothing in that family of yours!" he says, throwing his arm around my neck. "Little Einsteins, all of you! The talented tenth!"

He starts humming the theme song to the *Little Einsteins* cartoon, which I don't even how this twenty-year-old MAN knows. But then he throws in some hip rolls and snaps in time to the song, and I can't help but join in on his laughter. This is how my family shows love—by taking you down a few notches. And he's not even wrong. Etta will probably finish all of her bachelor's coursework before she's out of middle school, and Wally was valedictorian of his high school and went to UCLA on a full ride. My academic accomplishments mean nothing compared to them. And as much as they tried not to compare, that's always been clear in my parents' eyes too—especially Dad's. If I came home with an A minus on a report card, he'd fix me with a steely look and ask, "Now what happened here?"

"Jerry, I know you ain't out there singing when I told you to watch the grill!" Auntie Stacy calls, and his eyes get wide with panic.

"Gotta go!" he shouts behind him as he sprints to the kitchen.

I start to follow him, but then someone clutches my shoulders from behind.

"Have you seen him yet?" a voice says, and I spin around to see my cousin Reggie, short for Reginald. He's wearing his typical uniform of black jeans and a faded black T-shirt with something nerdy. Today it's *Static Shock*, whatever that is. Reggie is actually on my dad's side, Auntie Mae's kid, but all the family (and the people my parents call family) who've moved to California from the South treat Grandma Lenore's as a home base.

"Reggie, why you being all creepy?"

"First of all, congratulations. I know it was hard for you."

I shove his shoulder. "Y'all need to stop, I'm telling you . . ."

"Second of all. Well, I've been waiting by the door to catch you so you're not surprised. And don't shoot the messenger, but see . . . Marcus is here."

My stomach drops when I hear his name. Lord, haven't I been through enough this week?

Marcus is my ex-boyfriend. We dated for almost all of my sophomore year, but I've known him pretty much my whole life. We grew up going to the same Baptist church in downtown, and reconnected when we were both forced to be counselors at the same vacation Bible school the summer after freshman year. What started with making out in the craft closet turned into something much more serious. We were in love. We talked about getting married, about how many kids we would have, where we would live. All that shit! At fifteen! And he made me feel like he really meant all of it. Just like Jay, though, he was only with me until he found someone better.

"With Tapatha," Reggie adds. "He's here with Tapatha."

Tapatha. The light-skinned girl with hazel eyes and what my grandma used to call "the good hair" before we taught her not to. The girl Marcus started dating two weeks after he dumped me with some lines about how he didn't want to be in a relationship. When really, he just didn't want to be in a relationship *with me*.

"What are they doing here?" I whisper-shriek, because I'm not trying to get attention.

He shrugs. "You know your grandma probably invited her whole address book. And, uh, okay, don't turn around now . . . but they're right behind you."

Of course I turn around. And of course Marcus is looking right me. And *of course* he looks good. A fresh cut, tight jeans, a white shirt cuffed to show off his arms, and black Comme des Garçons Converse that only he could pull off. He has no business showing up here looking that good.

His full lips curve into a smile, and he waves. My whole body stiffens. I feel like I did last weekend at prom. Booger-y Jennifer Hudson vibes.

I grab Reggie's arm and pull him in the opposite direction. My game plan: avoid, avoid, AVOID.

And I manage to do that for the next couple of hours, which is no small feat in this house. Luckily, Grandma Lenore *does* seem to have invited every single soul she knows, so there's plenty of buffer. I make the rounds, get my cheeks kissed, and answer the same questions about NYU over and over again. And once we say grace and the food is served, it's even easier to pretend I don't see him as I fill my first, second, and third plates and eat with my cousins.

"I'm telling you, man, you can't be out here yelling that anymore. It's disrespectful!" Jerry is gesturing so wildly with each word that I'm worried the plate of key lime pie balanced precariously on his knees is going to fall over. "Kobe, rest in peace"—he kisses his hand and raises it to the sky—"wouldn't want to have his name shouted when you throw your trash away."

"You're acting like he's Jesus or something," Reggie, the offender, chimes in. He tried to do a hook shot with his crumpled-up barbecue-sauce-saturated napkin and started this whole debate.

"Well, you said it," Jerry says, shrugging, but then he looks around quickly to see if Auntie Stacy witnessed that sacrilege.

"If anything it's the most respect. It's an honorific," Reggie says. I know for a fact that he doesn't give one shit about this, that his interests skew more nerdy than basketball. He's just arguing to argue.

Reggie's older brother, Eric, snort-laughs. "So we just making up words now?"

"Actually, it is a word," Wally says. "And I agree with Reggie. It would be more disrespectful to stop yelling Kobe."

"No one asked you, Wally!" Jerry rolls his eyes and waves Wally away. "You never even played sports. Talking 'bout, 'Oh, I agree with Reggie.'" His imitation of Wally sounds like some reject *Downton Abbey* character. "Man, be quiet!"

What Jerry's saying is true. Dad didn't let Wally (or us girls) play basketball or any sports growing up, insisting that STEAM summer camps or after-school chess clubs and piano lessons were a better use of our time. But, still, Jerry doesn't have to be such a dick about it.

I look him up and down. "Don't be mad because your little cousins have a larger vocabulary than you."

"Oh!" Reggie calls, pumping the air. But Eric cuts him off. "Ask your boy, Wally! I bet he'd agree with us!"

Wally's "boy" is his longtime boyfriend, Kieran. They started dating their junior year of high school and stayed together long-distance through all of college when Kieran went to Duke. Eric thinks Kieran would know better because he was a basketball superstar in high school, and even tried to make a go of it at Duke but never got to start.

"Where is Kieran, anyway?" I ask, changing the subject. "Isn't he back in town by now? I just realized I haven't seen him yet."

I thought this was an innocuous enough question, but Wally is looking at me like I wrote my name all over his Jordans in permanent marker.

"We broke up. A while ago," he spits out.

"What?" I'm legitimately shocked. How come he hasn't mentioned this? I would think at least Mom and Dad would. They *loved* Kieran.

"What happened, man?" Jerry asks, apparently cool with Wally now.

"Yeah, I don't get it?" I say. "You two were, like, so solid. And I thought the plan was for him to move out here while you went to law school?"

Wally's eyebrows press down low, and he purses his lips. "I don't have time for that anymore," he says darkly, shaking his head. "You'll get it soon when you grow up. I can't mess around like you anymore."

With that, he storms into the kitchen, where the counters are covered with foil-wrapped trays. I feel like he punched me in the stomach. *Mess around like me?* What the fuck is that supposed to mean? I was just trying to understand what happened with his boyfriend of six years, someone who was basically a part of our family, and he's acting like I wronged him somehow.

"Whoa. Well, that was weird," I say, leaning back in my chair and looking at my cousins for validation. They're all staring back at me, wide-eyed, and it takes me a second to realize it's not about Wally but at something behind me.

"Hey, Lenore," the familiar voice says behind me. Warm and smooth, like an eighteen-year-old Aaron Neville. I don't have to turn around to know it's Marcus standing there. With Tapatha.

"Oh, hey, Marcus. Tapatha," I say, jumping up. Oh shit, am I not supposed to know her name? We've never, like, actually met. Are they going to know I stalk their socials now? "Gotta pee. Be right back."

I basically sprint to the bathroom and slam the door shut behind me. *Gotta pee?!* I could have gone to the bathroom without explaining to them what I'm doing here. Man. Why can't my mouth just slow down sometimes?

I slide myself onto the pink counter, next to the hand lotion dispenser covered in a knit cozy and the shell-shaped pastel soap.

Damn.

I came here to be celebrated (and okay, celebrate Wally too)—not to feel all these feelings I've been trying to push down all week. Not to be out here questioning whether love is real.

My parents are in love. I know that from the way they look at each other, all googly-eyed like they just met even after twenty-five years, and also the fact that they still get it on. Etta, seven years my junior, made that way too disgustingly clear.

The thing that Mom and Dad have, that Grandma Lenore and Grandpa John had before he passed. I don't think that exists anymore. Well, maybe for Tessa-and-Sam and Theo-and-Lavon. But then again, who knows what will happen to them in college? Maybe that makes me a bitch to think that, but I thought Wally and Kieran would last. I was sure Marcus and I would be together forever and now he's showing up to my graduation party with his arm wrapped around a girl with a stupid name like Tapatha. I even dreamed about Jay a little bit. . . . So, obviously my judgment isn't great.

I really think there are no one true loves or great, sweeping romances anymore. Maybe you just get to find someone who is good enough.

But why can't I even do that?

Someone bangs on the door, jolting me out of my thoughts.

"Lenore!" Jerry yells. "Listen, I, too, know the pure joy of taking a big-ass dump in the middle of the day, but you gotta line out here!"

I jump off the counter, feeling my neck warm up. I don't need him out here hollering about my bowel movements.

I open the door, and he throws his hands up. "There we go! Girl, what you need? Some Imodium? Some Lactaid? Pepto?"

"You play too much," I say, swatting his stomach, but I can't help but laugh as he pushes past into the bathroom, pointedly flicking the fan on before he shuts the door.

The laugh dies, though, when I see who's standing behind him. Shit.

Marcus just half smiles and waves, but Tapatha pounces on me like an overactive Chihuahua.

"Lenore! Hi! We haven't met yet, but I feel like I already know you! I love your jumpsuit. You have such unique style!"

"Thank you! I like your purse!" I say, pasting on my best fake smile. I don't really, but that's just what you say.

"Just so you know," Marcus says, taking a tentative step toward me with his right palm up, like I'm some unpredictable animal they've encountered in the wild. I hate it. "We're here because my grandma needed a ride. I don't know if you, like, heard, but they took away her license last month when she parked her car about a centimeter away from her beauty shop's window." He laughs. That same warm, rumbly one I know so well that stirs something in my stomach. I hate that too. "Anyway, I wanted you to know, so we don't have to make this weird."

Weird. Just like Jay. *Don't make this weird.* Why is everyone so concerned with things being weird? As if their comfort is all that matters and me feeling anything is *too much*. And lord knows, I felt EVERYTHING when I was with him. I was stupid. I showed too much emotion—even more after he broke up with me and I tried to convince him he was making a mistake, that it was true love. Meant to be. That's why I scared him away. I was weird.

My insides are swimming, and I get the irritating tight feeling in my throat that I know is warning me of even more irritating displays of emotion on their way if I don't get it

42

together. "Yeah, of course," I say. "That was forever ago, Marcus." I laugh, and it sounds hollow. But I know they won't be able to tell the difference.

"Oh, you two!" Tapatha cuts in, laughing too. Except her laugh is practically at a pitch that only dogs can hear and makes me want to claw out my eardrums. "It's so nice of you to be so considerate of each other over this little thing you had when you were basically kids. I love it!"

We weren't kids. We were having sex and planning our future kids' names, but go off.

"So, I heard you're going to NYU," Tapatha continues. "Marcus and I are going to Spelman and Morehouse. We're going to live in the dorms freshman year, but we're talking about getting an apartment later. Don't tell his grandma, though, because she would just die!" She slaps Marcus's shoulder and lets out another brain-scrambling laugh. "Now, are you scared to live in New York? I saw a video on Instagram of this rat—"

"Pretty girl, can I steal you for a minute?" Grandma Lenore swoops in like some jewel-toned-wearing dental assistant on *The Bachelor.*

"Oh, yes, please," I say, clutching her arm and letting her steer me away from my worst nightmare of a conversation. "Bye! So nice chatting!" I call behind me, and Grandma Lenore joins in with, "You have a blessed day now." Which basically means "fuck you" in respectable granny language. I want to cheer.

We walk into her formal living room and sit down on her fancy couch, the crinkly plastic cover sticking to my bare arms.

She leans in close to me, her spiky hair of the day tickling my cheek, and she takes my hand. Her skin feels soft and delicate like tracing paper.

"Now, you know that grandmoms don't have favorites," she says, her dark eyes sparkly with mischief. "I love you and Wallace and Etta all the same. But you've always been my special girl."

"I know, Grandma." I smile. She's the one person I've always been not only enough for, but *just right* for.

"And because of that," she continues, "I had to get you a special gift for this day. Now, I've seen all those honor classes you been taking, and you working so hard. And not just anyone would be brave enough to move clear across the country for school, especially to a school that's as big of a deal as I hear this one is. I want to make sure you know how proud I am of you, so I got you something."

The mention of how far NYU is, of leaving, makes me feel almost as sick as seeing Marcus and Tapatha did, but I push that feeling down and focus on the good feelings rising up.

"Grandma, you didn't have to get me a present to show me you're proud. This party is more than enough."

"Oh, hush up," she says, squeezing my leg. She turns and reaches over to the baby-blue cabinet next to the couch, and pulls out a gift bag stuffed with a cloud of tissue paper. "And don't get your hopes up. There ain't no car keys in here, but you won't need that in New York anyway."

"Yeah, right," I mumble as I reach into the bag and pull out a little piece of my childhood. It's pink and gray, with a gigantic flash attached to the top. It has the same scratch on the bottom from when I dropped it at Disneyland trying to take a picture on the Dumbo ride, and there's a chip of paint missing from the left corner.

"Is this . . . ?"

"Your old Polaroid camera," she finishes for me. "Yes, it is."

"But how did . . . I never knew what happened to it."

She laughs. "Oh, I'll tell you what happened to it! You were over here taking photos of Grandpa out in the backyard. You had a whole setup—put him in a three-piece suit and made him sit all up in the jasmine bush even though his allergies were acting up. But you couldn't get the light just right; the flash kept going off when you didn't mean for it to. So, you threw the camera down on the lawn and declared that you were done with photography. Next day, you moved on to your watercolor phase, and that was that."

I don't remember that. Like, at all. I figured that I just lost the camera or something, or that Mom and Dad stopped buying me film. But I guess that's not much of an explanation, either. I *do* remember how much I loved carrying that camera everywhere around my neck, how my brain and fingers still itch to capture moments in perfect little squares. Why did I give it up so easily? And for *watercolors*? I can't even recall a watercolor phase.

I guess I was hopping around, even then. I was signed up for a photography class at Chrysalis at some point—freshman year?—but I didn't like the teacher, Mr. Stabler, so I transferred to something else—printmaking, or maybe illustration. I've never wanted to commit to one thing, to get tied down to a specialty when it's possible I'd be better at something else.

"So, wait, you saved it for me?" I ask. Grandma Lenore's wide smile remains, but something flickers in her eyes.

"Your granddad did," she says. "Put it aside in his office and wouldn't let nobody touch it, even when we were cleaning out the place, you know, when we had to switch the room around." When he got sick and his office became his hospital room, she means. "Said you loved this here thing and would find your way back to it . . . eventually."

My throat gets tight again. Grandpa John's been gone for six years now, but I still miss him so much. It's almost like this is a present from him too.

"And before you say anything about me just giving you something that's already yours for a present," Grandma Lenore says quickly, her voice getting back some of its pep. "Your cousin Reggie helped me buy fifty-leven packs of film for this thing on the eBay, and those things weren't cheap. So, you better not be throwing this camera on my lawn no time soon."

"Oh, never! Grandma, it's perfect." I pull her into a hug, inhaling her coconut-and-lavender scent. "I'm excited to have it back. I've been thinking of photography a lot lately, actually."

"Well, look at God!" she says, slapping her hands together. "Something told me this was what you needed right now. And maybe you can even take some classes again in New York. You mama told me you're studying art there at that university of yours."

"Yeah, maybe."

"Now, why are you making that stank face?" she asks, narrowing her eyes at me. "Every time someone's mentioned New York today, you pull your lip up and scrunch your nose like you smell something funky."

I can feel that exact expression on my face, and I rush to smooth it out.

Going away to New York seemed like the sort of thing that confident, brave, loud Lenore would do. New York is where all the big artists live at some point, after all. But now that New York will be my reality in just a few months, this place so far from everyone and everything I know . . . well, I'm nervous. Apparently so nervous that Grandma Lenore can see it all over my stank face.

But there's no point in talking that through. No going back now.

"Maybe it's your greens?" I say with a smirk. Deflecting.

"Child, you better tread carefully," she says, giving me a stank face of her own.

"And anyway, I'm studying art, but not really," I explain. "Not in the same way I am now. My major is art history. So less doing, more analyzing, you know."

She looks me up and down. "That face because of my greens again?"

I cover my face and laugh. I've got to get that lip under

control. "Maybe. Maybe also because art history can be pretty boring, but I had to make a decision when I applied, and that just made sense . . . at the time." Once I decided on New York, and NYU specifically, I waited until the very last day, January fifth, to submit my application because I couldn't narrow down what I wanted to focus on. My portfolio was kind of all over the place to commit to one specialty, so this seemed like the best compromise. I got an A in AP Art History, and Ms. Ramiro told me it was something I should consider—plus I didn't have to submit any art samples to be judged. That's another reason why I didn't even consider ArtCenter or CalArts, the art schools in California that Theo was deciding between. "But I don't know," I continue, shrugging. "I guess I see it as more of a placeholder, though, as I figure out what I really want to do."

As I'm saying it, I hear how privileged I sound, talking about just figuring it out when my parents are basically paying a whole-ass salary to send me to this prestigious school. But I can't help it. I jump around a lot, I think, because I thrive on that spark that something brand-new brings. The excitement of the unknown, learning something new. It's hard to imagine committing to something for my whole life when I'm not even eighteen yet. And I need to commit, finally, right? With all this money involved. I feel guilty that I'm not more like Tessa, with her writing, or Sam, with his baking. Or even Wally. It's boring and predictable that he's following in our dad's footsteps to become a lawyer, but at least he's committed and passionate about something.

I talk a big game sometimes with my friends, but it makes me nervous that I can't commit to any one thing. That I'm so all over the place instead of sure and steady. Maybe that's part of the reason no one can commit to me.

"Seems to me like you've got time, pretty girl, and there ain't nothing wrong with throwing things out there and seeing what sticks," Grandma Lenore says. "You're going to thrive whatever you do."

When she says it, I can almost believe it. I sometimes wish I could carry her around in my pocket, when this confident and strong front of mine starts to fall. Which it's been doing a lot lately.

"Grandma, can you just come with us on Monday?" I ask. "I'd rather share a room with you than Wally."

"Me? On a cruise?" She slaps her thigh and lets out a loud laugh. "It's like y'all never seen *Titanic*. They warned you! But let me be quiet."

CHAPTER FOUR

"Mom said I have to act like a kid for an hour, so I need you to play this ridiculous board game with me." Etta is standing at my door, holding Life with one outstretched hand like it's going to bite her or something.

It's the next afternoon and I should be packing for our trip since we're leaving tomorrow. I should be reading the freshman guide that came in the mail from NYU a couple weeks ago and has been sitting under a pile of crap on my desk ever since. But instead I'm staring at the ceiling, half responding to Tessa's sappy *this is the beginning of the rest of our lives* texts, and questioning every decision I've ever made. That still doesn't mean I want to play Life with Etta, though.

"It's a mutually beneficial situation, really, because it doesn't appear as if you're doing anything of importance," she continues, and I turn my head to look at her. On the outside, she looks her age. A sweet yellow eyelet dress that Mom probably picked out for her and her dark hair pulled into a tight puff. But her eyes give her away. They're the eyes of someone closer to Grandma Lenore's age, someone who's been everywhere and seen everything and is waiting for you to catch up. That little old lady inside her is why Mom and Dad have to give her directives to "act like a kid." If it was up to her, she'd spend all day researching the migration patterns of monarch butterflies or the reign of Mansa Musa or some shit. She's not picky, as long as it doesn't involve interactions with others—especially others her own age.

"Please, Lenore," she whines, and I think I see a glimmer of the ten-year-old she is, begging her big sister to play with her. But then again, it's probably just something she learned in the human psychology online class she's taking through Long Beach City College.

"Fine," I huff, rolling off my bed. "But only if you let me take your picture."

She shrugs, settling herself down on my floor, and then sets her kid-sized Apple Watch knockoff for an hour.

I walk over to my desk to get the camera, sitting on top of the gift bag it came in. I've loaded in film, but I've been scared to use any of it yet. It feels like a precious resource because it's so limited. But I guess I should figure out if it works or not now, before committing to lugging it around in my carry-on all around Europe.

"Okay, look here." I hold it up, centering Etta in the viewfinder, and brace myself because there's probably an 89 percent chance that this thing will explode and take my eyebrows off in a blaze of glory. But it makes a click sound and then there's a *rrrrrrr*, like gears are turning, and a white-framed picture pushes out. I stare at it, waiting for the colors to slowly appear, and I realize, with a little embarrassment, that there's a tight feeling in my chest—I'm holding my breath in anticipation. It's silly, I know. This is just my camera from when I was a kid. Nothing like the nice models they checked out to students at Chrysalis.

But the picture delivers.

Etta's eyes are wide, surprised by the flash, and it's like the picture cut through all the layers to show her at her very core. The Etta who used to be my shadow and call me "Nor-Nor" and, like, eat her boogers and shit—before she started reading Ta-Nehisi Coates at six for fun. A moment memorized.

A smile takes over my face, so big my cheeks hurt. I've missed this.

Etta comes to my side now, to peer at the picture over my shoulder. "The composition is interesting, but the lighting is unfortunate. I don't understand the purpose of using such outdated technology when you could take a far superior photograph with a DSLR."

"Far superior photograph," I imitate her in a nasally voice, pretending to hold up a pair of imaginary glasses that she doesn't even wear with my pointer finger. It's a stupid joke, and she looks me up and down, making it clear she won't even dignify my childish behavior with a response.

I roll my eyes, and toss the picture and camera onto my bed. "Whatever. I like it."

She nods slowly, humoring me, and then sits back on the floor. "Can we begin? We have"—she checks her watch—"fifty-six more minutes, and you know they're going to check on me."

"Yeah, that's because last time you were supposed to 'act like a kid,' you ended up writing a ten-page paper on the villainization of Black girls in the Descendants movies."

"It was a solid thesis," she says as she begins to set up the board, taking out cards and cars and pegs.

"It was."

I clown on her sometimes, just to keep her humble, but my little sister really is brilliant. Like scary brilliant. But the thing with my parents is that even though Etta has a brain that's probably going to be stored in the Natural History Museum like some freaky artifact and sought out by the Nic Cage of the future—that's still not enough. They're permanently focused on her improvement, how she can be even better. Yes, she will probably hold a PhD by the time she's nineteen, but can she talk about the latest Disney Channel Original Movies with her peers? Has she mastered the Hasbro canon? Can she adequately explain what "a TikTok" is? There will always be a next step, a pushed finish line.

And it's like that for all of us. Wally and me can't be caught slipping either. But I guess it's fair because they hold themselves to those standards too. Dad has worked crazy hours all my life, and I don't see him stopping anytime soon even though he's reached partner at his law firm. And Mom started her own education nonprofit that was profiled in the *LA Times*. They're crazy successful, and expect us to be, too.

"Okay," Etta says, handing me a yellow car with a pink peg in the driver's seat. "First you need to select a pet."

"A pet? Since when does this game have pets?"

"I'm not familiar with the history of this particular board game, but feel free to research that independently after we're done." She arches an eyebrow way too skillfully for a ten-year-old. "Pick a pet."

"But what if I don't want one?" I wrinkle my nose. "I don't even get the appeal of pets anyway. Like, who's down with some creature creeping and pooping all around your house, and all . . . *licking* you or whatever. Why have we as a society accepted this as normal?"

"It's in the rules," she says, sticking a green puppy-shaped peg into my car. "Now are you taking the college path or the career path?" She motions to two separate starting points on the board.

"Oh, the career path for sure," I say. "It's shorter and you get your first paycheck sooner."

"Hmm," Etta says, sucking her teeth and shaking her head like the ninety-year-old granny inside her. She's much more deserving of her old-lady name than me.

"What?"

"If you take that path, it's highly likely that you'll lose the game. When you take the college path, your probability of winning increases because you get a career with a higher salary, which in turn provides you with benefits that will impact the entire game." Leave it to Etta to turn this ages-eight-and-up board game into a goddamn economics lesson.

"Sure, but even going to college, you could end up with a career you don't like, so then who cares if you're making more money? And then you're also going into debt before your life even really begins because you have to pay the bank for an education that might not even be valuable to you in the long run. And all this for an uncertain future? Nah, I'm starting over here." I slam my little green car with the mandatory puppy onto the board, knocking over a stack of cards.

"Hmm," Etta says again, pursing her lips this time. "While I'm curious to unpack that, I need this hour of kid time to count so I'm off the hook for the rest of the day."

"There's nothing to unpack," I spit out. "It's just strategy."

"Sure," she says, moving her little pink car to the starting line.

We start to spin and flip cards as we move through the board, Etta checking her watch every five minutes. I end up being a professional athlete (as if) and my sister is a secret agent (very possible). And yeah, her stack of bills is much more significant than mine, but that's not because she chose the college path. It's because she keeps getting stupid cards like "You win a beautiful forehead contest, collect ten million dollars," while I keep getting ones like "You're fired for sneaking your cat into work, pay a billion dollars and also you have no friends."

I get to another little stop sign, and Etta tries to hand me another peg, blue this time. "Time to get married."

I eye that thing suspiciously because I've been through too much this past week (hell, my whole life) to trust any more boys, even if they are plastic.

"Yeah, I'm not getting married."

"You have to," she huffs. "It's in the rules, Lenore."

"Well, I think we need to question the values of this game, then," I say, taking the blue peg from her and tossing it across the room. "Why do I need a husband to be successful? Some people just don't find a partner and fall in love and that's okay— it doesn't mean there's anything wrong with them. In fact, it means there's something wrong with the boys. Maybe you should write a paper about the misogyny of this game, huh? I won't tell Mom and Dad."

Etta blinks at me. The "hmmm" is unspoken this time but still very much present.

"Okay, maybe this is getting too real," I concede.

As if summoned by their names, our parents appear at my door, and Etta jumps to spin the rainbow wheel, clapping her hands excitedly. "Whoo boy, this is fun!" she laughs, fooling absolutely no one.

Mom is still wearing her church clothes from the early morning service she went to with Grandma Lenore. And Dad is in a navy suit because he's been at the office all morning. He always works at least one weekend day—he has for as long as I can remember. It sucks that he has to work so much, but this is actually an improvement because when I was really young, he used to go in both days. He had to in order to give himself a leg up as the only Black man working at the corporate firm. This vacation will be his first real one since Etta was born.

"Lenore, can we speak to you for a minute?" Mom asks, and her tone makes me look up and really take in their faces. Her brow is furrowed and her lips are pressed in so tight that they're nonexistent. And Dad looks tired because of course he does, but there's something else there. His jaw is jutted out, and his eyes are zeroed in on me.

What the hell? I just graduated! With honors! How am I in trouble already?

"We need to have a talk," Dad says, emphasizing those last two words in a way that's very familiar.

They don't just want to talk to me. They want to have a Talk. You know, like the Sex Talk, the Police Talk, and the Why We Can't Listen to "I Believe I Can Fly" Anymore Talk. Capital T.

"Sure," I say, looking over at Etta, expecting her to leave. But she spins the wheel again and moves her pink car along the board.

"I'm going to keep playing without Lenore then, because you guys told me that I only have to do this for an hour, and this counts."

I laugh, expecting Mom and Dad to join in, but they just look at me with their serious, scary faces. "Let's go into the living room," Mom says, leading the way.

When we sit down on the brown leather couches, Dad gets right to it. "We heard you talking to your grandmother yesterday at the party," he says, narrowing his eyes at me, as if I should know what this means.

I rack my brain. What did I tell Grandma Lenore? I don't think I outright admitted that New York terrifies me, but maybe I did? Is this, like, a *we told you so* thing? Both of them were against me going to college in New York. Mom actually lived there right after grad school, before she moved to LA, and she said I would hate the snow and the fast pace that's so different from California. And she was probably right. But eventually I won them over, especially once I leaned into what a prestigious school NYU is. But did they notice my stank face yesterday too?

"Is this because I made fun of her greens?" I say, trying to defuse the tension, distract. "You know I was just playing."

Instead of laughing, though, they look at each other, weary expressions taking up both of their faces.

Mom's fingers press together in a steeple. "It's about what you said, baby, about your major—the major *you* selected, for the record. You called it boring?"

"I believe you referred to it as a placeholder," Dad cuts in. "Until you figure out what you really want to do. Which was disconcerting because that's . . . breaking news to us."

"Oh!" I let out a small laugh of relief. This isn't as big of a deal as I thought. They just heard that I'm a little unsure about my major. "Well, yeah, that's true, but that's actually totally normal. I looked into it. You have to declare a major to apply—well, you don't *have* to, but it looks better on your applications. That's why I did it, to make sure I got in." I wait for them to nod their heads, to get that same proud look that filled me up when I first got the acceptance letter from NYU. To remember that their daughter knows what's up. But they still look stern as hell. I keep going, trying to sound light and confident. "But nothing is set in stone. You have until the end of sophomore year, really, to actually decide before it messes with your graduation timing or whatever. So I figure I have a little bit of time to try things out and take classes to figure out what I want to do. No big deal."

I put on my biggest smile, and fight the urge to do jazz hands after my little song and dance. Mom exhales and puts her face in her hands. Dad shakes his head as he studies the floor. They don't look like they would appreciate jazz hands.

"Lenore, baby," my mom says finally, but then she turns to my dad. They communicate something to each other with no words, just tight lips and eyebrows pressed together, something I guess you master after twenty-five years of marriage. Finally, they seem to come to a consensus, and they turn to me. I can read both of their faces immediately. Disappointed. And also, strangely . . . scared.

"Lenore, this has got to stop," Dad says, his voice stern. "The bouncing around. The indecision. Now that you're starting college, we need you to find some . . . focus."

"Wait, I'm confused," I say, searching their expressions for some sign that this is a joke. Why are they talking to me like this is some sort of intervention? Like I'm some kid on the Dr. Phil show desperately trying to spout out some catchphrase that'll get me a Sprite sponsorship or whatever. I had a 4.2! I'm not some meme-worthy mess!

"I think you know what we're taking about," Mom says, her brown eyes locking with mine. "You've never been able to settle on something for too long, and we . . . we *love* that about you! We love that you're talented at so many things. But we thought once you began your studies, that you could pick one path for yourself. It's hard to become an expert at anything when you move on so quickly."

She's right that I've been this way for most of my life. Just like Grandma Lenore mentioned yesterday—photography to watercolor to collages to whatever medium caught my attention next. I've always loved to explore and try new things. But I thought that was a good thing. Teachers at Chrysalis and all the way back to elementary school praised my ingenuity and creativity. College apps look for that, even—your hands in many pots, all the different ways you're a leader.

When did that change? You graduate and then *bam*, there's a shift, and a laser beam of attention on *only one thing* is all of a sudden the standard?

"You need to get serious. Life isn't fun and games anymore," Dad says. "Look at your brother. He hunkered down at UCLA and did what he needed to do. No messing around and trying to figure things out. He had focus."

60

The mention of Wally makes my whole body tense. They're always doing that, comparing the three of us, when we're nothing alike. And let's face it, next to them, I'll never measure up.

"That's not fair," I say, my voice sounding more whiny than I would like. "Wally is just doing what you did. That's the easy path."

Dad leans forward, elbows on knees, and points at me. "Now listen, nothing about Wally's path has been easy. Student government, internships every summer, a 173 on his LSAT. Your brother has worked for everything that he has. Hard work, sacrifice, and *focus*."

"Yeah, we all know how perfect Wally is. You don't have to remind me." I know I'm not helping my case with all the snark, but I can't help it. "You know what I mean, though. What Wally does, it's not creative. It's different for me. With art, I don't have to know right away what exactly I'm going to do."

This makes Dad stand up and start pacing, and Mom exhales all loudly again.

"Lenore, we've supported you wanting to be an artist," Dad says, and I hate how he says "artist," like it's "astronaut" or "zookeeper" or something. You know, like one of those precious but totally unrealistic future careers that kindergartners proudly claim.

But also, I can't be too mad because it's true. They have supported me 100 percent. They've paid for every day camp and after-school art class. Mom took me to Michaels every Saturday growing up and wouldn't say one word about buying the expensive acrylics. And my dad is the one who first heard about Chrysalis and said what a good opportunity it would be.

"We just think it's time to pick, Lenore. Narrow it down to what you're truly passionate about," Mom says. "I always thought it would be fashion, you know." She gestures to my outfit, a tiered lavender dress with bright red polka dots and a vintage (i.e., "borrowed" from Grandma Lenore) silk scarf tied around my neck. "And if that's what you want to do, we would be okay with that."

Dad stops pacing and gives her a look, but she shuts him down with her own.

"We would be okay with that," she repeats. "But you better work your butt off and be the best damn fashion designer there is out there."

I've taken a handful of design classes at Chrysalis, which got me unlimited access to the fabric closet so I could make whatever wild outfits popped into my head. Babydoll tops out of thrifted pillowcases. Floral-print wrap skirts. A baby-blue tulle ball gown that I still haven't found an occasion to wear yet. Making something beautiful from a sum of parts. I love it. But do I want to do that for the rest of my life? I don't know. How can I know?

I guess they can see that indecision written all over my face, because Mom's face shifts into a frown and Dad sits down on the ottoman, eye to eye with me.

"What I need you to understand, Lenore, is that we don't have the privilege to figure things out. To float around and see where things take us." His voice is low and steady. It hits me right in the chest. "It's not a fair race for us. We have to be better or we're behind, and part of that is being prepared and having a plan."

I don't need him to tell me who "we" is. Not just "we" as in our family, but the collective "we." All of a sudden, the severity of this hits me, and I feel ashamed for being surprised, for joking. Of course what they're saying makes sense. Of course they're worried.

"Black people don't get second chances in life," Mom says, sitting close to me and holding my hands in hers. "You know this, Lenore. And it's not right, and it shouldn't still be like that. But it's reality. So we gotta be ready on the first one. College is your first one, and we just don't want to see you waste it."

"You are too bright to waste it," Dad adds, putting his smooth palm to my cheek.

I can feel tears coming on, so I look past them out the window. The June Gloom is in full force; gray skies and dark clouds make it look like it's going to rain. It matches how I feel.

My parents have excelled so far beyond the barriers their own parents faced. None of my grandparents were able to go college, and my grandpa Wallace, who Wally is named after, had to leave school after eighth grade to work on his family's farm. But it was because of my grandparents' sacrifices that this was possible, like Grandpa John working double shifts as a janitor to save for Mom's college tuition or Dad's parents driving him two towns over to go to the best public high school. My parents, in turn, have sacrificed so much for Wally, Etta, and me. They have given us all their time and money so we could have the best futures possible, and because of that, they deserve excellence from us. We owe that to them. To be better than even they are.

But am I following through with my end of the deal? I got into a great college, yeah, but my plan is just to, what . . . wing it? Imagine if my parents had winged it. Where would our family be?

"I'm sorry," I say, and my mom's eyes soften.

"You don't need to be sorry, Lenore," she says. "We want what's best for you because we love you. We want you to know where you're going, so you don't miss this opportunity that's ahead of you."

"You need to be sure," Dad says.

"I will."

Dad looks me right in the eye, and it's hard not to look away. I feel like his sharp eyes are cutting right through me.

"By the time we get back from the trip," he says, "we want to know what your plan is—a major you'll *commit* to, what career you're working toward, everything."

"Okay."

We hug, and they tell me they love me and they're proud of me. But it doesn't cut through all the noise in my brain, not like their other words do.

When I get back to my room, Etta is there waiting for me.

They won't have to have this talk with Etta at graduation, that's for sure.

"Okay, the game's over. I kept playing for you, so we wouldn't waste time," she says. "You're a single mom of two sets of twins, you lived on a houseboat, and you died owing all your money to Countryside Acres retirement home. So, you lost."

Isn't that appropriate?

"Can you clean up? Because my time is up and I have some reading I need to complete by tonight." She taps her watch and stands up, leaving a mess of cards and pegs around her. "That was fun. Bye."

She walks out without even looking up, and I'm left alone with my thoughts.

CHAPTER FIVE

So here's a recap in case you're keeping track at home. Your girl Lenore is:

1) Doomed to be alone forever because, as my history clearly demonstrates, I can't seem to get a guy to stick around. Even when I keep things no-strings, more-benefits-than-friends casual AF. Even that isn't enough to entice someone to want to be with me.

2) Now painfully aware, thanks to my parents laying it out for me in no uncertain terms, that I am not, in fact, my ancestors' wildest dreams. No, I am possibly their worst, indecisive, privileged, flighty nightmare. And unless I can get my act together and figure out what I want to do with my whole damn life by the end of this trip, I'm going to be my parents' worst disappointment. 4.2 GPA be damned!

3) Currently confined on a plane, nonstop
to Rome, to be further confined on a cruise ship
with my two perfect siblings and those previously
mentioned parents who think I'm a mess—oh, and did
I mention they want me to figure out my whole life
by the end of this twelve-day cruise?!

My finger hovers above the send button. I mean, this is why I splurged for the Wi-Fi on the plane. Tessa went up to Northern California to visit her friend after graduation, and Theo was busy with family stuff, so I didn't get to see them yesterday night. And this morning was fully on some *Home Alone* shit— missed alarms, running and hollering—so I didn't even get a chance to FaceTime them to say goodbye. But I don't know . . . can I really unload on them like this?

I know Tessa and Theo would support me. Or at least, I hope they would. But this is a lot. And it's not what they usually get from me. I'm over the top, yeah, but I keep it steady, light. Easy. I'm the one to listen to problems and offer advice, not the one to share my own.

I scroll through what I wrote, highlighting the message with my thumb, and then hit cut. Let's try this again.

Hello from some indeterminate but fabulous location
above the Atlantic Ocean! Your girl Lenore is about
to have the best time ever gallivanting across the
Mediterranean. Will I eat my weight in gelato? Will

I run into the Kardashian-Jenners? (That fancy rich people beach is in Italy, right?) Will I re-create one of the epic dance scenes from Mamma Mia?! Will I fall down a flight of white stairs into the unnaturally blue ocean? Stay tuned!

I hit send before I can think about it too much.

"Hey, is your screen working?" Wally says, leaning into my already very small area and tapping the video screen in front of me. It comes to life, blinding me in the dark cabin.

"Why even ask?" I roll my eyes at him.

"Can we switch? Mine keeps freezing, and you're not even watching it," he says, gesturing to my phone. He unbuckles himself and stands up, not even waiting for my response. I wish again for the billionth time this flight that I had decided to sit with Mom and Dad across the aisle. Etta's position, sandwiched between them with her pink cat headphones, doesn't look so bad, when faced with Wally's incessant knee-jiggling, openmouthed pretzel eating, and now kicking me out of my seat, apparently.

"No," I say, returning my attention to my phone. I can see the three little dots, letting me know that Tessa is typing. But Wally moves even more into my space, nudging my knee.

"C'mon, Lenore, you bought the Wi-Fi! You can watch something on there. I cannot go the whole flight like this."

"Not my problem."

"Okay," he says, narrowing his eyes at me and sitting down. "I guess I have nothing else to do for these next nine hours but eat. Good thing the flight attendant gave me extra pretzels."

He grabs a bag from a disturbingly large stash in the seat pocket in front of him, tears it open, and then throws a handful into his mouth, taking slow, exaggerated bites.

"Whatever. You do you." I turn my body away from him. But he just moves in closer, sloshing his tongue around, smacking his lips. All it takes is for one crumb to fall on my shoulder before I jump up into the aisle.

"Fine, Wally! Ugh!" I scream. Mom and Dad turn toward us, and Dad raises one thick eyebrow. A question, but also a directive. Bennetts do not make scenes, especially when we're surrounded by a whole bunch of white people, like we are right now.

"Fine," I repeat, standing up. "Take it."

"Thank you," Wally coos, giving me a fake-ass smile as he slides over into my seat and starts scrolling through the movies. I move over him, making sure to step on both of his feet, and plop myself down into his middle seat. The old guy on my other side is snoring loudly, not even enjoying the window seat he's taking up.

I check my phone again and Tessa's dots have disappeared. She's probably busy with her other friend. They've known each other since they were toddlers or some shit, so it makes sense that this girl takes priority. I'm about to give up and zone out to my favorite Jamila Woods album when a bright light in the dark cabin catches my attention. It's Wally's phone in the mesh seat pocket, a text lighting up his screen.

I grab the phone and wave it in his face. "Looks like I'm not the only one who bought the Wi—" But the words get stuck in my throat when I see what the text says.

Please, Wally, just talk to me

It's from Kieran. And another message quickly appears on top of it:

I don't understand what happened

"What the fuck, Lenore," Wally whispers, ripping it from my hand. "Reading my texts? Really?"

"I didn't mean—" I start, but he's already jumping out of his seat. He throws me a death glare and then storms off to the bathroom, the phone clutched tight in his hand. Across the aisle, Mom looks worried and Dad gives me another meaningful eyebrow arch. I throw my hands up in response. It's not my fault Wally is making a scene.

This doesn't make any sense. Wally and Kieran have always been such good communicators. Like, I'm talking weekly feelings check-ins (that I accidentally walked in on once and roasted Wally about for months) and listening to Esther Perel's depressing marriage podcast for fun. That good. It's one of the reasons I thought they would last forever, because they seemed so mature, so in tune with each other. Starting their relationship in high school seemed like a blink in their long, long future together. And I was, low-key, always a little jealous that they found each other so early in life, that they could be settled and out of this garbage fire that is dating before they even hit their twenties. So I don't understand what could have led to them just being . . . over. And it seems like Kieran may be on the same page as me.

I consider texting him myself to get the scoop. I mean, it's not like he's a stranger. He spent Thanksgiving *and* Christmas with us last year! But that may just make things worse with Wally if he finds out. Better to slowly get it out of him.

I unlock my phone to see if their Facebooks give anything away (because they are actually on Facebook like dinosaurs), but I'm distracted by my messages. Tessa has responded. So I guess she wasn't too busy with what's-her-name.

Tessa: Oh girl, if anyone deserves this adventure, it's you! Please post lots of pics because Roseville is significantly less glamorous and I'm gonna be living through you.

Tessa: I wish you had taken that Tembi Locke book I tried to give you. From Scratch! It's set in places you're going. I checked!

I roll my eyes, not wanting to get into this "romantic research" thing she apparently still hasn't let go. Didn't she get the hint after what happened at prom that I am *so* not into this? But I guess maybe I am sending mixed signals, laughing it off and pretending like nothing's wrong. Would she lay off me already if I was honest and told her that I'm pretty certain I'm meant to be alone forever because I'm never going to be any guy's first choice?

Luckily, Theo chimes in, saving me from doing something cringe-y like baring my soul.

Theo: Isn't that book about her husband dying? I'm pretty sure my mom read it a couple years back because it was a Reese's Book Club pick. I only remember because she was crying so much after and made my dad go to the doctor.

Tessa: I marked the happy parts with post-its!!!!

Lenore: Your mom's a Reese stan?

Theo: Who isn't a Reese stan? She is universally appealing

Tessa: There are a lot of happy parts!! You can probably download an e-book. How many hours do you have left in your flight?

Lenore: She does have playing the epitome of privileged white lady DOWN. I think she must actually be really cool right?

Theo: Definitely. I think her work is intentionally subversive.

Tessa: Why is everyone ignoring me???????????

Theo: Because you're harping on the same note and not taking a hint

Lenore: Yeah, I love you but can you just give it a rest for now

Lenore: I don't want to talk about it

Tessa: Fine

Theo: By the way, Lavon and I went to the open mic at Viento y Agua last night, and it wasn't terrible.

Lenore: That's a ringing endorsement!

Tessa: I just want to tell you one more thing, and then I promise I'll let it go. You need to go to the Trevi Fountain and throw two coins in. If you do, you'll fall in love by the end of your trip. There are like loads of examples.

Theo: TESSA!

Lenore: 🗿

Tessa: I'm done. I'M DONE! Promise.

Lenore: Jesus christ I hope so

Theo: Do you feel proud of yourself?

Tessa: And throw the coins separately! Not at the same time

Tessa: Okay, I'm really done now

Theo: ANYWAY what I was trying to say was, at the open mic, we saw this guy. I think his name was Trainor? He had Frank Ocean performing "Moon River" vibes.

Theo: And he's going to be playing Buskerfest Labor Day weekend. We should all go! Lenore will you still be here then?

Lenore: I'm not sure. I have to look it up.

I know I won't be; I'm moving at the end of August to get all set up in the dorms before orientation. But I don't have the heart to tell them that yet. It makes it feel final. The life they're all going to have together after I'm gone.

Tessa: I hope you will be. And when you think about
it, Labor Day isn't even that far away. Like, weeks! 😰
This can be our last hurrah!

"Last" for me only. Because I am the one's who's leaving.
Very soon.

To study something that I haven't figured out yet.

To prepare for a future that's a blank, scary canvas in my
mind.

The prospect of trying to figure this all out by the time
our ship docks in Barcelona at the end of this trip feels so overwhelming and impossible. Dread sits on my chest, making it
tight and heavy like I'm locked into one of my aunt Stacy's
death-grip hugs.

Lord, maybe Tessa is onto something. Out of all the shit on
my plate, all the items on the long list of things wrong with me,
maybe it would be easier to focus on this romance bit. Well,
maybe not easy, because I definitely pissed off an old crone at
some point in my life and am cursed to only be a guy's stepping stone on their way to something serious. But a swoony,
no-strings-attached fling with a mysterious foreigner would be
a nice distraction from trying to figure out my whole damn
life these next couple weeks, at least. Tessa seems to think it's as
easy as throwing some change in a fountain and making a wish.
I could do that.

Lenore: Okay, I know I'm going to regret this, but
this Tembi chick did the coin thing? And then met an
Italian bb? Explain.

Theo: Why are you encouraging her???

Tessa: I JUST SCREAMED

Tessa: AND HIGH KICKED

Tessa: MY DREAMS ARE COMING TRUE

I'm outside in Rome for approximately two seconds before I am completely certain that Tessa has no idea what she's talking about

Rome is hot. Oppressively hot. Satan's-morning-breath hot.

And I'm convinced all the romanticization of this place that Tessa has obviously fallen prey to is a conspiracy to sell pink paperback books to impressionable young girls, because ain't nobody falling in love in this heat. Nope.

My under-boob sweat is significant. My shorts are out here trying to strangle my thighs, squeezing out a steady flow of sweat down my legs and into my gold gladiator sandals. And I'm estimating that I have a very short period of time before the two sweat sources combine and flood the cobblestone streets, giving Rome canals to rival Venice.

I want—no, I *need*—air-conditioning. Immediately. And it's barely even eight a.m.

"Okay, so we will begin the day at St. Peter's Basilica," Etta says, holding up a map that's almost as tall as her. "I've signed us up for a free tour, and it's in English—I've already confirmed. After that we're going to go to the Colosseum and the Roman Forum, which I know is a little bizarre, as we're not viewing them in chronological order, but from my research, I think the lines will be better this way. After that, we can take a quick lunch break, and if time permits, visit the Palatino before—"

"Hold up," I say, interrupting her. "You're talking about *just* today?"

"Correct." Etta blinks at me and continues to recite her memorized itinerary while I zone out.

Our ship boards tomorrow at the port in Civitavecchia, meaning we only have one day to explore Rome. So, I thought we would pick a couple sights, maybe stop for some cacio e pepe and definitely a few rounds of gelato. Not traverse the entire city! But of course Etta always has to make everything an extra, endurance-testing learning experience.

Luckily, though, Mom steps in and takes my side instead of marveling at her genius child. "This all sounds really enjoyable, baby," she says, squeezing Etta's shoulders. "But I would be just as happy to walk around and take it all in. I think all of us would, especially with the jet lag. Maybe you can narrow down your list, help us make a compromise?"

"Perhaps," Etta huffs.

"Perhaps you better," I say.

She shakes her head at us, no doubt lamenting what unrefined plebeians she has to put up with, and then buries her face back in her map.

"Thank you," Mom says with a smile. She grabs Dad's hand and leans into him, her eyes wide and dreamy as she looks around. "It's so beautiful, isn't it? I was worried it wouldn't live up to my expectations, after imagining being here for so long.

But this place really is special."

It was Mom's idea to take this trip. She has never been to Europe before—none of us have. But Grandma Lenore told me that when Mom was little, she used to cover her walls with pictures torn out of *Sunset* magazine and maps and old posters that their travel agent neighbor would give her. She talked and talked about all the places she would go. Of course, Grandma and Grandpa couldn't afford all that when Mom was young, and then there was college and grad school and a mortgage and some kids. But somehow, even with all their bills and impending college tuition, Mom and Dad made this trip happen. And this cruise around the Mediterranean makes it so Mom can see the countries she's always dreamed about. She probably would have been content backpacking or hopping cheap trains from country to country, but Dad wouldn't play with that. He won't even let us go camping, because like he'll tell you when he goes on one of his rants, "Why am I going to sleep in the dirt and call it vacation?" And honestly, I agree.

Looking at Mom now, I can almost see that little girl looking out into the big world. I hold up my camera that's hanging around my neck and snap a quick picture of her. The loud flash makes her jump, but then she winks at me.

"I've always loved seeing you with that camera," she says, and it makes me feel warm inside. But then Dad nods at it and says, "That could be a good major, huh? And it's practical. You could do weddings and family photos on the weekend, to have a steady income."

And then the warm feeling is gone.

"Sure," I say. I nudge Etta's shoulder. "You ready yet?" She peeks over the map at me to roll her eyes. "And where's Wally?" I ask, turning Mom and Dad. He didn't meet us in the lobby for the breakfast buffet, but I thought he would turn up by now.

"Oh, he's not coming," Mom says, the smile on her face a little strained.

"What?" I ask, immediately irritated.

"He says he's jet-lagged and was up all night," Mom explains. "Told us to go on without him."

"He needs to drink some coffee or something, then!" I say. "This is our only day in Rome, and he's going to spend it lying around! That's stupid."

"Cut him some slack," Dad says. "He's had a difficult year. It's not easy managing your senior year of college, all while studying for the LSAT and completing three separate internships. Your brother has earned the right to be tired."

"Yeah, whatever."

I think that's a stupid reason to miss a once-in-a-lifetime trip that my parents paid basically a million dollars for, but I don't want to push it in case Dad steers the conversation back to my academics. Maybe Wally's talking to Kieran, working all this out.

And hey, I'm in Rome! This is probably the most exciting trip I'll ever go on, and I refuse to let Wally's annoying attitude ruin it for me.

But approximately thirty-seven hours later (really more

like six, but it just feels like it), I'm a little less excited. We've tweaked our necks staring at the ceiling of St. Peter's Basilica, fought through crowds in the burning-hot sun at the Colosseum, and successfully talked Dad out of buying us all matching "Rome took a pizza my heart" T-shirts. And now I'm about ready to collapse on the Spanish Steps with hazelnut gelato on an IV drip. But I don't even think I could make it up them because my heels are bloody thanks to these stupid, beautiful gladiator sandals I wore due to my weakness for themes. And my ankles are swollen because cobblestone streets are charming as fuck but I can't see what their actual purpose is, outside of causing me to roll my ankles.

I'm done.

I'm grateful!

(Unlike Wally!!!)

But I'm done.

Luckily, the last stop of Etta's condensed, but still way too long, itinerary is the Trevi Fountain. I thought we got here earlier, but it was some other fancy fountain. There are a lot of fancy fountains in Rome.

Less lucky, however, is that this place is super crowded, like everywhere else we've been today. I can barely move without catching someone's selfie stick to the shoulder or grazing someone else's disgusting sweaty limbs.

How am I ever going to get close enough to seal my romantic future with a coin toss and/or just throw Tessa a bone?

"Oh, we have to take a picture here. I need a new profile

pic!" Dad says, pulling out his phone. "You scout a spot, Lenore. You're our expert photographer."

I fight the urge to roll my eyes at that, and I do what he says, searching for an opening closer to the fountain so you can see that instead of a sea of cargo shorts and Skechers. But instead of a photo spot, my eyes zero in on a boy.

He stands out. First, because there aren't a lot of Black people around here (my dad's only given The Nod once today to another family waiting in line to buy water outside the Colosseum). But also because he's gorgeous. Like so gorgeous that my heart skips a beat. Or at least it would if my body did corny shit like that.

He has high cheekbones, and thick tortoiseshell sunglasses sit on top of his wide nose. His skin is coffee with a dash of cream. And his hair is cut close on the sides, with a jet-black cloud of curls on top, falling into his eyes. He has on tight cut-off shorts, a black button-up with a pattern of silhouettes, and white Jack Purcells.

If I believed in romance like Tessa, he would be my leading man. No question.

"Now, how do I turn this off again?" Dad says, and when I turn around, I'm blinded. The flashlight on his phone is somehow always turned on, except when he actually needs a flashlight.

"Oh, I'll fix it," Mom says, grabbing it from him. "Honestly, Ed, you're such an old man sometimes."

I turn back to look for my dream guy, but he's gone. Of course he's gone. So much for that.

In his place is a woman loudly directing a photo shoot of her family in front of the fountain. "No, not that face! Make your cute face, Rebecca! Ha-ha-ha-ha! Laugh! Do a fake laugh!" She crouches down, wiping the sweat under her wraparound sunglasses with the back of her hand. "That is not the cute face!"

She has Big Karen Energy, like she has all the world's managers on speed dial. And all of her family are wearing bright orange shirts that read "The Arnold Family Italian Adventure." All of them—her husband, two sons, Rebecca with the not-cute face, and Grandma, who's looking like she's on the verge of heatstroke. Bright orange, I guess, in case they lose each other? But Karen's not letting any of those kids get lost, as much as they may want to.

"See, we need to get shirts like that!" Dad says, pointing at them. "To commemorate this trip!"

"Negative," Etta says.

"What you talking about, negative?" Dad says. "They're cool!"

"Okay, bye, I'm going to get closer to the fountain." I fight my way to the front of the crowd, inhaling an unpleasant mix of sunscreen and BO as I maneuver between people. I only get one "Hey!" but I avoid eye contact, and soon I'm standing right on the edge. The water is a bright turquoise, like the water at Disneyland, and there are tall white columns, and statues of people that Etta explained in detail but I forgot, hanging out on top of some rocks. It's pretty, I guess. But it doesn't look magical. I wonder how this coin thing started in the first place. Like, is the Trevi family out here every night collecting a fortune and laughing at all the gullible tourists?

I take a picture to send to Tessa. But then I realize it won't go through, because my parents gave me a firm "absolutely not" when I asked for the ten-dollar international day pass from our phone provider, insisting I needed to focus on my big decision. I take another one with my camera, leaning in close to capture all the change under the water.

Well, I guess I better get this over with. I dig in my purse for a euro, but someone bumps into me, knocking my arm.

"Excuse me."

"Yeah, no problem," I grunt, but when I look up, the Italian guy who just invaded my personal space isn't looking at me. He's looking at the skinny blond girl standing next to me, who was sitting on the edge of the fountain while her girl took approximately ten million pics of her staring off into the distance.

"Excuse me, bella, you dropped your cell phone!"

"Oh my god, thank you! Thank you!" she says, clutching her hands to her chest. "I didn't even notice. Oh my god!"

"It's no problem," he says, looking down at the phone like he's considering something suddenly, but I recognize the game. "Maybe you would like me to put my number in before I return it to you? I can show you and your friends around the Eternal City."

Oh lord. So it really does happen. These white girls just be walking around, being clumsy and irresponsible, and then, oops, they're suddenly racing around Rome on the back of their new boyfriend Lorenzo's moped.

Damn.

I return to the task at hand. Throwing my money away for a chance at what that lady just got, no biggie, free of charge. Right. I finally find a euro and toss it into the fountain. And then I just stand there. That wasn't it, was it? Was there something else I was supposed to do, like a chant or something?

Oh, wait! I was supposed to throw two coins. Tessa was very clear about that.

I dig around in my purse some more, but I don't have any more coins, only paper bills. I used the last of my euros on a glass-bottle Coke while I waited for Etta to finish asking our tour guide follow-up questions at St. Peter's.

Of course. Isn't that just like me. Unprepared, like my parents think. Too much and not enough at the same time.

And, goddamnit, one coin means I'm going to return to Rome!

But I don't want to return to Rome!

Not to be all ungrateful and irritating like Wally, but you know, as my thigh sweat gets dangerously close to soaking clear through these shorts, I can only think about going somewhere cold. Like Antarctica. Or my godmama Arlene's refrigerator. I'm not bougie.

"Oh honey, you're only going to throw one?" I turn and Karen is standing next to me, her bright orange squad nowhere in sight.

"I'm out of money." I shrug, turning to leave, but she makes this little squeak noise.

"Oh, no, no, no. We can't have that!" She starts digging around in the bag strapped tightly across her chest, and I throw my hands up in protest.

"No, it's okay. Really." The absolute last thing I want in the universe is charity from this lady.

But she presses a shiny quarter into my hand before I can get away.

"I can't watch you waste this opportunity. You're young, you're beautiful! Do it before you're tethered forever to a man who doesn't pick up his dirty socks and spends his evenings playing *Call of Duty*."

"Um . . . okay."

While she watches eagerly, I throw the second coin into the fountain.

"Now there you go! It's settled, honey. Oh, Italy is the perfect place to fall in love."

CHAPTER SIX

I had no intention of ending up at the *Mediterranean Majesty*'s teen mixer on our first night on the ship, but somehow, that's where I am.

Earlier today, when we were on hour two of waiting for our group number to be called to board, a white man with dreadlocks made his way over to our family, and I swear I saw him take us all in and come up with a game plan. He leaned back a little more and started to walk with a hitch in his step. Because of course.

"Yo, Bennett family! My name is Chad, and I'm the director of teen events. I've got a flyer here with some dope activities we got going on the ship these next twelve days."

I didn't respond because I was too busy throwing up a little bit in my mouth, but Mom takes the flyer, further encouraging him.

"It all starts tonight at the teen mixer. You're still a little too young, little mama," he said, pointing to Etta. "But this'll be the perfect way for big bro and big sis here to start the party. Responsibly, of course. It's gonna be lit!"

"That sounds like fun!" Mom said, looking alarmingly sincere, but as soon as Chad made his way to the next family, Wally and I burst out laughing.

"I would rather swim along the cruise ship to our next destination," he said.

"I would rather wear those matching purple Sail Away shirts that Dad tried to buy earlier."

"Hey!" Dad shouts. "He said he would add our names on the back for free! That's a deal!"

"I can't believe his name is Chad," Wally continued.

"Of course his name is Chad. That guy could only be born a Chad."

"Be nice," Mom said, swatting me half-heartedly.

"Be nice?" I laughed. "That guy burped up the entire Urban Dictionary on us."

"We are not getting lit with Chad, Mom," Wally chimed in. "*Nobody* should be letting their impressionable young teens get lit with Chad, all right?"

For the first time on this trip—hell, for the first time in a while—Wally and I were getting along. Laughing like we used to. On the same side. It made me hopeful for the rest of our time here, for the future once we've returned home.

But that hope was short-lived. Because once we finally got on the ship, stood in *another* line to get on one of the ten elevators, and walked down the navy crown-patterned carpet to our room, Wally was back on his bullshit.

"I have to share this tiny room with you?"

"Hey!" I said, but I was thinking the same thing. The room was tiny, basically the size of Mom and Dad's closet at home. I'm pretty sure I could reach the tiny bathroom sink from my tiny bed. Oh, and there were no windows, let alone a veranda, like the room we dropped Mom, Dad, and Etta off at on the way here. Here I was thinking their room was pretty small, but I would swap with them in a second.

"Well, do you want to watch something?" I flicked on the TV, but every channel was playing a safety demonstration. "Or we could go walk around, find something to do. Our bags aren't supposed to get here until later."

"Nah, I'm going to sleep until the stupid Sail Away dinner." He turned off the TV with the remote, and then turned off the light.

"Are you kidding me?"

"It's not my job to entertain you, Lenore. We may be sharing a room, but you're on your own for this trip. I'm going to be busy."

I huffed, trying to think of my response, something to hurt his feelings as much as he'd just hurt mine. But with the lights off, I could feel the boat rocking, and a wave of nausea hit me.

"Okay, well, I'm leaving," I said, standing up.

He didn't even open his eyes. "Bye."

And that's why I'm sitting alone at the teen mixer. To my

credit, I tried to find the brunch buffet, but I got lost on this big-ass ship. And when Chad found me wandering the fifth floor, between an intense senior bingo game and a divorcée speed-dating session, I didn't really have much of an excuse to say no.

"Are y'all ready to get this party started?" Chad calls from the front of the room, pumping his first in the air. There are a few half-hearted cheers, which seem to lift Chad's spirit. "That's what I'm talking about! Welcome to the Teen Club, your own personal escape from the parentals, where you can chill and be yourselves without anyone harshing your vibe. I'm sure I'll be seeing a lot of y'all during this voyage. Am I right?" Crickets. "Okay, all right, I see we've got some shy ones here. Well, I've got some jams to help you loosen up. Let's rock and roll!"

Chad tucks his C-curved frame over a set of turntables and starts playing an old Justin Bieber song. And I feel sick. But it's not just the sight of his limp, frizzy dreads bouncing in time to the music. No, the nausea that started in the room is even worse now that the ship has pulled from the port on its way to our first destination, Sicily. My head feels like it's swimming and my bubble guts feel like they're going to bubble right on up out of my mouth if I'm not careful. And like, I knew that we were going to be on a ship for almost two weeks. But I don't think I ever really thought about what that actually means. I hope I'm just adjusting and I'm not going to feel this way the whole time.

"Yo, turn this shit off!" someone shouts from the other side of the room, followed by an uproar of laughter. But Chad just points at them and smiles, transitioning to Ariana Grande while he flips on a set of rainbow lights.

I take a sip of my ginger ale and look around the room, assessing my fellow teens who I will be forced to interact with for the next hour or so until dinner—because I sure as hell am never coming back here again. I don't know what kind of crowd I was expecting exactly, but this looks about white.

There's a group of alabaster bros in pastel polos and khaki shorts in the corner, congregated around the air hockey machine. That's where the shout came from. I will definitely not be heading in that direction. Some more girls huddle nearby, sending the boys looks over their shoulders, in between intense-looking whisper huddles. And another crowd is sitting in front of an old *Riverdale* episode on the couches in front of a massive flat-screen TV. Exactly no one is dancing to Chad's booming music.

Just like I usually do when I enter a new space, I count the people of color. It's something that I do almost without thinking, calculating how much of a minority I am in any given situation—probably a habit left over from my summers spent being the only Black girl at bougie arts day camps. There are three East Asian kids, going to town on at the nacho buffet that's set up, and a couple Latinx girls, flipping through magazines and looking bored on one of the couches. No one else is Black in the room, which I can handle, but it's never a great feeling.

I know I should be social. Walk over and say what's up to

someone. Maybe make an acquaintance I could hang out with since Wally's committed to being a dick. But number one, I'm barely holding this possible puke situation down, and number two, I don't have the energy to put on that front right now.

If you asked anyone who's met me, they would say I'm an extrovert. But that's not my natural state. It's something I have to do intentionally—talking and laughing and being loud and cracking jokes—until I feel like my teeth and cheeks are buzzing and I need to rest and recover. It's all performative. It takes a lot of work.

I can remember the first time I made a conscious decision to make people like me. It was fourth grade, and even though the gifted and talented class starts in third, I was just beginning then. My mom didn't agree with the previous years' results, something about bias in the assessment. So she made them retest me, and look at that, apparently I should have been there all along. Except the kids in the class didn't accept me as easily—and it didn't help that their moms were whispering, too, about my mom going up to the school and "making a scene." No one wanted to talk to me in class or play with me at recess, it was a whole thing.

So, I decided to fix it. I told loud jokes that kept the whole lunchroom laughing. I memorized something unique about everyone and was always ready with a tailored, heartfelt compliment. I made everyone feel special. I wore outrageous outfits that made Ms. Chang, our teacher, smile as soon as I strutted into the classroom. I was goofy and social and charming.

I put on a show to make them like me. I was relentless until it worked.

Because, see, it's a little hard to hate someone who's making you laugh and making you feel good about yourself. If people love being around you, they stop worrying about whether you deserve to be there in the first place. And *listen*, I know I deserve to be in whatever room I decide to enter—my parents raised me that way, my mom told me that when I got added to that special class. But sometimes it's easier to just not fight, to pretend like the bullshit isn't there. If I'm bright and happy and hilarious, I can convince myself that people would be down with me regardless.

And I guess—no, I'll be real. I *know* this has trickled down into my relationships with my best friends. I know Theo and Tessa would accept me either way, or at least I hope they would. But also, I like knowing that I give them something they need. That I play a role in their lives.

It's not that it's not me. It is. But it's only part of me. And it's exhausting to keep it up sometimes. But I'd rather be exhausted than show the other parts that are there too: depressed and pissed off and self-conscious. Those parts would just send people running.

Of course, those parts are the ones bubbling up right now, along with my bubble guts, when I desperately need the other smiley, confident part of me. Because that's the only part of me that belongs at a goddamn teen mixer.

Yeah, I feel like I'm about to reenact a scene from *The*

Exorcist any moment now, but where else can I go? I'm not about to go hang out in Mom and Dad's room and have more talks about my future. And I'm pretty sure if I tried to sneak out the exit anyway, Chad would call me out on his stupid microphone, and I cannot handle that level of cringe right now.

"Whoa, how do you get your hair like that? I love it."

I turn, and one of the air-hockey-watching girls is now standing inches away. She has brown, wavy hair, tan skin that was clearly tanned explicitly for this trip, and a white babydoll dress. I'm worried she's going to reach out and tug one of my locs, but to my surprise, she has more home training than that.

"Hi, I'm Joelle. You should come hang with me and my cousins." I'm thinking I must be giving off better vibes than I thought, but then she reaches behind me to grab a Diet Coke from the cooler and I realize I'm just blocking the drinks.

I take a deep breath as another wave of nausea passes, and then get my face on. "Hi! I'm Lenore! Where are you from?"

"Bloomfield Hills, Michigan! What about you?"

"Long Beach. It's like right outside of LA."

"Long Beach!" she calls back, doing a Snoop Dogg impersonation, and my whole body tenses trying to keep my eyeballs that are desperate to roll in check. I mean, she could *at least* try to be original.

"Ha-ha, yeah. . . ."

"So, have you been to the gym yet? There are only five Pelotons! Five! For a ship this big . . ."

She begins to go on about the gym's entire equipment

inventory, which she's somehow had a chance to assess after only, like, an hour on the ship. And I listen and smile encouragingly, throwing in an "Oh girl, really" when it's appropriate, as it becomes increasingly clear that this girl's only discernible character traits are vocal fry and a love for exercise.

When she finally leaves, after giving me her room number to link up, I've firmly decided to go. The way things are headed, I am definitely going to blow chunks on someone's checkered Vans slides, and I just don't have the mental capacity to deal with that right now.

But then, something—or *someone*—catches my eye from across the room.

No. No, it can't be.

But . . . yes! It's him. The boy—the *beautiful* boy—from the Trevi Fountain. Walking into the *Mediterranean Majesty*'s teen mixer. For real.

How?

Why?

And even more pressing, what the fuck? Is this a nausea-induced mirage?

I blink a few times, but he's still there. Light brown skin contrasted with a bright white tee. He runs his hands through his curls and purses his full lips as he looks around the room from the doorway.

Damn, this coin shit really worked? I probably shouldn't tell Tessa or else her head will blow up like a balloon and float above me forever, making that smug smirk I hate. Except I actually want to kiss her smug smirk right now because this worked! It really worked!

Of course, it's probably not the best time to be seeing him when I look like a sweaty, sick mess. Unless he's got a thing for Gamora, I'll probably have a better chance if I sneak out now and hunt him down later when I've gotten myself together.

As if he can hear my thoughts, though, he stops scanning the room and his eyes land on me. Before I can even look away to pretend like I wasn't just gawking at him, he starts striding toward me with purpose.

My body shakes and then tenses. This is happening.

"Hey, I'm Alex," he says, holding out his hand. Up close, he has one of those faces that make people ask, "Where are you from?" Which I never would because I'm not an asshole.

"Hi. Lenore," I say, trying to sound all cool. But that's shot when I put my clammy-ass hand in his. Luckily, he doesn't wipe his hand against his jeans when it returns to his side because then I would have to just keel over and die.

"Okay, I know this is kind of crazy," he starts, and I feel my chest get all fluttery and shit. Is this really happening?

"Oh yeah? Well, I can be down with crazy."

He laughs, but he's not looking at me. His eyes are fixed on something across the room.

"Ha! That's good." His dark brown eyes return to mine, and I swear I'm about to start writing sonnets or something equally stupid about the color brown. I want to start searching for flecks of amber or obsidian to obsess about like every girl in those pink paperbacks. "'Cause, well, you see, my ex-girlfriend is on this cruise, too. She's actually across the room right over there. It's a long story, but our parents—they're friends, and they booked this trip together? But then we broke up, and it was after the no-return window. So we all had to come on this trip anyway. And I want her to see that I've moved on. Because I have! So, could you pretend that we're, you know, hanging out? Just for a little bit. Just to make her see that I'm definitely over her."

He takes a deep breath, obviously relieved to get that off his chest. And there's some embarrassment, too, in his expression, but mostly he looks hopeful. That I'll go along with this plan to make his ex-girlfriend jealous.

I feel like I've been punched in the stomach. I let myself think, even for a fleeting second, that this was finally my love story, that everything would happen for me just like it happens in all these ridiculous stories. I let myself believe in Tessa's bullshit. Even though I know better!

But again, I'm not the prize. I'm just a pawn, a stepping-stone to another relationship with another girl. Like I was with Jay and Marcus.

I get another rush of nausea, and something hot and bitter burns the back of my throat. I need to get out of here before I make this even worse by adding vomit to the equation.

"Nah, fuck that," I say, pushing past him and stomping out of the room.

CHAPTER SEVEN

"Why do you look like you're plotting someone's death?" Etta asks, wrinkling her nose.

We're in the elevator on our way to the big Sail Away dinner, and I'm still fuming. If this was one of Tessa's stories, what Alex did would be an exciting and promising beginning. If this was one of Tessa's stories, we'd fake date to make his ex-girlfriend jealous before realizing that it's not fake at all and fall in love and return to this same ship someday to get married and then have beautiful little brown-skinned babies who vacation in Italy every summer.

But it's not one of Tessa's stories, and instead, I'm just pissed. And nauseous.

"I'm fine," I say, a lot sharper than I intend. The lady in a hot-pink track suit standing in the corner, who threw her arm in to stop the elevator, looks like she may be regretting that choice right about now.

"Better not be anybody in this family plotting someone's death," Dad says.

"Actually," Etta says, "this would be the best place to plot and then carry out someone's death. It would be much easier to get away with it, as prosecution would be tricky in international waters and you could always throw someone overboard and make it look like an accident. I was reading that twenty-two percent—"

"Etta." Mom clamps her fingers together tightly, the universal motion for "shut your mouth."

Wally laughs, though he doesn't look up from his phone, and the hot-pink-track-suit lady stares at us with wide eyes, as if she's memorizing all of our faces for when the cruise police come asking questions later.

"I'm not going to kill anybody," I say again, but even I have to admit that I don't sound very convincing.

The elevator doors open, and we head to the Crown Room. Hot-pink-track-suit lady goes speed-walking in the opposite direction, but maybe she's in one of the other five dining rooms.

The Crown Room has shiny wood floors, with golden suns inlaid into them. There are at least fifty large cream tables circling the space, with navy velvet high-backed chairs, surrounding a black-and-white marble-tiled dance floor at the center of the room. The ceiling is painted dark, almost black, with swirls of stars and crowns creating their own constellations. And hanging down from the ceiling are giant chandeliers, casting the whole room in a warm, dreamy light. I expected this all to be kinda cheesy, but even I have to admit that this is pretty cool.

Mom stares up at the ceiling, a small smile on her face, and I find my fingers itching for my camera, but I left it in the room. I wonder for the hundredth time since we've walked onto the boat, how is this all on one ship? It all feels too big, too over the top to be floating in the middle of the Mediterranean Sea. But my rocking stomach reminds me that we definitely are. I say a little prayer again that this won't last past tonight. That I'll wake up tomorrow, miraculously adjusted—and if not, at least we can get off the ship for the day and explore the steady ground of Sicily.

"Welcome! How can I help you?" the hostess asks, her bright green eyes jumping between us. *What do you mean, how can you help us? We're obviously trying to sit down to eat?* But luckily Dad has better manners than me. "Five for the Bennett family," he says, gesturing to all of us.

"Oh, yes, here you are," she says. "I'll take you to your table."

We follow her through the dining room, maneuvering between tables full of people. Some already have a collection of empty champagne glasses, so that dance floor is definitely about to get some action tonight. Finally, we get to a table in the corner, label number sixteen, but instead of five place settings, there are eight.

"This looks a little big for us?" Mom ventures, and the hostess's face transforms into one of those plastic customer service smiles that she's probably mastered working on this ship. "Yes, sometimes we're able to seat families privately, if the request has been made far in advance, but typically smaller family groups will join with others for the entirety of the cruise. I'm sure you're just going to love your dining partners though—some families go on to become lifelong friends!"

She sounds like she's reciting from the *Mediterranean Majesty* manual, but it seems to be enough for my parents. "Well, all right then," Dad says, nodding and easing himself down into the seat that has the best view of the dance floor.

"And I have something special for you," the hostess continues, her voice going up five octaves. She places a pack of crayons and a paper place mat in front of Etta. I can see the brightly colored illustrations of chicken nuggets and cheese pizza from here.

"It seems like you're making a lot of assumptions about my culinary tastes," Etta says, looking the waitress up and down. The lady chuckles nervously, mumbles something about our server, Phillip, being with us shortly, and then makes her escape. But as soon as she leaves, Etta grabs the green crayon, and I can see her fingers itching to smash that word search.

"Wally, will you put that away already," Mom says, swatting his shoulder. "We're trying to have some quality family time here. You can write your long love letter to Kieran later."

So, Mom doesn't know about his breakup with Kieran yet. Hmm.

"Just give me two seconds. It's something for school," he

says as his fingers continue to move fast across his phone's screen. I don't know what he could possibly be doing because he graduated last month and he doesn't start law school until August, but his furrowed eyebrows and tight jaw make it look important. That's probably intentional, though. He's always trying to act like he's got to decide between cutting the red wire or the blue wire on a bomb, even if he's just responding to someone's comment on IG.

Mom turns to me. "So, have you given any more thought to what we talked about before we left, baby?" No, I'm actively trying to ignore it. "Your major," she clarifies, as if I've forgotten. "I thought that maybe seeing Rome yesterday, all that ancient art, may have inspired you. Do you think you might want to stick with art history after all? There's so much you can do with that."

"Yeah, I don't know—"

"But with a different focus, perhaps," Dad cuts me off. "The world doesn't need another person specializing in European art. You could focus on art of the diaspora. I could see you working as a curator at the California African American Museum. Or even better, the National Museum in DC."

"Wouldn't that be something?" Mom says, eyes dancing. "You know, when Dad and I were walking around earlier, I'm pretty sure I saw a business center that had computers. On one of the sea days, you could go on NYU's website and see what specialties they offer within the major. We would be okay with paying for a couple hours on the internet for that. It might make you more excited about it all."

"Okay, maybe, I could check—"

"I don't understand why this is some big thing for you." Wally is apparently done with his very important task and is zeroed in on me. "Picking a major is nothing. That's, like, bare minimum compared to what's on my plate. And you already chose art history, so why do Mom and Dad have to convince you?"

"Wally . . ." Mom warns, but it doesn't have the same bite it normally would. Probably because she agrees with him.

"Yes, I was going to major in art history, but now I'm not completely sure. It's a big decision, and I want to be sure." I eye Mom and Dad's wary looks. "And I will be sure. Soon. Before we get home."

"If you think this is a big decision, wait until you get to the real world," he scoffs, shaking his head. "You're going to have a rude awakening soon. You have it easy now, I'm telling you."

God, Wally's always been a smartass, but I feel like it's on a whole 'nother level this summer. I wish he would go back to his stupid phone.

I narrow my eyes at him. "Mom still washes and folds your underwear, so don't be talking to me about the real world, Wallace!"

"Lenore," Mom whispers. I know she's mad, and I'm going to hear it when we're not in a room full of witnesses. But Wally's cheeks going all burnt sienna is worth it.

"I think this is it, Mom. Table sixteen."

The voice comes from behind me, and it sounds familiar, but I can't place it. I whip my head around too fast and the world spins. So I'm swallowing down bile when I see his face.

No.

No, no, no.

It's Alex. And he's standing in front of our table, table sixteen. Which is apparently also his table. Because the universe hates me and wants to see me suffer.

I can feel my eyes bugging out of my head, and he freezes, probably because he's worried that I'm going to spill the tea on his douchebag behavior to his mom. Ha! Little does he know that he has nothing to worry about because I'm too mortified to reveal any of that to my family, especially Wally, who would never let me live it down.

The woman behind Alex, his mom, steps forward. She has the same deep espresso skin as my dad. Her black hair is in shoulder-length Senegalese twists that look perfect, like they were just done yesterday, and she's wearing a pastel purple shift dress with gold geometric earrings and strings of rainbow beads around her neck.

"Well, hello, all." Her eyes flick quickly to Alex, concerned about his sudden silence. "My name is Ronni, and this is my son, Alex, and it seems as if we're your new dining partners. My husband"—she pauses to look around—"well, he's around here somewhere."

"Ronni! Alex!" my dad calls with his arms wide, like they're old friends. "I'm Edward Bennett, and this is my wife—"

"Marla Bennett, good to meet you." My mom stands up and shakes her hand. "Now, you don't chew with your mouth open or put your feet up on the table or"—she leans in and whispers like she's going to tell a secret—"eat all gluten-free, right?"

"No, I eat lots of gluten. *Exclusively* gluten!"

"Well then, I think we're going to get along just fine!"

The old people all break into laughter, but Alex is still staring straight at me, his mouth hanging open. "You trying to catch flies with that thing?" Grandma Lenore would say, to break the tension, but instead I harden my own shocked face into a glare.

"Okay now, sit down, sit down," Dad says, gesturing to the table like we're having them over to our place for dinner. It's only then that I realize I'm sitting next to an empty seat. Surely, Alex will have the good sense to sit in one of the other two empty ones and leave me to sit next to his parents, but—no. Nope. He plops down right next to me. I keep my body rigid, refusing to acknowledge him in any way.

"Of course they've put us all together," Dad adds with a sly smile. "Can't keep the brothers and sisters separated!"

"Right, now!" Alex's mom laughs, slapping the table and not caring how loud she's being. I like her already. Too bad she has an asshole son.

"So, Alex, right?" Mom asks, turning her attention to him.

He nods. "Yes, that's right, Mrs. Bennett."

"These are our three, Etta, Wally, and Lenore, who is . . . mean-mugging you for some reason, *Lenore*—" She swats my shoulder. "You two look like you're about the same age, actually. She's seventeen—well, eighteen in a few days. How old are you, Alex?"

"I'm eighteen, Mrs. Bennett," he says, his voice smooth. "I just graduated from high school."

"Oh, you've got you some manners!" Mom says. And she's giggling. Giggling! "Please, call me Marla. We're cruise family now."

Um, she's never told any of my friends to call her Marla, but okay.

"A birthday on board, Lenore!" Alex's mom says, clapping her hands. "That is so exciting! We'll have to talk to the chef about getting you a cake. You know, I went to his macaron-making demonstration today, and . . ."

She continues on, but I get distracted by a middle-aged man with shiny black hair, pale skin, and a bright-pink polo walking up behind her. He approaches the table with purpose and pulls out the empty seat. I'm confused at first, but then it clicks in my brain—Alex's light brown skin, loose curls, and ambiguous features.

My dad's not so fast though.

"Excuse me, sir," he says, and my stomach clenches with the impending cringe. "That seat is saved for her husband. Which table are you looking for?"

"Dad!" I say through clenched teeth, and I see Alex wince out of the corner of my eye.

"This one," the man says. "Because I'm this beautiful lady's husband." He leans down to kiss Alex's mom on the cheek.

I feel the whole table freeze as we sit on the precipice of massive awkwardness.

"Oh! I'm sorry," Dad says, slapping the palm of his hand to his forehead. "Of course you are."

"It happens a lot," Alex's mom says, waving it away. "No worries."

"Still, that doesn't make it okay," Dad continues. He stands up to shake hands. "Ed Bennett. Nice to meet you, man."

Alex's dad grins, a twinkle in his eye. "Honestly, good looking out! Men are always trying to steal the seat next to my wife. We must stay vigilant." He extends his arm up like he's holding a sword. And Alex's mom shakes her head at the corniness, but the rest of the table falls into easy laughter, grateful for the excuse. "I'm David Lee. And I see we've definitely been put at the right table."

"Yes, we have," Mrs. Lee says. "Oh lord, honey, remember the Stewarts from the cruise last August?" She leans forward, looking around the table. "They were *the* worst, already legally divorced, but they were trying to make it work again. As if being trapped in a two-hundred-fifty-square-foot room in the middle of the ocean was the key to all their extensive problems, most of which they wanted to talk through with *us*. And their son—"

"Digestive issues," Mr. Lee cuts in, nodding knowingly with wide eyes.

"That's a nice way of saying he was letting the bugle play all dinner long. I don't know why the ship bothered to hire a band when he had it all covered!"

Mom and Dad laugh, which I scrunch my nose at. Usually they're too highbrow for fart jokes.

"So, y'all are old pros at this, then?" Dad asks.

"Well, that was only our second cruise," Mrs. Lee continues. "We like to travel in tour groups, too. Two summers ago we walked along the Great Wall, and then the summer before that, we spent a month in South Africa. . . ."

My parents are engrossed in the Lees' excited retellings of their travels, Etta is zoned in on the kid menu's puzzles that she turned up her nose at just a moment ago, and Wally is back to his phone. So, I guess Alex sees this as his opening to talk to me.

"I'm sorry. For earlier," he says, leaning in so close that I can feel the warmth of his breath on the side of my face. I want to throw up. Well, I already felt like I was going to throw up, but this isn't helping matters. "I wasn't thinking clearly. The breakup, between Natalia and me—let's just say it wasn't easy, and—"

"I don't need to hear your whole life story." I keep my eyes on the empty gold charger in front of me.

"I know what I did was wrong," he continues, and his voices sounds so full of repentance that I almost turn to look at him. Am I being too harsh? "But, also . . . you don't have to be so rude about it."

No, definitely not too harsh.

I whip my head around, and a few of my locs hit him the face. I wasn't planning that, but serves him right for getting so close. "How do you expect me to react?" I whisper-yell, so my parents don't hear.

He holds his hands up in defense, which makes my blood boil. "Listen, I know it wasn't ideal. But really, if you think about it, it was maybe even a little bit flattering? I mean, I picked you out of every girl in that room." His full lips pull into a half smile, his dark brown eyes sparkling. I'm sure that look is foolproof on all the girls, but not me.

"Oh really? Is that so? I didn't think about it like that, but now that you put it that way." I laugh and shake my head in mock amusement.

"Did you hear that, baby?" Mom asks, and I turn to see that all the adults are staring at us.

"What?"

"Look at them!" Mrs. Lee laughs. "Already getting along, thick as thieves."

"I was saying that the Lees are from Cerritos," Mom says. "Isn't this a small world? We go halfway across the world, and we end up sitting with people who live right up the 605!"

"And Alex, your father mentioned that you're going to UCLA in the fall," Dad says. "That's where our Wally just graduated from, and he's starting law school there next."

"Is that right?" Mr. Lee says. "You must be very proud. That's quite the achievement."

"We are, oh, we are," Dad says, beaming at Wally. Wally is typing on his phone, completely unaware. "What will you be studying there, Alex? Wally here double-majored in poli-sci and philosophy and graduated summa cum laude."

"Biology, sir," Alex says.

"Oh, what an excellent choice," Dad says, his eyes lighting up. "Now, what are you planning to do with that major? There are a lot of different paths."

I know my dad is just interested and excited, especially about a young Black man who obviously takes his education seriously. And he's asked every one of my friends and cousins the same type of questions. But I also can't help but feel like it's a slight to me.

"Well, sir, do you want the five-year, ten-year, or twenty-year plans?" Alex says, and all the parents laugh. He leans forward with his hands clasped, and he looks all proper like he's at a job interview. "My plan is to intern at the medical center and in a few research programs I have my eye on while I'm in undergrad. I wanted to do that this summer, but the positions were already filled by current students."

"And don't be modest, you already volunteer at the hospital," Mrs. Lee chimes in.

Alex smiles and nods in her direction. "I intend to take the MCAT, and then up next will be medical school, residency, passing my boards, et cetera, until I'm a licensed physician like my mom."

So, I guess Mrs. Lee is actually Dr. Lee? Which surprises

me because she just seems so . . . cool. Especially compared to her stuffy son.

"I would like to specialize in cardiology," Alex continues. "But I know I should leave a little wiggle room in the plan."

All the parents laugh again, and they practically have hearts shooting out of their eyes in Alex's direction. I wonder what would happen if I told the Lees what their golden child propositioned me to do just a few hours ago.

"Wally, I'd love to talk to you about UCLA sometime this trip. Get a graduate's perspective," Alex says, leaning forward, so he can see Wally past me.

"What?" Wally says, looking up from his phone.

"Wally, I've told you for the last time," Mom huffs. "Put that dang thing away."

"Right, sorry," Wally says, but he follows her directions slowly, like his eyes are physically attached to the thing.

"And Lenore, sweetie," Dr. Lee says. "Where will you be going?"

I knew I was coming next, but I was hoping something would interrupt this excruciating conversation. Where's the waiter already? Can we get some water? "NYU."

"Wonderful! It takes a special person to thrive in New York. How exciting!"

"And what will *you* be studying?" Mr. Lee asks.

Everyone turns to look at me, even Wally and Etta, and I feel like I've been called to the front of the congregation.

I take a deep breath and paste on the smile I know they

expect. "Art history. But I'm considering changing it."

"She's struggling to narrow down what she wants to do just yet because she's talented in so many areas," Mom rushes to explain.

"Lenore has always been our free spirit, but she's getting there," Dad laughs.

I feel my face burn because even though they're trying to help, it makes it seem so much worse. They're making it seem like I need defending, when I haven't done anything wrong.

"An artist! Wonderful!" Dr. Lee says quickly, repeating herself. "I wish my brain worked that way." I wonder if she really believes that, or if she's just trying to make me feel better.

I make the mistake of turning to look at Alex, and he's smiling. Smug. It's clear he's the winner here.

Of course the waiter chooses that moment to show up with drinks and the menus. I mean, damn. You couldn't have timed that five minutes earlier, Phillip?

The conversation, thankfully, drifts away from me and my future from there. There's a cheesy napkin dance and a big speech from the cruise director, followed by so many plates of food. But as our parents laugh and sip their constantly refilled glasses of wine over surf and turf, I still feel unsettled. It's not just the annoying way my parents talked about me in front of these people we just met. It's that I can feel each rock of the boat, as if I'm down on the very last level, drifting back and forth with each wave. I was keeping the seasickness at bay, but now it's overpowering. I push away my untouched plate of steak and start taking deep breaths, willing my stomach to hold down its only contents, that one ginger ale from earlier.

"Are you okay?" Alex asks next to me.

"I'm fine," I spit out, closing my eyes. That makes it worse.

"I'm guessing you're seasick?" he continues. "This is actually pretty common, especially the first few days. Did you bring Dramamine with you? Or Sea-Bands? There are also motion sickness patches."

"No, I didn't bring a whole pharmacy with me on this ship," I say, in between labored breaths. He can save his know-it-all schtick for the parents because I am not here for it.

"Okay. Sorry."

The lights go dim and disco balls drop down from the ceiling, casting swirling lights off the chandeliers and star-printed ceiling. Am I hallucinating? This is definitely my worst nightmare.

"Now, we'd like to invite you up to join us for our first dance of the night," the cruise director from earlier says over the intercom. "Don't be shy! I know you all know this one!"

The familiar peppy beat and whispers that start the "Cupid Shuffle" begin to blast out of the speakers. Mom is already shimmying her shoulders and snapping.

"Ooh yeah," Mr. Lee says, standing up and doing some hip gyrations that I didn't know he had in him.

My dad pops up too. "Yes! This is my song!"

The parents make their way to the dance floor, shouting

and waving their arms and carrying on, not even giving us a second thought.

I want to laugh, but the lights make the whole room spin. I stand up. I need to get out of here. I need air.

Wally doesn't even glance up from his phone, and Etta is now drawing a diagram of something with her crayons. Alex, though, looks up at me with an amused smirk. "Are you going to join them?"

"No," I say. The back of my throat burns. "But maybe you could with your girlfriend? Where is she? Or did you find another replacement?"

"I told you I'm sorry," he says, and he has the nerve to look offended. "And it wasn't like that."

"I don't care."

I rush out of the dining room, out of the lobby and giant elevator bank, out of the endless hallways until I finally reach a door that takes me outside. I push past people filling up cups of soft-serve ice cream on the pool deck and gulp in deep breaths of salty air.

After my stomach settles, I sit down on a sticky plastic chair and pull out my phone. But when I try to text my group chat with Tessa and Theo, it doesn't go through. Of course—there's no Wi-Fi or cell signal. My phone is basically useless out here in the middle of the ocean. I'm on my own.

But then . . . what has Wally been doing all evening?

CHAPTER EIGHT

I want to talk to Wally when he gets back from dinner, to figure out what he was really doing on his phone and maybe sweet-talk him into some answers about Kieran. I prop myself up on my pillows and everything, so the jet lag doesn't overtake me. But by midnight, he's still not back, and I finally, gratefully let my heavy eyelids droop closed. Being passed out is better than being constantly on the verge of vomiting, after all.

In the morning, he's there and not thrown overboard by one of the plentiful cruise ship murderers Etta warned us about. Thankfully, because that would make this trip even more of a downer than it's been so far, and Mom and Dad would for sure find a way to blame it on me.

I know he's there, and not swimming with the fishes, without even opening my eyes because his chain-saw snoring is making my whole head vibrate. It's so loud and oppressive that I almost don't hear the sound of the plastic white phone between our beds ringing.

I pick it up. "Hello?"

"Lenore?" It's my mom, and she sounds way too awake. "Where are you two? We were supposed to meet on the deck fifteen minutes ago!"

"Deck. Yeah. The deck." I wipe away my eye boogers and glance at the clock. Eleven. How did it get to be eleven? That means I slept through breakfast. Damn.

"You're just waking up, aren't you?"

"No," I say, but it comes out all garbled because apparently this is my first time talking in, like, eleven hours. "No," I try again. "We've been up forever. Went for a walk around the top deck together and watched the sun—"

"Lenore, don't even try it. I told your father we should have come get you earlier, but he said we should leave you be—"

"They're adults! They don't need us babying them!" I hear Dad calling from the background.

"Well, anyway, you and Wally have five minutes to get your butts down here. I don't want them to be waiting on us." She hangs up before I have a chance to ask who "they" are. Probably some cringe-y tour group she's signed us up for. Wonderful.

I swing my legs over the side of my tiny bed. "Wally! We're supposed to be outside!"

Silence.

"Wally! I know you're up because your snores have stopped trying to assault my eardrums."

Still no answer.

I take the decorative crown pillow off my bed and chuck it at his head. "Lenore! What the fuck?" Bingo.

"They're out there waiting for us, and Mom sounds pissed. We're going on a tour, I think, with the white-hairs and fanny pack enthusiasts. You gotta get up."

He mumbles, "Fine," and something else rude that I choose to ignore. I pull my suitcase out from under my bed (no space in this miniature room for an actual closet) and grab what I need. "Dibs on the bathroom. You better be ready by the time I'm done."

I brush my teeth, wash my face, and wipe down the stinky parts in record time. I wrap my hair up in a massive bun so I don't sweat to death again and put on a sleeveless black trench coat dress and tiny oval sunglasses that perch low on my nose.

This outfit seemed fire when I put it together last week, along with all of my looks for this trip, but now I'm not sure.

"Do I look European or like an off-brand Morpheus from *The Matrix*?" I ask Wally, stepping out of the bathroom.

"You know," he says, smirking, "that was the exact critique I was going to give you." He's sitting up in his bed at least now, but he's still in his plaid pajama shorts and white shirt. And I can smell his stanky morning breath from here.

"What are you doing? Let's go! Mom's going to lose her

damn mind if we're not down there soon."

He takes a deep breath and studies his hands. "I'm not going."

"What do you mean, you're not going?" I shake my head and start getting my purse ready. I put in extra film for my camera and sunscreen because I know I'll need it. "Stop playing, Wally, and get your butt up already."

He doesn't move, though. "I'm serious. I'm not going today. I don't . . . feel well." He lies back down and closes his eyes.

I look him over. He has giant bags under his eyes. Who knows how long he stayed out last night?

This isn't like Wally. He's always go, go, go. He never sleeps in and always gives me shit when I do it, talking about wasting the day or whatever. This will be the second day of this trip that he's choosing to lie in bed instead of exploring a brand-new city we've never seen before and probably won't see again. Something's wrong. It must be Kieran. They *were* together forever. Of course he's sad and wants to wallow in that. But then again, from the little I've snooped so far, it seems like he ended things? I don't know. Maybe he really is just tired after this most recent semester of overachieving.

"Well, what do you want me to tell them?" I ask finally.

"Tell them that. I don't feel well. Jet lag still, probably."

"Okay." I finish getting ready. Check my camera. Put on my black Ultraboosts, so hopefully my feet won't get destroyed like in Rome. When I'm about to leave, Wally's looking at his phone, his face illuminated by the bright screen. It makes him look even more dejected.

"Well, bye. You're welcome for handling things with Mom and Dad." He just waves, not taking his eyes off his screen. "Have fun talking to Kieran," I throw out the line, fishing for any information. Maybe he knows something about the Wi-Fi that I don't?

"I am *not* talking to Kieran. I need you to stop bringing him up," he says. His tone is firm, and I believe him. *But then what are you doing on your phone all the time?* I want to ask. I know I won't get any answers from him, though, so I just shrug. "At least brush your teeth before I come back. You smell."

When I step outside, I immediately notice the change in view. Instead of endless blue water on all sides, there are mountains peppered with buildings, washed gold in the bright sunlight. The main deck is swarming with people, so it takes me a while to find my family among the masses of other families meeting up for a day ashore. Maybe Dad did have a point with the matching T-shirts. They may be mortifying, but at least they would make this process much easier. I finally spot Mom, Dad, and Etta to the right behind a group of seventy-somethings in neon bathing suits and sarongs. Mom's head is swiveling, and she looks irritated. I know it's just going to get worse when I deliver the news about Wally.

"Lenore!" she hollers when she sees me, waving her arms around. As I make my way over there, the old ladies going to the beach move out of the way, and I see who's standing next to my family: Dr. and Mr. Lee and Alex.

I fight my face to keep its expression neutral.

"Finally!" Mom says, and she has a plastic smile stretched across her face that I know wouldn't be there if the Lees weren't present. She hates being left waiting, even in normal circumstances. So, I guess I should be grateful that they're here, but already my pulse is speeding up. Are they coincidentally signed up for the same tour as us? Am I going to have to avoid Alex and his smarmy, annoyingly perfect face all day? Hopefully it'll be one of those tacky, overcrowded double-decker buses, so at least I can get some space and not have to listen to any more of his fifty-year plan.

"Well, hello, Lenore!" Dr. Lee coos. She gestures up and down with her finger. "I love this look. Very sophisticated."

"Thank you, Dr. Lee." How did someone so nice create someone so irritating?

"Call me Ronni! Better yet, *Auntie* Ronni. After last night, your parents and I are old friends," she laughs, looking at my mom knowingly. "Pinot till we can't no mo'!" she yells alarmingly. "Am I right, Marla?" Mom wave her arms and does some weird whooping thing that I didn't know she was capable of, and then they bump hips, giggling some more. Some weird old-people bonding must have gone down last night after I peaced out.

"Better get used to that now that we're traveling together," Alex says, shaking his head. His striped button-up is French-tucked into his shorts like he just binge-watched the first season of *Queer Eye* on Netflix.

But wait, I'm confused. Traveling together? We're eating

meals together, yes, and I guess I have to suffer through this tour of Sicily in his presence, but that's a far cry from "traveling together."

"Oh, you haven't heard?" he asks, reading my face. He chuckles knowingly, and I hate it.

"The Lees have invited us along to join them on their private tours! For the whole cruise! Isn't that wonderful?" Mom says, her eyes bright with excitement.

What.

No. Please no.

The horror must be all over my face, because Dr. Lee comes to squeeze my shoulders reassuringly. "Now, honey, don't worry. These are not going to be those boring tours where we walk around museum after museum with those audio-guide things stuck in our ears, listening to someone drone on about things we don't care about. It's private, so we get to choose what we do! And I told them I want it to be fun! To really see the culture of each stop! Etta's already requested that we got to the—what was it again, sweetie? Norman's place?"

"Palazzo dei Normanni," Etta corrects her, not looking up from the massive guidebook her nose is buried in.

"Yes, that! We're going to palazzo it up!"

I smile, hoping it looks convincing enough. How do I tell this nice lady that I'm not worried about being bored? I just can't stand her cocky know-it-all son and am horrified that I now have to spend every one of these remaining eleven days in his constant presence.

"It was very generous of them," Dad says, nudging Mr. Lee with his elbow playfully. "But like I told David here, they're going to allow us to pay for half."

"And like I told you, it was already booked ages ago, and we got so many early-bird discounts that there's nothing for you to pay for!" Mr. Lee laughs, and Dad laughs along with him, but I can already see him calculating how to covertly send some money their way. Dad has been known to claim a restroom break and then sneak into the kitchen of a restaurant, just to make sure he gets the bill before one of my uncles.

"Tell you what, beat me on the golf course when we get back home, and I'll let you pay for the whole thing!" Mr. Lee says.

"Oh, you're on!" Dad slaps his back and laughs, all buddy-buddy. How did this happen so quickly? Does the Cupid Shuffle have magical powers?

"David! Ronni!" We turn to see two older Latinx women waving at the Lees like they know them. Next to them are their daughters, the two girls I saw at the teen mixer yesterday. I only have to look at Alex's wide eyes to know that the older one is definitely Natalia, his ex-girlfriend.

"Oh, those are some of our . . . friends," Dr. Lee says, glancing at Alex with concern. "We should go say hi. Would you excuse us for a sec?" She gives Alex a meaningful look and grabs his arm, the three of them making their way over.

"Why didn't you and Wally come down together?" Mom is twisting her neck around, trying to spot him.

"Because he's not coming," I say.

"What do you mean, he's not coming?" Dad asks, crossing his arms. He and Mom exchange a concerned look.

"I don't know." I shrug, trying to get a look at the Lees behind them. Dr. and Mr. Lee talk animatedly with the other couple, but Alex is a few steps back, biting his lip.

"He didn't tell you a reason?" Mom probes.

"Jet lag, I guess? I don't know. Y'all seemed to think that was an okay excuse in Rome." Natalia moves closer to Alex and says something. He nods and looks past her.

"We didn't pay to fly us all out here just for you guys to lie by the pool. You can do that at home!" Dad says. While he starts going on a rant about how we don't appreciate the priv- ileges we have, the Lees are hugging the other couple behind him. Alex goes to do the same with Natalia, but she takes one big step back. Whoa.

"Did he look sick? Dehydrated?" Mom continues. "Lenore, you should have told me this on the phone. I could have checked on him, but now there's no time."

"Hey, don't shoot the messenger! Take it up with your golden boy."

"Don't start all that," Dad huffs.

"I'm just saying." I throw my hands up. "I'm grateful to be here. I showed up."

The Lees rejoin us, and I'm not checking for Alex or anything. Because I repeat, I can't stand this boy. But I also can't help but notice how Alex's demeanor has changed. His confident—*too* confident—energy is now dejected and down. His shoulders are slumped, and he's studying the ground like it has some complicated formula written across it. What happened with this girl? They must have been pretty serious if their families were planning on traveling together. I would ask him about it. If I cared.

We wait in line and eventually make our way down a large ramp and off the boat. The port—"Stazione Marittima," a sign says—is even more chaotic than the deck. There are taxi drivers holding up signs and people in matching polos trying to sell tickets to one of those big red buses I thought we would be on today. Men with deeply tanned faces walk around carrying boards covered in souvenirs, calling out to the tourists and holding up *Godfather* bobbleheads to entice them. It's loud and hot. I hear more languages than I can place. But I feel peace. The ground is no longer rocking. My stomach is settled. I take a deep breath and look up to the sky, feeling the sun on my face.

"You look happy," Alex says next to me. "Feeling better now that you're on land?"

I quickly replace the smile on my face with a scowl. There's no way I'm going to admit that I was seasick, especially not when he tried to mansplain a cure to me last night, like he was already a doctor. He doesn't need any more encouragement that he's right and perfect.

"I'm just . . . excited to explore all of Sicily today," I say.

He looks confused, then grins. He covers his mouth with a fist and snorts out a laugh that he was trying to hold in.

"Lenore, you do realize that Sicily is a ten-thousand-square-mile island," Etta says, appearing next to me. "It is an autonomous region, not a city. Today, we're only seeing Palermo."

"Whatever." I roll my eyes and feel thankful that my blush is always covert, just for me. "You know what I mean."

This time yesterday, I was trying to get away from Alex as quickly as possible, and now, somehow, I'm pressed up against him, thigh to thigh, in the back seat of a luxury van.

I managed to avoid him for most of our time at the Palazzo dei Normanni, sticking close to Etta as she harassed our tour guide, Angelo, with questions and corrections and sneaking away to take pictures of the glittering gold mosaics and painted wood ceilings in the chapel. But when we were herded back to the van, I got distracted by these tourists feeding the pigeons like they were some rare, exciting species, and then boom, the only spot left was next to Alex. Of course.

I try to focus on the sights out the window as Angelo speeds along to our next destination—the cream, rust, and peach buildings, looking like something from another time; the courtyards lined with palm trees and manicured shrubs. I try to imagine what today would be like if Tessa's stupid coin trick worked and I was exploring Palermo with a boy who I liked, instead of my family, a boy I'm pretty close to hating, and his family. But next to me, Alex's leg keeps jiggling up and down, knocking me out of any flicker of a fantasy.

Does he realize his leg is practically shaking the whole car?

Is he doing this just to annoy me? Probably so.

And even worse, he smells good. Not like sandalwood or a running stream or some other ridiculous smell that all the boys in Tessa's stories have. But just normal good. Like his mom buys the expensive detergent *and* fabric softener. Every few shakes, his legs brush mine, the smooth dark hair tickling my bare skin. And because of the air-conditioning that Angelo has blasting, my legs are covered in goose bumps. Does he feel that? Does he think it's because of him? Because it's definitely not. God, he probably does. He probably thinks I'm working myself into a tizzy just being so close to someone so accomplished, a *future doctor.*

"Are you okay, bro?"

His leg stills. "Uh, yeah. I'm fine."

"Sure." I purse my lips and nod my head. "Then can you stop bouncing like you're a toddler that has to go potty?"

"Sorry."

I turn to look back out the window.

Our next stop is the Teatro Massimo, the biggest opera house in Italy and the third largest in all of Europe, Etta informs us, reading again from her big book.

"While the Palazzo demonstrates the Arab-Normal style of architecture that was prevalent in Sicily in the twelfth century, the Teatro Massimo is a combination of neoclassical and Renaissance styles," she explains as we walk up stone steps and past giant columns. "Also, did you know that the opera house was famously used in the closing scene of *The Godfather: Part*

III? Never seen it, but it appears as if a lot of people died in it."

Angelo looks like he's reconsidering all his life choices that led to him being here, with our tour group.

A rush of cool air greets us as we enter the marble-floored lobby, even though it's crowded with passengers from our cruise ship and the others who were docked at the port this morning. Angelo gathers everyone in a corner, giving us an overview of what we'll see on this tour. And as much as Dr. Lee promised we wouldn't be doing the boring thing, this sure seems like it.

"Can I just . . . wander?" I ask my parents, holding up my camera.

My mom looks around, surveying for possible dangers, I guess, before turning to Dad with raised eyebrows and a shrug.

"Yes, that should be all right. . . ." Dad starts, but then he turns to Alex. "Would you mind hanging out with her, son?" When he sees my outraged face, he quickly adds. "Hey, the buddy system can't hurt, right? We are in a foreign country, Lenore, and I want to make sure you're safe."

Okay, and what is this skinny boy going to do about that? He ain't no Keanu Reeves.

But instead I just grimace and make my escape. "Well, come on then."

I weave through the groups of tourists quickly, heading toward the double doors leading out of the lobby. The plan is not to lose him, like, *intentionally*, but I mean, if he can't keep up, then maybe my dad should have selected a better chaperone to protect his precious daughter.

The next room has high ceilings that seem to stretch an extra two stories and intricate carvings on almost every surface. I want to stop and appreciate the extra-ness of it all, how even the floor being scuffed up by all these ugly tennis shoes has a beautiful pattern of inlaid marble—there's some meaning, some important philosophy of life in that. But if I stop to consider all that, I'll be trapped making conversation with Alex. So, I keep it moving. I don't even turn to look back. Through two more doorways and past a particularly large tour group in matching lavender shirts, and then I've made it inside the theater.

All of my snarky thoughts about this being a boring stop today fizzle out as I enter the grand space. Rows of crimson velvet chairs stretch out before me and up toward the ceiling in gilded boxes, with matching lush curtains draping over every opening and framing the stage. Bright lights make the gold walls sparkle even more brilliantly, all the way up to the domed ceiling, where giant paintings of half-naked musicians across a blue sky are arranged into the shape of a flower. The whole place is dripping in wealth and opulence, like I'm in some goddess's jewelry box. I want to photograph everything, even though I already know that no camera, especially not my Polaroid, can truly capture all this beauty.

I walk down the aisle, and turn into one of the rows of chairs, half expecting someone to stop me because they can sense that I don't have a trust fund or own a ball gown or whatever. Thankfully, though, I go unnoticed among all the other people drifting wide-eyed through the auditorium. I pull my camera up, centering the grand stage in the viewfinder, but then change my mind. I can already find a much better photo of that on their website. Instead, I tilt my camera downward, so it's framing the rows of chairs in front of me. The flash goes off, somehow so bright and loud even in this space, and I get a warning look from an official-looking man a few rows up.

"Oh, so that's not just an accessory?" a voice asks, and I feel the chair next to me move under the weight of someone. I don't need to turn to know who it is.

"Why would I be carrying around this big-ass thing just for a look?"

"I don't know." Alex shrugs. "It *does* look cool."

When I don't say anything else, he adds, "Sorry, you didn't lose me. But don't worry, it's for purely selfish reasons. I'm under no illusions here that anyone but you would be the one to do the protecting if shit went down." He pinches his arm as if to show off that it's wimpy, but it looks fine to me. I feel my mouth wanting to curve into a smile, but I hold on to that resting bitch face with a vengeance.

"So you really don't have a major?" he tries again, obviously trying to keep this conversation going. And of course, he picks the literal worst topic ever.

"I do. Like I said last night, it's art history. I'm just . . . probably going to change it."

"I didn't realize that people actually did that," he says, talking easier now that I've encouraged him with a few words. "Started school not knowing what they're going to do, I mean.

I know, of course, that the undeclared option was there. But I thought it was for show, like it wasn't a *real* option."

I switch from my resting bitch face to my active bitch face, and his eyes go wide like a cartoon woodland creature caught in a hunter's crosshairs.

"I only meant I didn't think those people got in," he rushes to explain. "Because it's so hard to get into good schools without having your angle, you know, setting yourself apart. That's what my school's counselor drilled into us. But I guess you weren't undeclared. Like, not on paper, even though you kind of are in practice." His eyes meet my cold stare, and for some reason he keeps going instead of, I don't know, running away or bursting into flames. "But you obviously did set yourself apart somehow. You must have had really good grades to get into NYU . . . hey, why are you making that face?"

I side-eye him.

"Not the face like you're thinking up ways to murder me, because I've gotten used to that. But the face like you smelled something bad. When I said NYU."

Just like Grandma Lenore said. Lord, my face needs to chill.

"No. Face. Is. Being. Made."

"Whoa, okay," he says, holding his hands up. "I take it back."

We sit in blessed silence for a while. He studies the ceiling, and I watch my picture as it slowly develops. I'm plotting a polite way to get up and find my family, because even a boring tour is better than this. And right when I've decided to say fuck it to politeness and make my escape, he starts back up again.

"I was surprised, anyway. I don't know you, obviously, but I can see that art history doesn't seem right."

"What do you mean by that?" I ask, my tone sharp. Everything he says feels like a little dig at me, and it's making my whole body feel tense. Like I have to be ready to fight.

"Shit. I'm sorry," he says, and he actually looks contrite. It catches me off guard. "I don't know why things keep coming out wrong when I talk to you."

"Yeah, I don't know why either," I say, but the words have less bite than before.

"It's just . . ." He gestures to me. "You seem like someone who makes art, doesn't just study it. And before you bite my head off, that's firmly, unambiguously a compliment." I try to hold in my smile again, but the right side of my mouth is a traitor. "Also I was watching you and you looked bored out of your mind at the Palazzo, with all that art there . . ."

"You were watching me? Okay, creeper."

"Not like that," he sighs. "Whatever." I can see he's considering giving up on this conversation. And even though that was all I wanted a moment ago, now I want to keep it going. The jet lag must be making me loopy.

"Maybe I want to study a different type of art. You know, there are plenty of scholars in European art already, and someone needs to study all the other contributions." But I know that's not it. I'm parroting the suggestions my parents brought up before. "And I *do* make art—painting and illustration and fashion design. I'm good at all of it, too. Really good. I actually just graduated from this exclusive arts high school, and I dipped into most of the conservatories there." I take a deep breath and decide to take it a little further, be a little more real. After all, I'm never going to see this guy again after this trip. "But I don't know . . . I'm not sure what feels right. What my real passion is, for the rest of my life."

He raises his eyebrows, surprised that I'm choosing to say more than a few sentences to him. "I don't know if it needs to be all that, though. Maybe you're making it harder than it has to be? It's just a major." My mind flashes to what Wally said yesterday at dinner, and it stings. Maybe this was a mistake.

"Easy for you to say, Mr. Ten-Year Plan."

"Yeah, I know what I want to do," he says with a shrug and a sarcastic smile. "That's not a bad thing."

"Even if you're right, you don't have to be so irritating about it." I roll my eyes and find myself returning his smile. "You've found your passion. That's what I'm trying to do."

"My passion?" He lets out a laugh with his head back and slaps his knee. "Biology isn't my passion. I don't even know if being a doctor will be. My passion is having job stability and being able to pay a mortgage."

I bite my lip. "Yeah, well, I don't want to settle for something that just pays the bills. That seems like a depressing way to live my whole life."

"Hey, not everyone who doesn't want to pursue art is some unenlightened, repressed pod person."

I gesture to him like he did to me before. "Ha! Could have fooled me."

"Well . . . okay then." His voice is small, and he looks down at his hands, like he's offended or something.

And I'm confused. I thought this was hate-fueled (or at least strong-dislike-fueled) banter. Like we can't *really* hurt each other because we'd have to like each other first to even care what the other person is saying. And I definitely can't hurt him because it's so clear he doesn't respect me. But Alex looks wounded by my stupid joke.

Am I just projecting my own shit on him? Making him out to be the villain because I'm stressed out about my drama?

"Anyway, my parents want me to be more like you," I venture again, unsteadily. "They actually gave me until the end of this trip to figure it out. Pick something to study, a whole damn life path, and stick with it."

He looks up. "The end of *this* trip?"

"Yeah."

"Wow." He runs his hand through his curls, and I try not to think about what they feel like. "So are you making any progress?"

"No!" I side-eye him. "It's day two, man!"

He laughs, and his leg bumps into mine again, just like in the car. I turn away because I definitely can't take looking him in the eye when that happens, and I see Dr. Lee at the front of the stage, being twirled around by Angelo while my parents, Mr. Lee, and that whole group of lavender-clad tourists clap.

"God, were we switched at birth or some shit?"

He covers his face, his cheeks red. "I mean, you can have her if you want her."

After the Teatro, Angelo takes us to a café for lunch. We sit outside on the patio, eating plate after plate that Angelo orders with expertise—thick bread studded with plump tomatoes and onions, salad with fried eggplants, and bowls of pasta topped with cheese and sardines. After dessert (cake with dark chocolate and hazelnut), I'm ready to roll out of there, but my parents and the Lees are calling for another glass of wine, laughing and telling Angelo stories about their wild night last night. It feels like Alex, Etta, and I are the parents chaperoning our giddy teenagers.

"You ready to go? I think there's still time to visit that cathedral before we have to get back on the boat," Alex says, obviously on the same wavelength as me. Though a quiet church might not be the best place to bring this bunch.

"Why don't you kids go explore?" Mr. Lee says, watching with amusement as his wife fills his glass to the very top.

"Yes, meet us back here in an hour," Dad chimes in, as if he wasn't just nervous about me walking around a theater an hour ago. "It'll be fun."

Etta looks up and assesses me and Alex, and then returns her gaze to the book on Sicilian theater that she picked up in the gift shop. "I'm fine."

Alex stands up and shrugs. "Shall we?"

The option doesn't sound great, but neither does staying here and watching my parents get loose. I stand up too. "I guess."

We start walking down the street, and we're both quiet. I mean, I hated this guy this morning, and now I might think he's okay, but that doesn't make us suddenly great conversation partners. It's so awkward, and I'm considering turning around because seeing my mom dance in her seat and attempt Italian may actually be more enjoyable than this, when Alex finally breaks the silence.

"Did we just get ditched by our parents?"

"Yes. Yes, I think we did."

"Does that make us losers?"

"I mean, I'm not a loser, but I won't get in the way of your self-assessment."

He stops suddenly. Oh no, did I hurt his feelings again? But also, he needs to stop being so sensitive. I see his face, though, and he's still smiling.

"Let me go in here real quick," he says, gesturing toward a corner store with his thumb.

"Uh, okay."

He runs inside, and I hold up my camera again, surveying what's around me through the viewfinder. There's a tall cream building with green-shuttered windows across the street. Vines drape out of window boxes, and laundry hangs from each iron balcony, the myriad of prints and fabrics making a rainbow of colors. I walk closer to get a better look, trying out different angles until I get the perfect one so I don't waste this film.

"There you are. I thought you ditched me," Alex says, appearing at my side.

"Maybe I should have." I click the buttons, and the mechanical sound signals my picture is coming out. "What were you doing, anyway?"

"Just a quick errand," he says, patting his backpack. "The guy told me there's a big market around the corner. That would be a good place for photos."

"You speak Italian?"

He shrugs like it's nothing, and it probably is to him. Just one of many classes and extracurriculars. "I speak enough."

I follow him down the street and around the corner, and I soon realize that "big" was an understatement. This market is another world. Red, orange, and green awnings cover stalls selling everything you need for a feast—bright citrus, juicy tomatoes, and a rainbow of produce. Swordfish and tuna sparkling in ice. Giant barrels of spices. Sausages and other cuts of meat swing from hooks. It seems to go on forever.

"Whoa," I say, wide-eyed.

"Right?"

"Okay, I know what we need right now." I make my way down the crowded aisle, eyeing each stall as the owners hold up samples of their cheese and olives, until I finally find what I'm looking for.

"Two," I say, holding up my fingers. "Per favore," I add. I might not speak Italian, but I can get by. The tan man behind the counter has a full head of dark hair, despite the fact that he must be at least seventy. He nods, takes my euros, and then gets to work. He takes two pastry shells, fills them with custard, sprinkles them with powdered sugar, and then wraps them in paper before handing them over the counter to me.

"Grazie," I say, and he says something back to me with a huge smile, but I just smile and nod because I've already used up the extent of my Italian.

"Here," I say, handing one of them to Alex. "I may not know shit about Sicilian geography, but even I know that we need to get a cannoli while we're here."

I take a big bite, and my eyes roll into the back of my head. It's flaky and creamy and perfect. It's everything.

When I look at Alex, though, he's not eating his. He's staring at me.

"You can really eat," he says, and he's smiling, but I feel suddenly self-conscious.

"Yeah? So?"

"It's just last night, at dinner. You barely ate anything. I think I saw you take maybe two bites before you left."

"Okay. Again, creeper," I say, rolling my eyes. "And that was last night when the whole boat was rocking and my stomach was threatening to vacate everything in it. I have to make up for the lost time now."

"Ah, see! I knew it!" he shouts. And he points his finger at me. "You *were* seasick!"

His smile transforms. High eyebrows, lips pressed together

into that same know-it-all smirk. I can't explain why it bugs me so much, but suddenly whatever easiness was slowly growing between us feels like it disappeared.

"And, uh, actually," he continues. "Eating too much right now might make it even harder to adjust when you get back on the ship, so—"

"What, have you been waiting all day for me to admit that?"

"No," he says, a little chastened. "But—I was—I *am* just trying to help. Why couldn't you just admit that when I was asking you about it? Instead of acting like I didn't know what I was talking about."

I sigh and shake my head. So much for being wrong about this guy.

"Well, congrats. You're right again, Alex." I turn back toward the café. "Let's go see if they're done yet."

CHAPTER NINE

The next day is a sea day, which means I'm trapped on the ship holding in vomit while our boat heads toward Greece. When I turn down checking out the waterslides with Etta and Dad because hurtling down a twisted metal tube and being thrown out into the abyss seems like the literal worst option in the world, my mom suggests yoga.

"It'll be good for you," she says when she drops by our room to check on Wally and bring me another few cans of ginger ale. I don't even know if they're helping at this point or just adding to the sloshiness of my stomach. "Deep breathing, focusing on the present. It might help trick your body out of feeling this way."

Yeah, sure.

But I decide to go anyway. Our room is too crowded with Mom in here fussing over Wally, feeling his forehead and making sure he's not sick. He promises her he'll be on our outing tomorrow, but she still knocks on our door three times before lunch. Plus, anything has got to be more effective than staring at the ceiling and praying for land while my head spins and my skin gets all clammy. I got up five times last night and sprinted to the toilet, sure that this would be the time I finally puked. *Hoping* it would be. Because then maybe I could get it all out and move on with my life. But nothing.

Hell, maybe yoga really will make a difference. I need to be open.

As I walk into the wellness room on the fourth deck, though, I see that all of my initial skepticism was correct, as usual. I've somehow walked onto the set of a yogurt commercial.

Everyone is white. And I'm the youngest in the room, by at least twenty years. But also the least in shape? They all have perfectly toned arms and visible clavicles and muscle-y Lululemon-clad legs. One lady is doing some weird stretch on the floor where she pushes her butt straight up in the air and presses her legs above her head, I don't know, for funsies? Like, chill, people, you're not getting extra credit for being weirdly flexible. Also, if I even thought about doing that leg thing right now, I would definitely break something. And then vomit.

I almost nope right out of there, but a man sitting in the front on a throne of folded blankets waves to me.

"Welcome, traveler," he says, holding his arms outstretched. He has long blond hair that falls onto his shoulders in greasy clumps, pulled back with an indigo-dyed headband. He's wearing a tank top and leggings in two different shades of moss green and has toenails so long that they must be a political choice. He looks like Teen Events Director Chad's crusty older brother.

"Please, choose a mat and sit down. We are about to begin." His voice is so serene, his expression so peaceful, that my body follows his directions before I've even made the conscious decision to do so. And just like that, I'm locked into an hour-long yoga session with Wellness Chad and his boneless middle-aged followers. I can see how people end up in cults.

"My name is Phoenix Asher." Yeah, okay, bro. "Today I will be acting as your guide as you go on a journey to discover your body, mind, and—welcome, traveler. Please, choose a mat and join us."

And what? What else will I discover, Phoenix? But he's distracted by someone else entering the studio. And when I turn around, I'm real distracted too.

It's Alex.

Of course it's Alex. Probably gearing up to "um, actually" Phoenix and his followers on the correct way to do poses. And wearing tight black pants he has no business looking so good in. Out of anywhere he could be on this massive boat, he's here.

I made sure to sit as far away as possible from him at the table last night. And our only interaction this morning at breakfast was when he saw me grabbing a pastry from the buffet and made a judge-y face, mumbling something about germs. But if I'm actively trying to avoid someone, it's just my luck that he'll end up on the only remaining mat in the room, way too close to mine.

"I didn't know you practiced yoga," he whispers to me as he sits down. He arranges his legs in an intentional way—like everyone else in the room, I realize.

"I don't just practice it. I do it."

"Oh yeah?" He's smirking and I want to smack it off his face.

"Now, if we could have all individual conversations end, as we will be taking this journey together," Phoenix says. His voice is calm and light, but his message is clear: shut up. The lady with a white bob in front of us, who was folding herself clear in half a moment ago, turns to give us a dirty look.

"We will start by sharing a little about ourselves because, as I have shared, this is a collective journey." Why does this guy keep dropping the word "journey" like he's a *Bachelor* contestant? Is he going to ask us if we're here for the right reasons next? "I would like everyone to share their names and their current experiences with yoga, as I begin to take in your energy." He waves his hands, as if our energies were a scent he was wafting toward his nose.

"I will go first. I have been practicing yoga since the day I left the womb and entered this world, in a perfect child's pose, but it wasn't until I met my guru, Doug, that I came to have the relationship with yoga that I do now."

Doug? Doug is . . . not what I was expecting. Like, I'm not trying to be all ignorant or whatever, but there are a lot of names

I would assign to gurus before Doug. I press my lips together so no giggle slips out. While everyone else's faces remain solemn, I can't help but notice that Alex is smiling too.

"I met Guru Doug when I needed him most," Phoenix continues. "The Blockbuster I worked in had just shut down for good. My five roommates held a house vote and decided they no longer wished to live with me. I was lost. But then Guru Doug found me and guided me into a pigeon pose that changed the course of my life. As Guru Doug says, 'Everything happens for a reason.'" I try so hard to hold in a laugh, but one escapes. I turn my head to the side and pretend that I'm coughing to hide it. Um, pretty sure Guru Doug isn't the only one who says that, Phoenix.

"Anyway, that's enough about me. I would love to hear about you, my students and fellow travelers, now. As Guru Doug says, 'We're all in this together.'" Is he serious? Yes, he's serious. Must. Not. Laugh.

The lady in front of me waves her arm around. "I'll start! I'm Roberta, and I'm celebrating my thirtieth wedding anniversary on this cruise." There are a few *awww*s and someone even claps. "I began practicing yoga when my youngest went off to college, and I am really most experienced with kundalini yoga—"

"A practitioner of kundalini yoga almost led me to an untimely death." Phoenix's voice is venom and eyes are narrowed at the woman as if she may be that very person in disguise. I can't help it. I lose it. And Alex, next to me, laughs too, holding up a fist to his mouth as his body shakes. Apparently we're the only ones who find this funny, though. All the ladies shoot us chastising looks and then turn, wide-eyed, to listen to Phoenix's harrowing tale about being forced into a pose for too long while the blood rushed to his head. The white-haired lady peppers his tale with several *I'm so sorry*s as if she was involved in this conspiracy to assassinate Phoenix with yoga.

"We will begin with some breathing exercises," Phoenix says after he concludes his story, apparently no longer interested in learning about his students' energy. He guides us through a few rounds of breathing in through our nose and then out through our mouths, which turns out is actually pretty good for my nausea. I close my eyes and focus on each breath and start to feel better. Maybe yoga is okay after all, even if it attracts some weirdos. But then apparently the breathing part is over, and Phoenix says it's time for some sun salutations.

"Inhale as you raise your arms to greet the sun, lean your hips forward, and arch your back. And then exhale. With your knees slightly bent, your chest forward, you will fold in. It's okay if you can't yet reach your toes. Don't force it. Wait for your body to tell you it's ready. As Guru Doug says, 'Good things come to those who wait.'"

As we all bend forward, I hear the unmistakable *pffftttttt* of someone letting out energy. Some fart energy. I turn my head to the side, searching for the culprit, and see that Alex is looking at me wide-eyed. "It wasn't me," I mouth.

"Make sure you're breathing. Take a big inhale here and

come back up halfway, flat back." I follow Phoenix's instructions, and my head passes through the fart cloud. I can taste it. Fucking Roberta.

I hear a small laugh and know that Alex watched the whole thing.

"I would like to remind all of my students to remain in the present and refrain from any expressions that may take others away from their journey." Is Phoenix calling out Roberta's rank emissions? Roberta doesn't need to be put on blast like that. But I sneak a look up and see that no—he's giving the evil eye to me and Alex as he paces around the room between us.

"Now, we're going to exhale and bring both feet back into plank. Shoulders over your wrists, backs straight. I know this pose can be difficult, but like Guru Doug says, 'No pain, no gain.'" In front of me, there's another telltale *pffftttt*. "We'll hold this plank for ten, nine—feel your energy, focus on your breath—eight—make sure you're not locking your arms—seven—this is all part of your journey, like Guru Doug says, 'Life is about the journey, not the destination'—six." My arms burn because he is definitely not counting in any normal way, and I bring my knees down. "Five—there's no shame in going into a child's pose if you need to, accept your limitations—four, three . . ."

I don't know what child's pose is, but I'm pretty sure Phoenix just yoga-dissed me.

Finally, he guides us into something called cobra that's a little easier, and then into a dog that's looking up or whatever, which seems to unleash something in Roberta, and a steady stream of stank floats my way. Next to me, Alex smirks and covertly waves his hand in front of his nose.

"Can you control yourself?" he whispers, raising his lip in mock disgust. Or maybe it's real disgust because Roberta has definitely been gorging herself on kombucha or kale or something else that makes your toots rancid.

"Whoever smelt it, dealt it."

"What are you, five?"

"Actually, I wonder if that's some of Guru Doug's wisdom."

Roberta chooses that exact moment to let a loud one rip, and Alex's face stretches into shock and then total joy as he lets out a loud laugh. I can't help but join in, falling out of the dog pose that I'm pretty sure I wasn't even doing right in the first place.

"It seems that some people are not yet ready to take this journey," Phoenix says, glaring at us from the front of the room. His expression is grave. "I hate to throw out passengers before we have reached our final destination on the path to peace, but like Guru Doug says, 'It is what it is.' Please leave the wellness center immediately."

He points to us and then the door, to make his point explicitly clear. Alex and I meekly gather our things and follow orders. As soon as the door shuts behind us, though, we explode with laughter. Alex falls forward, slapping his knee. My cheeks and sides ache. They can probably hear us inside, but I can't control it.

"Fucking Roberta," I choke out between giggles.

"Fucking Roberta!"

But as quickly as the laugh burst out of out, we're suddenly silent. Self-conscious. Remembering yesterday and the day before, remembering how we still hate each other.

Because we do still hate each other. Right? We haven't been healed by some weirdo animal poses and Roberta's magical farts.

Except, when I'm looking at him now, it's hard to feel the same way I did just an hour ago. All the fury and irritation and annoyance seem to have dissipated, like the top of the bottle that was holding it all in popped off.

I guess I was kind of a jerk to him for no reason. Yeah, what he did at that teen mixer was stupid, but after that . . . well, I can admit: I was trying to pick fights. Setting him up in this competition that I'm not even completely sure he knew was going on. Is it really so bad that he needed to be right about the seasickness? I mean, he's smug. He's a little too smart for his own good, too big for his britches, as Grandma Lenore would say. But maybe that's not the end of the world. He still lost it over something silly like an old lady's farts, same as me. Maybe that can be some common ground, if we're stuck together until the end of this cruise. It *would* be nice to have a friend on this trip, since Wally is ignoring me and Etta is being Etta.

"Listen, I'm really sorry. About yesterday," he says, taking me out of my thoughts. "I wasn't trying to be an ass, but . . . I know it doesn't matter what I was *trying* to do."

"I'm sorry, too," I say, and his eyebrows rise in surprise. "You're not . . . as bad as I'm making you out to be."

He smiles. "Can we just start over? And agree to see the best in each other going forward? You know, assume good intent."

"It's not like I was actively trying to assume the worst," I say, my lips curving into a sly smile too.

"Yeah, I know that, but I think we're going to have to make a concerted effort toward the other direction. Or else we're going to end up throwing each other overboard before we reach Barcelona."

"Etta *did* say that a cruise ship is the perfect place to get away with a murder."

"You know, from what I've seen of her so far, that does not surprise me."

The boat rocks, and another wave of nausea rolls over me. I close my eyes and will it to pass. Inhale through my nose, exhale through my mouth. Phoenix and Guru Doug would be proud.

When I open my eyes, Alex is studying me, concern in his eyes.

"I have something for you in my room that could help." He smiles playfully and raises up his hands. "Because I'm only trying to help! Will you walk there with me?"

"Boy, I just got through telling you that a cruise ship is the perfect murdering spot, and you're trying to take me to your unattended room. Red flag!"

A crew member happens to be walking by in the hallway,

his arms full of towels, and Alex waves him over.

"Excuse me, sir. My name is Alex Lee and this is Lenore Bennett. I am bringing her to my room—room 817—with completely innocent, non-murder-y intentions. Can you alert the authorities if she's reported missing? Again, that's Alex Lee. Get a good look at my face."

The guy looks confused, then annoyed, but then he pastes on the customer-service smile that everyone on this ship seems to have mastered when they're fielding complaints about the unlimited soft-serve machines or the pressure of the jets in the Jacuzzis. "Of course, Mr. Lee."

"We good?" Alex says, turning to me when the guy leaves.

"Okay, fine."

Alex's room is on the eighth deck, three decks above our rooms. And he's not stuck in a little box with no windows like me and Wally. No, when he unlocks his door, the glittering ocean greets us through the huge sliding glass door that leads to his veranda. The room is still tiny, which is made very clear when we both try to maneuver around his bed at the same time and accidentally bump hips. My whole body tightens in embarrassment and he jumps back, nearly falling into his shower. But it's less tiny than our tiny. And that view makes being stuck on this cruise seem not all that bad.

"Living large, huh?" I say.

"Well, I mean, Mom and Dad booked this like two years ago, so they got a discount. And I would have been fine sleeping on the pull-down bunk bed in their room, but I think they want to have, like . . . adult private time, so that's why they put me—"

"Chill, it's not an insult. I was just commenting on your sweet room." I smile. "We're assuming the best of intentions, remember?"

His cheeks turn red, and he runs his hands through his curls. "Yes, right. Okay, well, I have a couple things to give you." He walks to his couch—two steps from the bed—and unzips the backpack he was wearing in Palermo yesterday. He pulls out a paper bag that I recognize from the liquor store, and then presents me with two pink sweatbands decorated with a single white plastic button on each.

"First, these."

"And what are . . . these?" I ask, studying them. "Because, like, assuming the best or whatever, this was a very kind gesture. But I gotta tell you, these aren't really my style."

He laughs. "They're Sea-Bands. I mentioned them that first night? Well, they didn't actually have name-brand Sea-Bands in that corner store, but these are the Italian version, I guess."

"Uh, okay."

"The way they work is this little white thing here." He points to the bracelet. "When it's on your wrist, it'll press down on this acupressure point. It's called the Nei Guan, and when you, um, stimulate that point it helps with nausea."

He must sense the eye roll I'm holding in because he takes the weirdo sweatbands from me. "Here, let me show you."

He takes them out of the package and then reaches out for my wrist, but stops himself. "May I?"

My stomach flip-flops, reminding me that I'm only doing this because of impending vomit. "I mean, yeah, whatever."

He flips my hand over and touches a spot on my wrist, gingerly, delicately. My stomach freaks out some more. "This is the point right here. So we're going to slide these on." He stretches the bracelet over my hand. "And then there you go. It should start working soon."

He's very close. I can see each one of his freakishly long eyelashes, feel his breath on my arm. And my heart starts beating double time, like it's going to thump right out of my chest. Can he hear that? He's definitely close enough, and he's going to get the wrong idea. What kind of weird shit is this bracelet doing to me? And why is he still holding my wrist?

"Aren't you supposed to be a man of science?" I say, breaking up whatever was just going down, and he steps back. "I mean, magic bracelets that cure nausea? They can't be teaching this in medical school."

"Hey, a good doctor embraces all forms of medicine. And you can get some Dramamine in the gift shops on board if you really want it, but it's going to make you fall asleep and have a dry-ass mouth. But maybe you're into that." He shrugs playfully. "Give it a few minutes, okay? While we're waiting, thing number two."

He goes over to the miniature table in front of his couch and grabs a stack of papers. He's about to hand them to me, but then he pauses and pulls them close to his chest, takes a deep breath.

"First, just as a refresher, the very foundation of our budding friendship is that we assume the best of intentions. We both agreed to uphold this."

"Yeah, are we going to have to review that fifty million times every conversation? Because that's going to get tired."

"I just want to make sure we're on the same page here. That you're not going to, you know, storm out or slap me or something."

"Boy, what type of papers you got there? Because I can't be promising to 'assume the best'"—I hold up quotation marks—"if you're about to show me some plan to blow up the waterslides, or, like . . . porn."

"No! No, no, no!" he shouts, his cheeks flaming. "It's not that. I would never show you porn. Never!"

"Uh, okay." I can feel my neck burning too. "So then what is it?"

"God, I'm making this so much worse." His fingers tangle in his hair. "It's just that, I was thinking about what you were saying. About your parents wanting you to figure out your major. Soon. By the end of this trip. And so, I went to the business center last night, and . . . you know, printed out these questionnaires. My guidance counselor used them, I remembered, when we did group sessions sophomore and junior year."

"Okay . . ." I swallow down my first reaction, which is

annoyance. Because, like, why is he trying to get involved and insert himself in this decision I have to make? Does he think he's some expert in getting your life together at seventeen? I mean, yeah, he probably is. But still.

Assume the best. Assume the best. That's what I agreed to. So . . . that would be . . . lord, this is fucking hard. *That would be* that he actually wants to help me? Without judgment? HIGHLY unlikely, but I'll go with it. For now.

"Why would you do that?" I conjure up all of my non-bitchiness to make sure the words aren't accusatory but neutral.

"Yeah, I'm sorry if this is overstepping. I'm not trying to do that *at all*," he says. "I was just thinking about you, and it's a really hard decision, you know? Especially with such a quick timeline. I wanted to help if I could. You don't have to look at them if you don't want to."

He starts to put the papers back on the table, but I snatch them out of his hands. I glance at some of the titles. "What Should You Major In?" "The Comprehensive Quiz." The stack of papers is thick. Printing these probably wasn't cheap.

"But like . . . I guess what I'm wondering is, what do you expect in return?" I can't totally forget how we met, the stupid fake-dating thing he tried to get me to go along with, like we were in some Netflix movie. Is this some ploy to get me to help him with that?

"It doesn't need to be mutually beneficial," he says, and I search his brown eyes for something calculating, false, but I can't find it. "I can help you without needing something back. That's what friends do."

Is it? I'm always falling over myself to help my friends, but do they do the same for me? Without expecting something in return? I don't know. And how does he say friends like that? So it makes my whole body warm up and my chest feel like it's a shaken-up Coke bottle waiting to explode. I've definitely never felt that way with Tessa or Theo.

"Well, thank you." I look around the room, anywhere but his searching stare, his stupid lips, and catch sight of something else falling out of his backpack: a couple bags of chips and some sort of egg.

"Are those for me too?" I ask, pointing at them.

"Nope. Definitely not."

"But I thought we were friends?"

"Yeah, but we're not share-my-snack-stash friends yet." I fix him with my best glare, and he laughs. "Kidding, kidding! You can have some . . . I guess."

I grab one of the bags of chips and look at the label. Most of it is in Italian, but I can understand the picture. "Ketchup? You're out here hoarding ketchup chips?"

"It's not hoarding. I'm gonna eat them!" I wrinkle my nose in disgust. "They're probably not *that* bad. And it's just something I like to do when we travel. Find all the different, interesting snacks and try them. I don't know. It's fun." He shrugs. "That's what I went into that store for yesterday, and I just got lucky that they had the Sea-Bands too. And, oh, look at this." His eyes light up as he picks up the egg thing. "It's a Kinder egg. These are *illegal* back home."

"Oh my god. No!" I make my eyes go wide, imitating him, but I can only keep it going for a second before my laughter takes over. It is kind of . . . charming how excited he's getting over some snacks. "And okay, wow—so your corner store trip wasn't purely altruistic? It was really for illicit chocolate and ketchup chips? So—" I gasp. "You're not actually perfect!"

"I'm far from perfect."

"Oh yeah? Well, tell my parents that. 'Cause you were talking about your volunteer work and your freshman year internship last night at dinner, and they were side-eyeing me *real* hard."

"No, they were not."

"When's your birthday? Where were you born? I was joking yesterday because your mom is the coolest, but maybe we really *were* switched at birth and my parents can get the perfect child they need. Finally. To complete their perfect trinity."

"September eighth." He raises a finger. "But you know, there's also the whole half Korean thing. . . ."

"Damnit. June twenty-second." I suck my teeth and snap my fingers. "And I reeeeeeally wanted to be able to raid your mom's closet."

"But wait," he says. His eyebrows press together, and I immediately regret this turn of the conversation. "That's in . . . two days? I remember your mom mentioning it at dinner now. What are we doing to celebrate?"

I roll my eyes. "If we're not share-our-snacks friends yet, then I really don't think we're at the celebrating-birthdays-together-type-friends level. Do you?"

He considers that, and then throws his illegal Kinder egg my way. "We're on our way. Look at us! Who woulda thought? We just needed to get you a little less nauseous, so you could tolerate being in my presence."

"Hey, I'm still nauseous. Your bands aren't magic." But as soon as those words leave my mouth, I realize they're not true. My head is clear. Nothing burns at the back of my throat. And my stomach is . . . not normal, but at least not sloshing around anymore.

I haven't felt like throwing up for at least twenty minutes now, and I can tell by the smile tugging at Alex's lips that he can see it.

"Oh, not magic, you say?"

"Shut up. Also, thank you."

CHAPTER TEN

The exact moment my alarm goes off the next morning, a sliver of bright light cuts through the darkness and then disappears with a click. I hear heavy footsteps.

"Are you a murderer?"

"If I was a murderer, how exactly do you think I would answer that, Lenore?" Wally says, and I can hear the scowl on his face.

I see the outline of his lanky figure walk over to his bed and place something under his pillow. Then he clomps over to the bathroom, shuts the door, and a moment later, I hear the spray of the shower.

I turn on my light and see that his bed is perfectly made. Like he never even slept in it last night. He was here at one point, sitting on his bed in the dark and watching the cruise's activities channel with concentration that it didn't deserve. I didn't tell him to turn it off because I didn't want to start another fight, so I fell asleep when the video hyping up bingo cycled around for the second time. Did he go to sleep after that? Did he go to sleep *at all*? And where was he just now? Wally isn't one of those irritating people who work out in the morning, and he's not sentimental or sappy enough to watch the sunrise.

I shouldn't. I know that. But I'm also too curious to . . . not.

I jump up and listen at the bathroom door to make sure the water is still running and he's actually moving around in there and not just using it to cover up that he's taking a dump. And then I walk over to his bed and lift up his pillow to see what he put under there.

But it's not a love letter or a bloody glove or something even remotely interesting. It's a fucking *Norton Anthology of English Literature*. A textbook!

Man, I remember when Wally used to be cool. He's the one who took me to my first concert in middle school, Kendrick Lamar at the Forum, and showed me what shampoo to use to get the weed smell out of my locs. He campaigned his senior year to get Bixby High to let go of their prom king and queen titles in favor of something gender neutral, and won with Kieran. Issa Rae followed him back on Twitter. Only for a few weeks, but still!

And now he's out here reading William Blake for fun? What happened to him? When did he become so . . . boring?

The shower shuts off, so I shove the book back under his pillow and hop over to my bed. I'm sitting there, looking way suspicious, when he walks out of the bathroom, a towel wrapped around his waist. There are large bags under his eyes, and maybe I'm just looking for something, but he seems skinnier, too. His ribs jut out more than I remember.

"Are you going to get up already?" he asks, annoyed. "We're supposed to meet them in thirty minutes."

Are you okay? I want to ask. *What happened with you and Kieran? Do you want to talk about it?* But instead I just say, "I'm up. I was waiting for you to be done."

He rolls his eyes. "Well, I'm done."

We have to take a tender boat into the shoreline instead of just pulling up like we did in Palermo, and once we're there, we meet our tour guide, Adonis—legit, that's what he said his name was. I mean, maybe he was fucking with us, but I'm not about to question him. Anyway, Adonis says we're not even done with the journey yet, and that to get to the port of Thira, we have three options: cable car, donkey ride, or walking the 580 steps to the top.

I crane my neck all the way back, squinting at the zigzag path that goes up the mountain to the buildings stacked up on the cliff like a pastel layer cake. There's no way we're doing *that*. And the donkeys have sad eyes and look like they're a few steps away from selling their story to the *Blackfish* directors. So, I think it's pretty obvious that we're going to ride the cable car up the mountain real quick, giving us more time to feast on spanakopita and baklava and, like, grapes or whatever. But then Alex says, "I'm going to walk."

I snort-laugh. He can't be serious. But then I look at him, forehead all scrunched in determination as he studies the winding trail. He's serious.

"You want to come with me, Lenore?" he asks. "It'll be fun."

I shake my head. "I'm not trying to exercise on vacation. Or plummet to my death off the side of a mountain."

He shrugs. "I see it as an opportunity to really see Santorini. To understand the culture of the island, you know? And when will we ever get the chance to have this view of the Aegean Sea again?"

"I'm sure the view at the top is just fine," I say.

But my dad is nodding his head. "I like that outlook, Alex. I would be right there with you if I didn't have this bad knee." His knee seems plenty fine when he plays golf every other weekend, but okay.

And it's not just my dad, either. Mom, Dr. Lee, and Mr. Lee are all looking at Alex as if he said something profound, even though he really sounded like he was quoting one of the travel brochures on the boat. It's stupid. And even more stupid, it makes me say, "I'll walk with you."

"I knew I could count on you," Alex says. He lifts his tortoiseshell sunglasses and winks at me, and I realize this was exactly his plan.

"Hey, Wally, do you want to walk with us, too?" Alex asks, turning to my brother. "I'd love to pick your brain about UCLA. I'm supposed to turn in my dorm preferences, and—"

"Nah, I'm good." Wally gives a wave and stalks off to the line for the cable car. Mom and Dad exchange a concerned look, but neither of them call him on it.

"I want to come!" Etta shouts. "Did you know that the steps were the only point of access until the 1980s?"

But Mom grabs her shoulders. "It's not safe for you, baby."

"And it's safe for me?" I ask, already regretting my decision.

"You'll be fine, Lenore." She waves me off. "Have fun."

"See you two in an hour!" Mr. Lee calls.

"An hour? This is going to take an *hour*? Yeah, I've changed my mind."

But no one is listening as they leave us for the luxury of the metal buckets that are going to shepherd them safely to the top.

I turn to Alex and he's cheesing. "You ready for this?"

"I've been tricked. Manipulated! Bamboozled!"

"I think you're giving me too much credit."

A gust of wind blows off the ocean, giving us a reprieve from the heat and rustling Alex's curls in this romance-novel-cover way that I try to ignore. But the air also carries a stench like no other.

"Oh no, what is that?" I say, looking around wildly, as a smell worse than the public bathrooms at Seal Beach back home fills my nostrils. "Roberta? Roberta, is that you?"

"I think it's . . . the donkeys," Alex says, his confident demeanor breaking. "You know, the donkeys' . . . business."

"You mean the donkeys that climb the same trail we're about to walk up? The five hundred and eighty steps that they *definitely* can't get to the end to without dropping their business!" I shade my eyes and peer up at the winding path, clogged with donkeys and tourists. "And from the looks of that, there's going to be a lot of business."

"Six hundred, sweetie." A sixty-something white lady in a matching blue tank top and capris appears next to me, seemingly out of nowhere. "TripAdvisor says there are six hundred steps."

"Um, okay, thank you," I say, plastering a fake smile on my face as she pulls her husband over to the line of people waiting for donkey rides, ready to drop more unrequested pieces of information on other unsuspecting travelers.

"Six hundred!" I say, narrowing my eyes at Alex, who seems to find this all way too amusing. "I thought it was five hundred and eighty!"

"What's the difference?" He shrugs and begins walking toward the stairs. "Twenty more won't kill you."

I follow after him, trying to breathe through my mouth as the donkey-poop scent gets stronger. "Yeah, but they may drive me to kill *you*."

He throws his head back and laughs. "It'll be over before we know it. Plus, it gives us more time to do these." He pauses before the first step and pulls a stack of papers out of his backpack. "I notice you conveniently forgot them in my room."

"Oh, lord." I push past him and start climbing the stairs. Now he's trailing after me. "Forgot. Yes. That's definitely what I did."

"We have a long journey ahead of us."

"Okay, Phoenix."

"We might as well make this—watch out!" He grabs my waist, pulling me to a halt.

"What the fu—" But then I look down and see that my gold platform Teva sandals, that I had to drive all the way to a pop-up shop in North Hollywood for, are inches away from a steaming pile of donkey shit.

"Oh. Thanks." His hands are still on my waist, and I can feel the pressure of each individual finger. My lower stomach aches in . . . gratitude. "You can let go now."

"Yes, right." He springs back. His cheeks are flushed already, and we've only hit maybe ten steps, tops.

"And I guess I'll do your stupid questionnaires. But no guarantees I'll figure out my life plan by the end of this booby-trapped trail."

"Of course. It just might be a good start. There's only nine more days on this cruise, not counting today, so your deadline—"

"Well, get on with it then!" I wave my hand and skip a few steps ahead.

He straightens the papers in front of his face, climbing after me. "Number one, do you have a vivid imagination?"

"Yes. I just graduated from an art school, I told you that."

He nods. "Number two—"

"Don't you need to write my answers down or something?"

"I have a really good memory."

I roll my eyes, but then smile. "Of course you do."

"Number two," he continues. He moves in closer to me to make way for donkeys carrying a family of three who all have the same bowl cut. Alex doesn't even look up from the paper. "Are you a positive person or do you often feel blue?"

"I don't know." How honest am I going to get here? "I try to be positive, but I have my Frank Ocean moments."

"Number three. Do you prefer to stay in the background or stand out?"

He looks up from the papers and meaningfully looks up and down at my outfit. "Well, I know the answer to that."

I'm wearing a flower-print vintage romper, pointy cat-eye sunglasses, a hot-pink padded headband, and the aforementioned hard-earned gold Tevas.

"Hey, it's going to look real good against these white walls." I put my hands on my hips and then hunch my shoulders forward in my best supermodel impersonation. "You're taking my picture for the gram, by the way."

He arches an eyebrow. "Oh, am I?"

"Yeah, luckily there's no smell-o-vision, so I'll just look like a dewy, glow-y queen and not like the BO monster that I will soon become."

"You're not a monster."

"We still got like four hundred steps, bro."

He lets out a low snort. "Probably more than that at the pace you're moving at." He hops a few steps in front of me, dodging a tour group and a couple donkey-poop piles that look fresh. "Okay, next one. Are you in tune with other people's emotions?"

"Yes."

"Do you feel most comfortable in order or mess?"

"I love mess!" I say, holding my hands out and smiling all big like Marie Kondo in that meme.

"When given a chore, do you complete it right away or put it off?"

"I don't know. Both?"

"Do you have difficulty understanding abstract ideas?"

"Ugh, why do I feel like this test is judging me?"

"Because it is. That's the point!"

I roll my eyes again, and he flips to another page. "Okay, I think I already know your response to this one, but I'll ask it anyway. For consistency. Are you the life of the party, or do you hang on the wall?"

I open my mouth to respond, but then press my lips together.

My friends, the people at school, the boys I've dated—I know how they would answer this question. Loud, sassy Lenore is definitely the life of the party. But is that really how I am if I have to make a conscious choice to do that? If, after I've been that Lenore all day, I have to go home and recover because my brain feels scrambled and my face feels prickly? It's definitely a part of me, but it's not all I am. It's not my natural state.

How did I get to this point, where I have to perform for everyone around me? Am I going to do that for the rest of my life? Who am I going to be when I move across the country, away from everyone I love and everything I know, and start my life over?

My heart's beating fast, and I can feel my face getting hard. I don't want to do this right now.

"You know what, these corny-ass questions are not it." I grab the papers from him, not roughly but assertively, and fold them. "I know you have 'the best intentions' "—I put up quotes with my fingers—"but I'm huffing in way too much donkey shit and my thighs are burning and I'm sweaty and we just need to cut this."

He stops walking, takes a deep breath, and his lips curve into a small smile. "Well then, I guess we can rule out any majors and careers that require physical activity."

"Boy, you better be quiet," I laugh, and playfully shove his shoulder. He stumbles backward, eyes going wide, and then catches himself. I bite my bottom lip and stare at him guiltily. I *really* wasn't trying to do all that.

But then he bursts into laughter too. "Wooooooooooow!"

"It was an accident! Mostly! Assume the best!" I giggle as I jog up stairs, and he chases after me, until we're both falling over, laughing in between big gulps of breath. Two men with leathery tan skin pulling donkeys behind them give us curious looks as they pass by, and I wonder what we look like to them. Can they tell we just met a few days ago? That we hated each other until yesterday? It's crazy how things became so easy so fast.

"Okay, yes, we can be a little less formal," Alex says, when we finally stop huffing and begin walking again. "Plus, the next questions are about your emotional intelligence, and I know how you're going to react to that."

"CORNY. ASS."

"Those are actually some of the questions that tripped me up the first time I took one of these tests and kept me from getting 'doctor' listed as one of my career possibilities," he says. "So I just took it a couple more times until I aced it."

"Oh my god!" I laugh. "Pretty sure that's not how that's supposed to work. Do you ever get tired trying to be so perfect?"

"You sound like my guidance counselor." He shrugs and smiles. "But do you want a doctor who's not a perfectionist?"

I point at him. "Touché."

"Well, so, let's get right to the point then: What are you really good at?"

I suck my cheeks in and fix my eyes on the ground. That question knocks me over like a wave at the beach. Am I *really* good at anything? I'm good at a lot of things. But am I *really* good? Am I the best, like Etta and Wally and my parents are the best at what they do? Like Alex apparently is? Maybe that's why I hop around so much, so I can hide that I'm average.

I take a deep breath, swallowing down those feelings, and paste on a big smile. "I'm good at a lot of things, okay?" I say. I throw in a snap for emphasis. I know how to play this.

"I know you are." He grins, but then his eyes narrow and he scratches his cheek. "But I mean, specifically."

"I make clothes," I say, pressing a finger into my palm. "And just, like, styling, in general. I'm okay at painting with acrylics, and I got really into block printing for a while there. I know my way around Final Cut Pro and InDesign. And art history, of course, but more modern stuff is my jam. Like, Basquiat, yes, Vermeer, let me take a nap. And yeah . . . that's just some of what I worked on at Chrysalis. That's the art school I went to."

The words slowly sputter to a halt. Thankfully. I used to be able to list all these things and feel confident about it, but now it feels flighty, chaotic. No wonder my parents are worried.

But Alex doesn't have the judge-y look I expected. Which is good, because if he did I was going to push him off this cliff, for real. "Okay, problem solved," he says. "Major in one of those things, then. Honestly, this was faster than even I expected."

I sigh. "Just because I'm good at something doesn't mean I want to do it forever. Or even commit to studying it for four years of college. Plus, I can't switch from a BA to a BFA with a form. It's more complicated than that."

He nods, but doesn't say anything.

"Hey, do you mind if we stop for a second?" I ask. We've reached a bend, and my whole body feels like it's on fire. I haven't done this much exercise since we took the Physical Fitness Test in ninth grade, and I'm pretty sure I failed that.

"Sure. Yeah, of course."

We walk over to a rest area that is thankfully void of donkey-poop piles because apparently those poor things don't get to rest. I put my hands on my hips and really take in the view: the curves of the stairs we've already climbed snaking down the mountain. The bright sun sparkling off the brilliant blue sea. I guess this might have been worth it, just to see Santorini like that. But I will never, ever admit that to Alex.

I turn my camera on, the loud mechanical sound getting Alex's attention. I can feel his eyes on me as I crouch down to get the perfect angle for this shot, the water stretching out into forever.

"Why not that?" he asks. I click, and a picture cranks out of the top.

"Why not what?" I ask, playing dumb.

"Photography. Why don't you major in that? The way you look when you have that thing—" He gestures to my camera and shrugs. "Well, you seem happy. Peaceful."

I think back to the story Grandma Lenore told me at my graduation party. How I gave up on photography because I couldn't get things just right. And I guess that's my pattern, isn't it? I'm scared to commit to anything fully because I might not be the best. I don't want to risk being vulnerable, like, *really* put myself out there, because then I wouldn't be cool, calm, collected, and *confident* Lenore. But I can't say all that to Alex.

"I like it," I say finally, with a shrug. "But I'm not the best at it. And BFA programs are really competitive."

Alex's eyebrows knit together. "But isn't that the point of college? To, you know, learn? You don't have to be the best." He stops, smiles, and laughs at himself. "I mean, *I* like to be the best, but that's my problem. It's not a requirement. You just have to be interested and show some promise, and I'm sure your years at your art school would have been plenty enough experience."

"Yeah, I don't know." I jab a thumb back toward the stairs. "Do you want to keep going?"

He nods, and we start walking again, but the playfulness that was there before is muted. I feel like he's finally seeing me for who I really am, instead of the front I put on, and maybe it's disappointing.

Finally, after a while, he claps his hands together, face bright with a toothy smile. "Okay, let's switch gears here. Maybe if we approach this in a different way, we'll get better results, you know?"

"Spoken like a true nerd."

"Hey, not going to argue with you there," he laughs. "So, what drew you to NYU? Or New York in general? Maybe that can help us figure it out."

"Us," like this is a joint struggle. But it's starting to feel like one? And that's not terrible.

I try reeeaaal hard not to make the face that I apparently always make when someone mentions New York, but I can feel the stank there. And if I dig down deep, if I'm honest with myself—I know why that is. Should I be honest with Alex too? It'll probably be easier than admitting any of this to someone in my real life.

I take a deep breath, and let it out: "I don't really like New

York. I mean, I *get* why people like New York. It's diverse, it's exciting. There's always something going on. But we visited last August, and there are just so many people and the streets smelled like trash and no one smiles at you. And after one day outside walking around, I felt like I wanted to pull some Rip van Winkle shit and sleep for a hundred years. I kind of . . . well, I didn't just not like it; I *hated* it."

I feel lighter, like I threw off a heavy, itchy fur coat.

"But I don't get it. If you hate New York, why didn't you apply to schools somewhere else?"

I press my lips together. I've been asking myself this same question. "I don't know. It just seems like I have to be in New York or LA if I want to do anything, and I also hate LA."

"You hate LA? You live in LA!"

I fix him with a mock-serious stare. "Eh-hem. I live in Long Beach. You know it's different."

"Okay, true, true." His face is serious, focused, like he's trying to solve a serious math problem or compose the perfect thesis statement. I can see him over his textbooks in a few months, being a total nerdy star. "Why not a gap year?" he asks. "Give yourself some more time to figure out what you *really* want to study, where you *really* want to live. A year won't make a difference in the scheme of things."

I let out one laugh, loud and clear. "That's some white people shit. My parents would lose it!"

"Malia Obama took a gap year."

"Boy, I'm not Malia Obama!"

"Well, obviously," he laughs. I try to slap his shoulder and he dodges me. "But it should be an option for you. You really don't think your parents would understand?"

"Oh, I know they won't." I think of their faces if I dared to bring that up, and even just imagining the disappointment makes my throat feel scratchy and tight. "There's pressure to, like, be our ancestors' wildest dreams or whatever. I love that phrase and it's inspiring, but it's also so goddamn intimidating. And my siblings are doing that, they're the wildest of wild dreams, like, totally killing it—but then there's me. The black sheep. Well, actually I hate that because black is a good thing. The, like, *puce* sheep."

Alex nods. "My mom has that phrase in a frame up on her office wall, and I guess I've always seen it as, I don't know . . . some sort of challenge? But I get the other side of it, too." His brow furrows and he shakes his head. "But you're hardly the . . . puce sheep, Lenore. You got into a good school, you—"

I hold my hand up, cutting him off. "But that doesn't matter!" I'm getting louder than I want to be. I try to swallow down those feelings and try again. "It's not enough. My parents expect more from me. And I can't even be mad at them because they just want the next generation to do better than them, and that's fucking *hard* because they've done so well. They're the embodiment of Black Excellence and they—*rightfully*—want their kids to be too."

I realize my eyes are wet and want to kick myself for getting this emotional. He doesn't know me like this yet—hell, no one really does. I hope my glasses are hiding it all, or else he's going to be running for the hills.

I put my foot out to keep climbing, trying to put some distance between us so he can't see how embarrassing I'm being, but there are no steps left. We've reached the top. The universe is on my side.

"Oh, look, we're here. I wonder where they are."

"Lenore, we can keep—"

"It's good. I'm good." I wave him away. "Hopefully they have some gyros waiting for us because I'm hungry."

After taking a tour around Thira, Adonis drives us in another big, black van to Oia, the beautiful town that you see all over brochures and travel books and white girl influencer's Instagrams. We're finishing up another wine-fueled lunch on a café's gray stone patio, shaded from the afternoon sun under a canopy of fuchsia bougainvillea.

I'm quiet, sipping my glass-bottle Coke, barely following the conversation, but then I hear my name and:

"—surprised too," Mom's saying. "Look at our girl following through!"

Dad laughs and slaps the table. "I thought she was going to change her mind and try to hijack a donkey halfway!"

Everyone explodes in more laughter, and I try to join in but it's fake. It doesn't feel good to be a joke to them right now. Or, like, ever.

Alex is sitting next to me, and I can feel his eyes on me. He's probably thinking about my answers to those stupid questionnaires and what a mess I am. He's probably internally cringing about how I cried and tried to hide it.

When he taps my arm, I prepare myself to go off, but when I turn to look at him, he's smiling at me. And not an irritating, placating one, either. The kind that warms you up.

"Do you want to go for a walk?" he whispers, so I have to lean in closer. "We can take a picture of your outfit at that church with the blue dome. I'm prepared to do as many takes as we need to and not complain once."

A peace offering.

I smirk at him. "You just want to go find some weird flavored chips to add to your collection."

He throws his hands up. "Yeah, that too. You caught me."

We walk out into the bright sunshine together.

CHAPTER ELEVEN

The next day is my birthday, and the ship is docked in Athens. Alex, for some reason—even though we just met, even though we don't really know each other—is on me to make a plan for the night.

"What are you doing after dinner?" he asks as we all trail after Etta at the Acropolis. The tour guide doesn't even make an attempt to exert his trivia-knowing dominance, and looks at his phone instead.

"Not that you should have to plan it. I just wanted to get a pulse check, you know, see where you're at," he clarifies, while we're sitting down for coffee and crepes at Little Kook, this fairy-tale-looking café with over-the-top decorations that change all the time. Right now it's decked out in a *Wizard of Oz* theme, with green glittering walls, giant poppies sprouting from the concrete, and rainbow banners shading the alley where it's located. Every thirty seconds, a white girl in a maxi dress pretends to look around while her boyfriend takes fifty-leven pictures for the gram.

"How do you feel about balloons?" he leans in to ask me as we bake under the hot sun at the Temple of the Olympian Zeus.

"I hate them."

"Duly noted."

It's not that I don't appreciate what Alex is trying to do. It's nice or whatever. But I'm weird about my birthday. It's hard not to get your hopes up. To wish that someone will read your mind and do the exact perfect thing that shows they see you to your very core, that you matter to them as much as they matter to you. But that never, *ever* happens.

Like, last year, Tessa and Theo planned this big surprise bonfire for me at Sunset Beach. They invited everyone from Chrysalis. I'm talking *everyone*, like even the pink-haired girl from my ceramics class who I've only said what's up to once. But the thing is, I hate bonfires. I hate how the smoke smell hangs around in my hair for days. I have no interest in eating a hot dog that's been cooked over the fire. We ain't cave people! Plus, it was so exhausting to talk to that many people, to remain on for hours. I would have much rather just chilled with the two of them (Sam and Lavon could have come too), and, like, eaten Double-Doubles and watched a bad movie. And see, now I sound ungrateful, right? I should appreciate that my friends made an effort, blah blah blah. I know that, of course. But that's why I feel like it's better to have no expectations, no celebration at all. Let this day pass like any other.

"I can't believe our baby girl is an adult now!" Mom says at dinner that night. Her lips are pressed together and her brown eyes are watery as she looks across the table at me.

"Technically, I am your baby girl," Etta butts in. "If we're being precise with our language."

"Shut up, Etta," I say. "And did you know, dear parents, that the drinking age in Greece is eighteen? So, what are we thinking, champagne? Waiter? Waiter?" I raise my finger up and swivel my head around the room.

"You better put that hand down," Dad says, raising an eyebrow. "The Bennett drinking age is forty-three, and that trumps whatever Greece says."

"Forty-three? Wally has a beer!" I say, holding my hands up. "How is that fair?"

But Wally isn't even paying attention to us. He's typing furiously on his phone, doing who knows what because we definitely don't have service.

"It's not champagne, but I have something planned to celebrate," Alex whispers to me as the parents move on with their conversation.

My eyes go wide, and I look around the room. "These waiters better not be about to sing happy birthday to me, or do that weird napkin dance thing." He smiles and waggles his eyebrows. "Oh my god, Alex. I will die. And then my ghost would come back to kill you. I'm serious."

I grab his arm tightly. "Abort mission. Right now! Before this night ends in tragedy."

He laughs. "No, it's definitely not that." He leans in a half centimeter closer to me, but it feels like much more. "It's something after dinner. For just the two of us."

My stomach does a weird flip-floppy thing. I adjust the Sea-Bands around my wrists, but that doesn't seem to help.

We agree to meet on Deck 4, out on the promenade. I change into this yellow lace dress with big puffy sleeves, and then feel stupid and change back because why in the world am I changing just to hang out with Alex, and then change back into the yellow dress again because I look fire in it and really it's stupid to not wear it because of Alex. It's a journey.

The sun is setting when I walk out onto the promenade—five, okay *ten*, minutes late because of the dress indecision. I squint and shade my eyes as I scan the deck, looking for Alex. We spot each other at the same time, locking eyes, and his face crinkles up into a full-on cheese. My stomach does that weird flippy thing again. Stupid, unreliable Sea-Bands.

I'm relieved to see that he changed, too. A crisp white button-up, black pants cuffed at the ankle, and brown leather brogue oxfords. The light makes his skin look like it's glowing rose gold.

"Hey, birthday girl!" He holds his arms out as I approach, and it takes me a few moments to comprehend that he's reaching for a hug. Okay, so I guess we hug now.

I move in close, breathing in his clean laundry smell, and then I realize, with horror, that he can probably hear me smelling him, like some creeper. So, I jump back quickly, suddenly fascinated by the ground.

"Sorry I'm late," I say. "CP time."

He blinks, and his cheeks go red. "Um . . . are you allowed to say that?"

I look up at him, searching for the joke, but he's totally serious. "Yes, I have a permission slip, signed by the ancestors and passed down from generation to generation. Don't you?"

His brow is still furrowed, and I laugh. "I'm Black. I can say it," I clarify. "And, hey, you're Black, so you can too!"

He bites his bottom lip, which I've noticed he does when he's sifting through something in his mind, trying to find the right words to say. He motions to the right with his head, and starts walking. I follow.

"Yeah. Yeah, of course. That makes sense. I probably err on the side of a little too cautious," he says finally, rubbing the back of his neck. "I think it may be a biracial kid thing. Because, like, for *me* saying it, I guess it's just—okay, sorry if this is weird, but I'm gonna get a little deep for a second?"

I smile. "Proceed."

"My friend Michael says I do this too much. Overthink something small in my head and take it way further than anyone was trying to go. I guess those emotional intelligence questions maybe weren't too far off in their assessment of—"

"You're rambling. Get on with it already!"

He nods. "It's just that I have this racial imposter syndrome, you know? It's hard to know where I fit in."

"Oh, so we *are* getting deep here."

He smirks. "Hey, you asked for it!"

"I did, I did. Well, let me help you here." I stop walking and make a show of looking him up and down. "You Black."

His head falls back in laughter, and the sound warms me up. He starts walking again. "How can you be so sure?"

I shrug. "Because that's how the world sees you. It's not like people are going to ask to check your credentials. Your Black card doesn't have percentages on it."

"So that's how it works?" he says. "However I'm perceived is who I am? I don't know how I feel about that."

"What?" I give him the side-eye. "You have a problem with being Black?"

"No, no, it's not that." He shakes his head. "But it feels . . . weird, you know? To deny a whole other side of me. Like, I went to hagwon—that's Korean school—every Saturday until I was a freshman in high school. My parents host Lunar New Year for the family every year. I'm just as much Korean as I am Black."

"Yeah, that makes sense. I get that," I say. "I guess I was just thinking of my friend Tessa. She's biracial too, but she calls herself Black. Then again, her other half is white, so . . . ."

We look at each other and both shrug at the same time, which makes us both then burst into laughter.

"So," he says. "When you first saw me, then . . . you thought I was Black?"

Well, when I first saw you, I thought you were super hot, a leading

man straight out of the love story Tessa has been planning for me.
When I first saw you, I was inspired to waste two perfectly good euros
by tossing them into the Trevi Fountain. But, of course, he doesn't
need to know all that. He didn't see me until the teen mixer,
when he tried to use me to make his ex-girlfriend jealous. "Yep,
Blackity-Black-Black." I nod. "But now I know, Korean too."

He throws his head back in laughter again. I love that I've
inspired that, but I also want to push those weird feelings down.
"Man, sorry for getting real serious, real fast."

"Yeah, are we going to break down the one-drop rule
next? The three-fifths compromise? I couldn't have asked for a
better way to spend my birthday." I smile. "But you don't have
to be sorry. I like hearing what you think."

He smiles back, eyes bright. "Well, thank you."

"Wait, where are we going anyway?" I realize I've been
following him blindly. Down the promenade, into the ship. It's
easy to just let go with him.

"Well, we're here."

He gestures in front of him to the entrance of the ship's
arcade. Which, I didn't even realize that the ship had an arcade,
but I'm not surprised—this place is basically a floating Mall of
America. I walked past a movie theater, an escape room, *and*
a go-kart track on the last sea day. The arcade has black walls
with neon geometric carpet and flashing lights from a line of
machines. It's filled with tweens and kids who should definitely
be asleep in their rooms already, or at least in the daycare center,
not here wildin' out with their hands full of tokens.

"The arcade?" I ask.

"The arcade!" His face lights up, but then flashes with worry. "Oh no, did I totally screw this up? Do you have beef with *Pac-Man*? A dark past with *Dance Dance Revolution*?"

"Oh, no! It's just that I was expecting . . ." What was I expecting? A stroll to watch the sun set? A candlelit dinner at the bougie restaurant on Deck 7? *Get out of here with all that*, I tell myself, shaking my head as if I can physically make those thoughts go away. That's not what this is. "It's perfect! And get ready to get your ass kicked in *Dance Dance Revolution* because my past with that game is filled with victories."

"Oh yeah?"

"Yes, I am a pro at dancing with my legs, exclusively." I do a few kicks and a jump to prove my point, and he laughs.

"I'm prrrrrretty sure you're supposed to move your arms, too, in that game."

"Ha! Rookie mistake." I bump him with my shoulder as I run past into the room, and he follows after me, calling, "*DDR* Diva coming through!"

Two hours later, we're sweaty and giggly and token-less, staggering into the bright light outside of the arcade. My ears are still ringing from all the beeps and buzzes of the machines, and my cheeks ache from smiling so much. My lies about my *DDR* prowess were exposed right away, after a kid who looked like he was barely out of Pull-Ups challenged me to a dance duel and beat my score by an embarrassing amount. So, we skulked over to this motorcycle driving game, where I reclaimed my pride by beating Alex in ten straight races. It was only because he wasn't willing to run over the grannies and little big-eyed bunnies on the side of the track. But still. They're not real! And then we played a few rounds of air hockey, where we gathered a bit of an audience because our yelps and shouts were so loud.

"That was fun, Alex. Really, thank you," I say, squeezing the off-brand orange-and-hot-pink Pikachu he spent a good twenty minutes trying to win me from the claw game. "I don't usually like my birthday much, but this . . . it was just what I needed."

"You think we're done?" he asks, his brown eyes locked on mine.

"I mean, I assumed," I sputter. "You probably have other stuff to do tonight . . ."

"Yeah, I've got big plans to watch the same two English movies they cycle on the TV and sit alone on my balcony, staring out at the ocean and contemplating my existence."

"Hey, that sounds like a wild night. I wouldn't want to keep you away from that—"

"Come on," he says, taking my hand. An electric charge shoots up my arm, and I hope he can't feel me shiver. "Let's go."

We take the elevators down a few floors to Deck 2, where I haven't been yet. Alex is still holding my hand, acting like this is a perfectly normal thing friends do, when he leads me to a little fifties-style diner, sitting there all anachronistically, like it was plopped down by a time machine. Because even in the freakin' Mediterranean, Americans need their burgers and fries, with a side of rose-colored nostalgia.

"Ta-da!" He holds his hands out, dropping mine. I fight the urge to reach out toward it, because apparently my brain is going all haywire and sending weirdo messages to my body. "I feel like we need a late-night snack after all that professional-level *DDR*-ing."

"That kid was a plant. Word got out about how good I am, and they needed to bring me down."

"They?"

"The DDR suits, obviously."

"Yes, *obviously.*"

We claim a mint-green pleather booth, and order fries and milk shakes piled high with whipped cream—cookies and cream for me, salted caramel for him. As we laugh and trade jabs, I study him. The way his full lips slowly curve into a smile. The flutter of his long, dark lashes. How his curls bounce when he throws his head back and laughs, usually just once, "Ha!" And how my stomach does that floppy thing and my brain tells me to keep going, keep inspiring more of those, because each one feels like an achievement.

I'm not stupid. I know where these feelings are heading. I've felt this way before in the beginning with Jay and Marcus and all the other unworthy boys. But Alex isn't like them. At least, I don't think he is, though clearly my judgment isn't great. He *seems* different. Respectful and kind. And genuinely interested in me—what I have to say, my mind, I mean. I don't know about . . . the rest of me.

But. BUT. We have a week left on this cruise. And then he

goes off to UCLA, me to NYU. He goes home to all the other options he probably has, like the gorgeous Natalia. It's just like me to be catching feelings for someone I have no future with. This fits my destructive, pointless pattern.

"So you said you don't like your birthday," Alex says, dipping a french fry in ketchup. "Why is that?"

"Nah." I shake my head. "I don't want to talk about that." I know that whatever I say, it won't come out right. I'll sound ungrateful, picky.

"Oh yeah?"

"Yep, and it's my birthday, so I get to decide."

There's a small smile on his face, and he nods once in agreement. "Well, okay, then."

"Anyway, I just got through baring my soul to you yesterday, so I think it's your turn now. And listen, bro, I've got some serious questions for you." I lean in, making my eyes wide, and he looks nervous. "We're friends now or whatever, so I've gotta ask." I pause for effect and I see his Adam's apple bob. "Did you really think that fake-dating mess would work? Like, *really*?"

"Ha!" His head falls back. Another point for me. "I mean . . . maybe? I don't know. I really wasn't thinking clearly."

"Well, that was obvious." Something stormy passes across his face, and it reminds me of the way he looked when we were docked in Palermo and he saw Natalia. He had the same look last night, when she walked past our table in the dining room on the way to the bathroom, waving awkwardly. There's still some feelings there . . . but what kind? Is he still into her? I decide to press on the bruise a little bit more. You know, just out of curiosity.

"What happened with you two?"

"Ahhhh." He puts his face in his hands, and when he looks up again, the storm has cleared for the sunshine of his smile—tentative, with flushed cheeks. "I'll tell you, but you have to promise not to laugh."

"I will promise no such thing."

He rolls his eyes, and then takes a deep breath. "She . . . she said I wasn't real; like I was playing the part of the boyfriend in a movie instead of being myself?"

I press my lips together, holding in a cackle. "So this fake-dating plot of yours was actually . . . totally in character?"

"No!" His cheeks flame some more. "Well, I guess maybe . . . yeah."

I let the laugh out then, and he joins in, shaking his head at himself.

"So what does that mean, exactly?" I ask. "What did you do?"

"I don't know, just like the normal stuff." He shrugs and takes a long drag from his milk shake. "I put these notes in her locker every day, reminding her what I loved about her. I walked her to all her classes, sat with her and her friends at lunch, even when it meant ditching Michael sometimes. I posted about her *every* WCW. . . ."

I feel a pang of jealousy in my chest, but I push it down. Stupid.

"I, you know—I did what I was supposed to do." He nods once, and his jaw is set.

"Well, that doesn't sound very romantic," I start.

"What do you mean?" he asks, throwing his hands up.

"I did what had to be done," I say, putting my fists on my hips and imitating his serious tone. "You sound like you were checking items off a to-do list, not actually feeling some type of way for this girl! Going through the motions of what you thought was expected . . . I don't think relationships work like that."

Says the person who threw coins into the Trevi Fountain to find love.

He shakes his head at me, incredulous. "So you're on her side?"

"Uh, I'm on the right side," I say, holding my finger up. He wrinkles his nose, but then his face settles into a grin.

"What was the last straw, then?" I ask.

"It was this spring—"

"Oh no," I cut him off. "Don't tell me you did a promposal!"

"What's wrong with a promposal?" he mumbles, eyeing the table. "Not that I did one? But you know, just. For science."

"So she dumped you because of your promposal."

He looks up at me, exhales loudly, and then nods. "She dumped me because of my promposal."

"What did you do?!"

"Have you seen that really old movie, *10 Things I Hate About You?*"

"Pour one out for Heath Ledger," I say, dumping the rest of my milk shake from the tall metal cup into the fancy glass cup.

"Well, I got the idea from that. The whole bleacher scene. 'Can't Take My Eyes Off You.' She was at soccer practice, and I called in a favor from my friend in jazz band, had them play the song. I didn't sing because that would have been mortifying for all of us, but I held up a big sign. . . ." He stops, taking in my side-eye. "I guess it was a little ridiculous, yeah, but I thought . . . girls liked that sort of thing. But Natalia said I wasn't being authentic."

"News flash," I say, waggling my fingers. "Girls aren't all the same. I mean, I would have loved to see your Heath Ledger cosplay. Actually, can I get a performance right now? I'll sing backup." His eyes go wide. "I'm kidding, I'm kidding! But I guess I get why someone would hate all that attention . . . maybe you didn't really get to know her and what she wanted."

I worry I'm going too far, that he's going to get defensive and peace out on this night, maybe even this whole friendship, but instead he nods.

"Yeah, you're right. I know you're right. And that's why I'm single." He leans back in the squishy booth. "And I'll just go ahead and make myself look even more pathetic by admitting that Natalia was my first girlfriend. I didn't grow into these ears"—he pushes them forward even more—"until sophomore year. And when I wasn't doing schoolwork or volunteering, my social life was pretty much just playing Xbox and watching *Law & Order* reruns with Michael. So when I finally figured it all out with Natalia, I guess . . . I didn't want to lose her."

"And then you lost her anyway. How tragic." I smirk. "And are you sure you grew into those Obama ears?"

He snorts out a laugh and shakes his head at me. "Okay, so now that I've thoroughly embarrassed myself, it's your turn to share, right? I feel like there's some good stories in your romantic past."

I shrug. "Nah, I'm good."

"You can't let me just confess all of my terrible boyfriend flaws and then give me nothing."

"I can't?"

He looks me right in the eye, a challenge there. I stare right back at him, and we stay like that, not blinking for who knows how long. But then his eyes start to cross, and he sticks his tongue out, making the most ridiculous face ever. And I start laughing, losing the staring contest. I put my hands up in defeat.

"Okay, fine. Fine! But let me skip over my long and cringe-y history of fuckboys and declarations of 'I don't date Black girls.' Or worse, 'I only date Black girls.'"

He raises his eyebrows. "Yikes."

"Yeah. So, we can just begin and end with the most recent asshole, Jay. He sums up my shitty romantic luck pretty well."

I tell him all about the months I wasted with Jay, keeping things on the down low so he wouldn't get in trouble with his parents. And then all about the prom night from hell, when I thought we would be meeting up and then seeing him with the girl his parents apparently had no problem with.

"Wow, what a dick," Alex says.

"Yeah, and that's an understatement."

"You don't deserve that, Lenore." He shakes his head. "What the fuck." He crosses his arms, and his face scrunches up in anger. And I feel . . . touched? It's only been a few days, but I can tell that he genuinely cares about me already. It's not a front.

"Has he tried to contact you at all? Since then?"

"Uh, I don't know." I try to say it all casually, like it hasn't even occurred to me, but of course it has. "My phone doesn't work, and I haven't checked my email. But it's whatever. I don't care about him."

His warm brown eyes lock with mine, but it's different from the silly staring contest before. I feel like I've suddenly become transparent, and he can see all of my mushy, gooey insides. All of the embarrassing shit I keep in lockdown from everyone else.

"It's okay to care," he says finally. "It's okay to not be okay about it."

I bite my lip and look down. Why does that all feel totally possible when he says it? I spend so much of my life trying to be the Lenore people expect. Letting things rolls off me, too confident and self-assured to care. But that's not all of me. That's just the side of me that's easy to be around. What would happen if I showed the other side, the side that's pissed off and sad and hurt and not so easy sometimes? What would happen if I showed that side to Alex?

When I get the courage to look at him again, he's sticking a candle in the top of my milk shake and lighting it with a Zippo that appeared out of nowhere. The candle is wobbly, because duh, it's in a milk shake, and he has to flick the lighter over and over before it finally catches.

"Boy, what are you doing? You're gonna burn this place down!"

He nods. "You're right. Let me call the waitress over here to bring a cake instead. Do you think they know the Stevie Wonder version of 'Happy Birthday'?" He holds up his hand. "Ma'am!"

"No. No! You better be quiet." I grab his hand to pull it down, and he laces his fingers with mine, squeezing once before letting go.

I can feel my cheeks, my neck, my whole body burning, and I blow out the candle, hoping that will extinguish whatever's going on inside of me.

My eyes are heavy as we stumble back to the upper deck, and when we make our way outside, I see that it's much later than I thought. How many hours have we spent together tonight? It's passed in a blur. The air is warm, and it feels like we're wrapped in the blanket of the starry sky and the dark ocean. It's hard to see where one begins and the other ends.

Alex sits on a deck chair, and pats the one next to him. So I sit down too, tucking my weirdly colored Pikachu behind my head like a pillow. I can see that Alex is sleepy like I am, his eyes heavy-lidded. And it makes sense after the full day we had in Athens, and this night of video games and food and whatever strange feelings are brewing between us.

"Do you still hate your birthday?" he asks, reclining his chair, so it's all the way flat. He interlaces his fingers across his belly and turns to me.

"Maybe a little less."

"Just a little? Damnit. I knew we should have hit up pool-side bingo."

I shake my head. "You can't always be great."

He laughs and closes his eyes, and I do the same. I know we should get up, go back to our rooms. It's past midnight, and my dad would lose it if he knew I was out this late with a boy. But I don't want to move just yet. I'm not ready for this to be over.

"So, you're a Cancer then. Mmmm."

I wave my finger above me. "Uh-uh. Don't do that. I hate when people find out your sign and then they act all smarmy like they can see you naked or something."

His eyes pop open at that, stricken, so I quickly add, "Plus, you're a man of science. How can you believe that bullshit?"

"How can you not believe it when it's so right?" He smiles. "I'm a Virgo, which means I'm incredibly intelligent and organized. I like a plan. I'm a problem-solver. Tell me that's wrong!"

I roll my eyes. "Okay, so yes, I'm a Cancer. What does that tell you about me?"

"You're creative and passionate." He closes his eyes again. "You can be guarded at first, very guarded in this case." A smile starts to spread across his face, and I close my eyes so I won't see it. Those stupid, perfect smiles are affecting me too much. "But inside," he continues, "you feel things very strongly. You're sensitive and soft. You just don't let many people see that."

I know he's just talking about astrology, but why do I feel like he's reading me? Why do I feel like he's cracking me open again? There has to be a catch. There has to be something wrong with him that I'm not seeing. Because this . . . I don't get to have this.

I keep quiet. I'm scared that if we keep going, I'll be proved right. Something will ruin this night that was nothing like I expected, but everything I was too scared to want.

So, we lie there in silence, and I can hear his breathing getting deeper. I feel peace roll over my body as sleep pulls me closer. But as my mind gets hazy, I can't help but ask, "What do the stars say about us, huh? Do Virgos and Cancers get along?"

He doesn't respond at first, and I think he must have passed out. Should I shake him awake? We're not supposed to be here this late. Finally, though, he whispers. "Oh, they do . . . they have the potential to be something really great . . . really special."

"See? It's bullshit."

His quiet laugh mixes with the water rolling against the boat, rocking me to sleep.

CHAPTER TWELVE

I dream that I am waiting for something. No, someone. Definitely someone. My palms are sweaty, and my stomach has that familiar, irritating fluttery feeling. And just when that someone is finally approaching, when I hear that warm laugh, I open my eyes to see . . . Wally.

"Good morning, sunshine."

I spring up from the plastic chair, knocking my Pikachu pillow to the ground.

"No. It's not morning."

"Oh, it's morning, little sister."

I blink frantically, my eyes adjusting to the dim light. The sun isn't up yet, but it's definitely morning. Shit.

"What time is it?"

Something passes over Wally's face, so quick that I barely catch it, and he shrugs. "I don't know."

I look him over and realize that he's wearing the same

clothes that he had on at dinner last night. What's he doing out here this early? Or did he just never go to sleep? That would explain why he has those deep bags under his eyes that somehow have gotten even darker. They're a sharp contrast to the wide smile that's now spreading across his lips.

"You and Alex here have a wild night?" he asks, gesturing to the chair next to me. Alex is stretched out with a smile on his sleeping face. His shirt has rolled up, and his hand is resting on his surprisingly toned stomach. All of the confusing feelings from last night swirl in my chest.

"It's not like that, Wally," I say, swatting Alex's leg, so he'll wake up and stop looking so frustratingly appealing.

"Sure."

Alex yawns and stretches his arms out all slow and cute, like he's a fairy-tale character waking up from an enchanted sleep, but then his eyes open and he jumps up at attention when he sees my brother.

"Um, hi, Wally." His whole body braces as if he's waiting to be punched. But I know that Wally doesn't care like that, not anymore.

"Whatever. I won't tell Mom and Dad," Wally says, giving me a hard look. "But you two better be on deck ready to go. I'm not going to cover for you."

With that, he turns and walks into the sliding doors, leaving all my questions about his nighttime wandering unanswered.

"Well, that went better than it could have," Alex says.

I sigh, shake my head. "Yeah, I guess."

"You know, you sleep with your arms crossed like a vampire," Alex continues. "Like . . ." I turn to him, and he has his arms in an X across his chest, with his eyes closed and his tongue hanging out.

"No, I don't!" I say, slapping his arms away.

"Uh, yes, you do." He purses his lips and nods with his eyes wide.

"How did you see me sleeping? Wally woke us up!"

"I woke up at some point, when it was still dark. These drunk moms woke me up, woo-hoo-ing and twerking. I should have taken a video. It was something."

I throw my hands up. "And you didn't get me up? We should have gone back to our rooms! You trying to get me murdered by my dad? Or I take that back, you would be the one getting murdered."

"I don't know." He looks a little bit chastened. "You looked . . . peaceful. It was nice."

I feel my heart speed up, and I'm suddenly aware of what I must look like. My eyes are itchy, so my mascara and eyeliner are probably smeared everywhere. I can smell my own stanky dragon breath, and my dry skin is probably making all of yesterday's CC cream flake off like I have some weird infectious disease.

"Yeah, well, I don't look so peaceful anymore," I say, gesturing to my face. "You know in movies, when girls be waking up all glowy and perfect, and it's so fake—not that we're, like, waking up together, but—"

He cuts me off. "Lenore, you look great."

My heart beats even faster, and I can feel it all the way in my throat. I look down at the ground.

"Anyway, we better go get ready." I gesture past the guard-rail, where we can see the approaching port of Mykonos, with its bright white buildings peppered across the hills. "I don't know what time it is, but it looks like we're getting close."

"Yeah, yeah."

"Thank you," I say, stealing a glance at him real quick before looking back out at the water. His curly bedhead does weird things to my stomach. "For last night. That was my best birthday in . . . a while."

"You don't have to thank me, Lenore. That's what friends do."

The parents don't have some big itinerary planned for the day (much to Etta's frustration). Instead our driver takes us over to the north side of Mykonos, past a tavern and a cute little church, dropping us off at a golden sand beach with sparkling turquoise water. On the plus side, it's not crowded with loungers and umbrellas packed in tight for tourists, like the beaches we passed closer to the cruise ships. On the—well, I don't want to say negative side, but definitely *naked* side, apparently bathing suits are optional here.

"Oh! Oh my lord!" Mom says with wide eyes, hands flying to her mouth as a leathery-skinned man with things hanging that have no business hanging in public comes strutting by us.

I take that back. This is firmly in the negative zone.

Dad rushes to cover Etta's eyes. "Maybe this is not the best choice for our beach day?"

Etta throws his hands off and crosses her arms. "Dad, this is no different than the statues and paintings we have seen so far on this trip. And I've read that America's stance on nudity is quite puritanical compared to the rest of the world—"

"Yes, you're a Puritan until you're sixty-five!" Dad says, putting his aviator sunglasses over her eyes. "Lenore, you too! Eyes on the sand."

"Oh, loosen up, Edward!" Dr. Lee says, laughing. "Maybe we should all join in. When in Greece!" She bumps Mr. Lee with her hip, and he chuckles along with her.

Alex's whole body goes from brown to scarlet in a millisecond. "Mom, no. I'm pretty sure that's child abuse."

"Alex, you're eighteen, not a child," she says with a smirk. "And relax. I'm only kidding. Mostly."

We lay out towels on the end of the beach, as far from the congregation of naked people as possible. And my parents get over the naked thing pretty fast, running out into the sea with the Lees, splashing and diving and giggling like teenagers. But the four of us stay planted on the sand. Etta starts talking Alex's ear off about the Terrace of the Lions in Delos, where she wanted to go today, so I turn to Wally, who's lying flat with an arm covering his eyes.

"Thank you again. For not saying anything, I mean. We weren't doing anything. But you know that Dad wouldn't see it that way."

He uncovers his eyes, and I see that the deep bags are still there and his eyes are pink.

"I didn't do it as a favor. None of us need the drama right now."

"Okay," I say, swallowing down the pang of hurt his tone causes. "Listen, Wally, I know you don't want to talk about it, but I just . . . I'm worried about you. You're not acting like yourself since we got here, and you're not sleeping—"

"Just save it," he says, standing up and putting his sunglasses on. He pulls out his phone. "I'm not doing this. I—I'll be back later. I'm gonna see if I can find some food." He turns and makes his way up the sand, not looking back.

"Whoa," Alex says behind me. I turn, and his eyebrows are raised. He was listening to the whole thing. "Whoa" is also what my brain is shouting. A whole Sunday choir is in there, stomping and hollering out "Whoa!!!!!" with hands raised to the sky. Not because of what a dick Wally was to me, though. No, because sometime during that conversation, Alex took off his shirt.

And he looks good.

Real good.

More good than he has any business looking. I mean, he's a nerd. Where did he get toned arms and a flat stomach like that—lifting beakers or some shit? It's not right!

"I'm sorry he talked to you like that," he says, his face full of concern. Right. I'm just supposed to have a normal conversation with him like this. Okay.

"I don't know what's going on with him," I say, looking down at my hands so I can focus. "He's not usually like this. He . . . he broke up with his long-term boyfriend, but I think he's keeping it a secret. My mom and dad don't seem to know. And he's been up all night, every night, since we've been here, and just so . . . so goddamn moody. I wish he would talk to me. We used to be so close, and I want to help him."

God, I'm rambling. I look up to see if Alex is losing interest, but he's nodding and his eyes are totally locked on me, like he's listening intently. I'm still getting used to someone doing that.

"Maybe he's stressed about the fall," Alex says. "Law school is no joke. But it's not cool that he's taking it out on you." He reaches in his bag and pulls out sunscreen, and oh man, nope. Can't handle that. My eyes shoot back to the ground.

"Yeah, I get that," I continue, taking deep, steadying *I will not ogle Alex* breaths. "I'm stressed about all the changes coming, too, though. It's something we could bond over, maybe. If he would just talk to me." But I guess it isn't the same. He's worried about his very much focused and planned life. I'm a mess because I have no plan at all, and Wally's made it clear what he thinks of that. I squeeze my eyes shut and shake those thoughts away. "Plus, Kieran—that's his boyfriend. Well, ex now, I guess. He was going to move back to SoCal and everything, so they could live together during Wally's three years. What happened to make Wally throw all that away?"

I make the mistake of looking up at Alex again, and he's still listening, perfectly attentive, but now he's apparently rubbed his chest and arms with sunscreen? And his golden-brown skin is glowing??? I feel like Abu in the Cave of Wonders. My arm is twitching to reach out and touch even though I know, firmly, that I SHOULD NOT DO THAT. AT ALL.

"Um. Yeah. Okay." My brain is short-circuiting. Anxiety and hurt about Wally, this weird thing stirring in the bottom of my stomach for Alex. These are too many feelings to be feeling all at once.

"Obviously, I'm no expert at this. Only child here," Alex continues, like the way he looks right now is all totally normal. NO BIG DEAL. "But maybe just give him time? Let him come to you? The bond that you guys have didn't just disappear, you know? He's probably taking time to process this, that's all."

"Yeah. Yeah, you're right." I sigh and rub my face, resetting. "It just sucks that he can't like process it with me or whatever." I take a couple more deep breaths. "Anyway, I'm done with that emo moment."

"You don't have to be. If you don't want to be." He nudges my arm, and my whole body tenses. Those goddamn butterflies are back. A flock of them! A swarm!

"Do you want to go swimming?" he asks. "Take your mind off it?"

Oh, you mean take off this lace muumuu thing and frolic with you in the waves in what is basically our underwear? Yes, I very much do. But also NO. No, I very much don't.

"No, I'm good," I say, looking off down the beach. Of course, then I make direct eye contact with a white-haired couple letting it all hang out. Thank you, universe.

"Ooooooohh," Alex says, sounding way too excited. "I know what you want."

I hear him rustling in his backpack, but I'm scared to look up. Those words have sent my mind down all kinds of porno-y roads. But, no, Etta is still here. And there are our parents in the water, doing their best impersonation of Lindsay Lohan dancing in that one video. Get it together, Lenore!

"What's that?" I ask tentatively, and he answers by throwing bags of chips into my lap.

"Greek snacks! Look what I found! The chips in the green bag are oregano flavored and the blue bag is tzatziki." His eyes light up when he talks about his snacks, and it's so cute I want to scream. "And look at this chocolate bar! It's all bubbly and weird, like . . . alien eggs or something. But the cashier said it was the most popular, so I think we gotta risk it."

"You're really selling me here, man," I laugh. I put my hands out. "Gimme some of that alien chocolate."

The next day is another sea day, and Alex and I decide to skip poolside Family Feud with the rest of the crew and meet up at the business center for the Wi-Fi. His parents have bought him one of the expensive-ass unlimited passes that my parents refused to even consider because apparently that's what happens when you're an only child.

"Aren't you a little overdressed?" Alex says with a smirk,

gesturing at my outfit as I enter the room. I'm wearing a scarlet-red dress with hot-pink embroidery and bell sleeves.

I pose and then shrug. "It's a moment."

"Mm-hmmm." He lets out one of his loud, perfect laughs. I find myself feeling grateful that we're the only two in the room, so it's just mine to enjoy.

"And the camera?" he asks.

"You never know when the inspiration will strike." I hold it up over my eye, and he frames his face with his hands, cheesing. "Nah, not worth the film," I say, and he rolls his eyes.

"Okay, and just for that, I have the tax for using my internet privileges today," he laughs, turning his attention back to the computer. He types something.

"Tax? What are you, the troll under the bridge?" I ease myself into the chair next to him, and see what's on his screen. "Okay, yes, definitely troll-like behavior." It's one of the major-deciding quizzes that he had printed out before and that I had given the ax to in Santorini. "I thought we moved on from this, man. And we were making such good progress! I only hated you, like, thirteen percent at this point."

"Thirteen percent, huh? And I thought I was at least down to five. Maybe ten, tops." He smiles, and I shoot him back my best active bitch face. "Listen, the best tests are responsive; they change with your answers. So I feel like I couldn't give you the best testing experience before. Plus, it smelled like donkey shit, and even worse, you had to listen to my annoying voice. . . ."

He bumps me with his shoulder. "Please will you just try it? Worst case, you waste five minutes. Best case, all of your problems are solved."

I want to be annoyed, but then he does this fluttery thing with his long eyelashes. And I know he's trying to be funny, but it makes me want to do whatever he asks. Like, until the end of time. And I guess he is right. What's the worst that can happen from taking one of these silly tests?

So, I bump him out of the way and snatch the keyboard from him, grumbling the whole time so he knows I don't like it. But I answer each question, many of them repeats from the ones Alex read to me on the steps in Santorini, thoughtfully and honestly. And by the time I get to the last one, thirty out of thirty, I'm feeling almost hopeful, even. Like, maybe this stupid internet quiz will figure out my major and my life path for me. Maybe it was this easy all along.

But then I click submit, and the results pop up. "You should major in the arts!" The arts. That's it. For real. And then there's a long list of possible majors, everything from art history to graphic design to photography. Everything I've already considered.

My expectations weren't high, but like, damn. Can you narrow it down for me at all, internet survey? What will I feel fulfilled doing forever? What will I be the best at? What will make my parents—and me—happy? These are the questions I need answers to.

And soon. The end of this cruise, and my parents' deadline, is less than a week away.

Alex looks over my shoulder, eyes dancing with excitement, but then he visibly deflates when he reads what's on the screen.

"Well . . . that sucks."

"Yeah, no kidding," I snort, clicking out of the window. "Can I use your internet now, your trollness?"

"Yeah, yeah," he mumbles. And then, "I'm sorry."

"It's not your fault." I shrug, logging into my email. "And hey, it's not like I'm in a bad situation. I'll go to NYU. I'll study art history. Lots of people would love to do that. It's not the end of the world if I'm not, like, ecstatic about it."

"You deserve to do something that makes you ecstatic though."

I turn to him and shrug again. "Like you said before, though, when we were in Sicily, maybe it doesn't have to be all that. My passion. Maybe I just need to pick something that I know I'll be halfway decent at, and stick with it long enough. Like my parents keep telling me to do. I don't need to be in love with what I'm majoring in."

"I did say that." His eyebrows press close together. "But maybe I shouldn't have. It makes me kind of . . . sad? That my pragmatism has rubbed off on you. That's what I want for me, but it doesn't have to be that way for you."

"I mean, you make the pod person life look so appealing," I say with a wink. He smiles, but it doesn't reach his eyes. "And again, this conversation we're having, it just feels so . . . privileged? Like, my ancestors were fighting for the right to even go to college and I'm whining because the major I chose doesn't, like, give me life? I need to just get over it and put my head down."

His brow furrows even more, but then he starts to nod slowly, like I'm convincing him. I've almost convinced myself too.

I turn my attention back to my screen, and he logs on to the computer next to me. I start sorting through the emails I've gotten since I last checked it on the plane. I delete lots of summer sale emails from my favorite stores, skim and then respond to a couple of congrats e-cards from distant aunties, and I'm about to open one of the many messages from Tessa, when I see a name I wasn't expecting.

Jay Parikh.

My brain rushes to catch up with the words I see in the preview.

What's up, Lenore! Just wanna see when you're gonna
be back. We should . . .

My heart thumps in my chest as the cursor hovers over the message. We should *what*? What!

But instead of finding out what kind of mess he's spouting to try and reel me back in, I click the little trash can icon. And then empty my trash folder, too.

Jay doesn't deserve access to my mind or my heart anymore. I'm not sure when I truly and fully started believing that, when

I became certain that I would no longer be giving that asshole any more of my energy.

Was it after that night with Alex? When he—*as a friend*—planned such a perfect night for me, far beyond whatever boy I've been talking to even attempted?

I don't know. It feels good though. I let myself take a deep breath.

"Was that from the prom guy?" Alex asks, apparently still reading over my shoulder.

"Mind yo' business!" I swat him, and he laughs and goes back to his computer.

I turn my attention back to my email and start sifting through the ones left from Tessa. She has taken it upon herself to message me for progress reports on my "love journey" every day, including tips and tricks from her favorite stories. Because of course she has.

I'm about to respond to one of her increasingly frantic dispatches when a notification pops up on my screen.

Tessa Johnson is inviting you to a video chat.

I look around the business center. It's still just me and Alex in here, but still. I'm not sure if I want him hearing all this, and I don't have headphones.

Messages start rolling in.

I can see that you're online!

Hellllooooo little green dot talk to me

Resistance is futile.

I click accept, and the two beaming faces of Tessa and Sam

appear on my screen, pixelated but good enough.

"Lenore!" Tessa squeals.

"Hey!" Sam says.

"Hi, guys," I say, and Alex looks over, raising his eyebrows in interest.

Before I even have a chance to tell Tessa that he's there, though, and hopefully subtly warn her against talking about this "love journey" business, she's off. "Okay, so have you been reading my emails?? I haven't heard anything from you FOR DAYS! And I even sent a check-in to Etta, too, but she didn't respond. You think she'd check the contact page on her blog more—"

"Etta has a blog? About what?"

"She, like, critiques academic articles that she gets off JSTOR. Your sister is a genius, did you know that? Anyway, I was worried you got kidnapped or something, by some Italian lothario, sweeping you away on his moped. But I guess that would be good for our purposes, wouldn't it? Maybe he's a reformed pickpocket, worked the Trevi Fountain circuit, but then he saw you throw your coin in and it unlocked something inside him—"

Alex leans over, wide-eyed, probably trying to see who exactly is spouting this ridiculousness, and Tessa spots him.

"Wait, who's that?"

"This is my friend Alex. We met on the ship. Our parents have really hit it off," I say, gesturing for him to come closer.

He waves. "Hi, Lenore's friends!"

Tessa's eyes light up, and I immediately regret this decision. "Oh. *Oh*. I see that you're further along than I thought."

I drag my hand across my throat, which I think is the universally accepted signal for "Shut up, Tessa," but she keeps going.

"I knew the coin would work!" she shouts with glee.

"No, it's not like that," I start to say, but she cuts me off. "Praise Jasmine Guillory and Alyssa Cole and all that is holy, you are living in the middle of a vacation romance!"

My eyes bug out in horror and my neck burns. But then the sound abruptly cuts out. Her mouth is still moving, but we, thankfully, can't hear any of the romance crap she's spouting. At the bottom of the screen, it reads: Tessa Johnson is muted. And next to her, I can see that Sam is giving me a thumbs-up. Sweet, discreet Sam for the win.

"That's weird. We can't hear her," Alex says.

"So weird."

"What was she talking about, anyway?"

"No idea."

She goes on for a minute more, with a lot of excitement and even one case of jazz hands, before Sam subtly reaches over and unmutes them.

"Anyway, I just love you, Lenore," Tessa says with a smile. "I'm so excited for you."

"Thank you, girl. I love you too."

"So, what are you two doing in this . . . white room, anyway?" Sam asks, obviously trying to change the subject. "Shouldn't you be out exploring—where are you now? Greece? France?"

"It's a sea day," I say. "We just left Greece, and the ship's heading back to Italy next. What's our next stop again?" I turn to Alex.

"Naples," he says. "Today I'm annoying Lenore and making her take quizzes to find out her true destiny." He laughs, but when he's met with Tessa's and Sam's confused stares and my subtle shake of the head, it peters out.

Another topic I was trying to avoid. Jesus, when did a simple conversation with my friends become such a minefield?

"Oh no, it looks like our time on the internet is running out! Damnit! Every minute costs like a million dollars. It's so ridiculous. Anyway, I love you guys! Bye!"

"Well, call us again when you can. When is the—" I click out of the window before Tessa can finish her question.

When I turn to Alex, he's looking at me with amusement, but also concern.

"They don't know how uncertain you are, do they?" he says slowly. "Or how much you don't want to live in New York? And this deadline your parents gave you? Have you talked to . . . uh, Tessa? About any of it?"

"No, but it's, like, a recent development." His eyebrow arches to signal he doesn't buy that. "It's just . . ." I try again. "It's too much to get into with Tessa. You saw how she's kind of a steamroller. It's easier to just be . . . easy."

"Isn't she your best friend, though? I mean, you told *me* all about it."

I did tell him. And I didn't even really hesitate. Why is that?

"Yeah, she is, but . . ." I turn my attention back to the screen. Log myself out. Shut the computer down. "I don't know. It's different with you."

"Oh yeah?" I can hear the smile in his voice.

"Yeah. Because, well, we're in a bubble. Who knows if we'll even see each other again after next week."

I know it's more than that. What, I'm not exactly sure yet. But I'm scared to analyze it—to look too close, too much, until all the shininess loses its luster.

I turn to face Alex, and he's biting his lip, frowning. But when I pull my camera up to my eye, his face shifts back into a grin. I center him in the viewfinder. His shiny curls, the parentheses framing his smile, his brown eyes lit up the way they always seem to be when we're trading jabs. I push the shutter button, capturing him just as he is, right now.

CHAPTER THIRTEEN

". . . and so we've all made it through the scanner, they've done the pat-down on me because they always do, all right? But our bags *still* aren't out. So we're looking around and then the TSA agent comes up behind me and is all, 'I need you to come with us,' and the other guy, the one behind the machine, is looking at us all crazy, with these big ol' bug eyes like they're going to pop out of his head." My dad has everyone's attention at the dinner table—even mine, and I know how this story ends. "So I say," he continues. "I say, 'Who? Me? Because, all of my respect, sir, but your colleague over there has just inspected me more thoroughly than my wife has done in months.'" He pauses as everyone laughs, an expert at working an audience. It's why he's such a great trial lawyer.

"But then the man's face gets real serious, and we follow him right quick because we're trying to get to my parents' place in Florida, not be some viral video on the Facebook. And they bring us over to this table, and I'm expecting—well, I don't know what I was expecting, but it definitely wasn't Lenore's My Little Pony backpack." He winks at me, and Alex whips his head around and waggles his eyebrows in my direction, taken with this plot twist. "'Sir, is this your backpack?' he asks me, and I told him, 'Well, it's my daughter's, as I'm more partial to Pinkie Pie than Rainbow Dash.' And my man doesn't even crack a smile. Instead he starts grilling me, talking 'bout, where are we headed? And is this really your family? I was respectful, all right, because I could tell it was getting serious, but what I really wanted to tell him was, 'Do you see their paddle feet? Of course these kids are mine!'"

Another chorus of laughter, and Alex pulls the tablecloth up, trying to see my feet. I swat him away, letting my hands linger longer than they need to.

"But then he puts on these gloves, and starts pulling stuff out of Lenore's backpack. And that's when I started to actually get worried. Because, you see, we didn't help her pack the thing. Etta was little, we were still getting used to having three of them, and then traveling across the country for the first time? She was on her own! But instead of crayons and Barbies, my man starts pulling out pliers and foil and an old phone charger and this metal wire and I think even a hammer—"

"There was *not* a hammer, Dad," I interrupt him, and he waves that away with his fork.

"And I was cracking jokes before, but now I'm speechless, because how can I explain all of this stuff in our ten-year-old's plastic backpack? Honestly, it could have gone either way, and one of those ways was us not flying to see my mama for her big birthday. But!"

I feel the tension and see everyone lean in, like I've watched the jurors and the audience and even the judge do when Dad's in court.

"Lenore starts crying, talking 'bout how it's the materials for a mixed media sculpture she's working on. Just like that, 'mixed media sculpture'! At ten! So, she's bawling, snot dripping down her face, and the guy—all of the people working there!—they felt bad, so bad that they were apologizing to us, gave her a handful of these lollipops that had the American flag on them."

"Did she get to keep her materials?" Dr. Lee asks.

"Oh, no!" Dad says with a laugh, slapping the table. "But they did drive us up to our gate and give us priority boarding. We were still in coach by the bathrooms, but at least we got to get there first!"

The whole table joins in with Dad's raspy chuckles, and I roll my eyes but laugh too. This is one of his favorite stories, and he tells it in large gatherings all the time. I haven't figured out exactly how I feel about it—after all, the butt of it all is my art inconveniencing my family, right? But I also like being the center of my dad's attention, which doesn't happen often as the middle, average child.

"Excuse me, I can't *not* say hello." I look up to see a middle-aged woman with tan skin and feathery black hair. She looks familiar and I'm struggling to place her when Natalia pops up next to her.

"Mom . . ." she says, looking around uncomfortably, "they're trying to eat."

"Oh, I'm not going to ignore our good friends just because of some little lovers' quarrel," she says, and Natalia's cheeks turn pink. Alex suddenly finds his steak incredibly interesting.

Dr. Lee shoots Alex a sympathetic look before turning to my parents. "Marla, Edward, these are our friends from back home. Jasmin Rodrigo-Hernandez and her daughter, Natalia."

"Oh, wow, what a small world! Nice to meet you both," Mom says, giving them her signature sparkling smile.

Mrs. Rodrigo-Hernandez leans in and shakes my parents' hands. "Not such a small world. We were supposed to go on this trip together, actually, until . . . well. Anyway, Natalia and Alex went to high school together. They've known each other since the first grade!"

I can see that Mom is about to probe that "until . . ." but I shake my head at her, and she presses her lips together.

"And now they'll be off to UCLA together in the fall. Can you believe it, Ronni?" Mrs. Hernandez says, clutching her hands to her chest. "Our babies are all grown up!"

They're going to the same school in the fall? Now that is a fact that Alex has conveniently left out. I feel a pang of something—irritation? Worry? But I shake that away. I don't have any claim on him. If anything, I'm intruding on their story, if their lives have been this intertwined for this long.

". . . our son, Wally, just graduated," I snap back in to hear Dad saying. He's all lit up like he always is when he gets a chance to brag about Wally. Instead of basking in it like he usually does, though, Wally is staring at his hands. "What is it you're studying, Natalia?"

"I'm double-majoring in political science and sociology," she says. "And I hope to go to law school right after undergraduate."

Of course she just gave the best possible answer in my dad's eyes. He claps his hands in delight.

"Oh, wonderful! Wally here will be starting at their law school this fall." Dad glows with pride as he looks at Wally. I'm pretty sure he's never looked at me that way. "And I'm with Sidley & Jones. Here let me give you my card—for when you're in the market for an internship." He hands it to her, and I can see her eyes widen in recognition of the big firm my dad works for.

"Thank you so much, sir," she says with a dazzling, all-teeth smile. It's easy to see why Alex did everything he could to keep her. She's beautiful, and apparently super smart too—the kind of girl guys treasure.

"No problem," Dad says, shaking her hand. "I love to see young people of color succeed. I can tell you have a bright future ahead of you."

And I know he doesn't mean it that way, but it feels like a torpedo sent straight for me. Because when he's discussing my future, there's just worry and concern. But for Natalia, it's so obviously clear skies ahead. I swallow down something hot and tight in my throat.

"Well, anyway, we'll get back to our table before dessert arrives. My wife will eat all my tiramisu if I'm not there to claim it!" Mrs. Rodrigo-Hernandez laughs. "I expect you to save me a dance at the formal dinner in a couple days, David. I know you've got those moves!"

Mr. Lee shimmies in his seat, and they all laugh. Mrs. Rodrigo-Hernandez and Natalia wave before heading off to the other side of the dining room.

I turn to Alex, expecting to see him pining after his long-lost love, but instead his eyes are zeroed in on me.

"You okay?" he mouths, nodding toward my dad. I'm shocked, and a little mortified, that he picked up on all that. I guess I wasn't keeping my face under control like I should be.

I nod quickly and wave it away. "Yeah, I'm fine."

"Maybe she can shadow you through a day at law school, Wally," Dad continues.

"I don't know, I'm going to be pretty busy," Wally says dismissively. I'm not jealous of where Wally is in life—I know I have no interest in being a lawyer like Dad. But I guess I am jealous that he gets to treat all the attention and pride and Dad looking at him like the goddamn star-eyed emoji all the time like it's nothing. It's every day to him, so it's no big deal.

"Yes, of course, of course," Dad says. "The first year of law school is no walk in the park, and it just gets harder from there.

And especially with Kieran back in town—that's his boyfriend. They've been together since high school," he explains to the Lees. "Well, there's going to be a lot on your plate. Tenfold what you had this past year of undergrad. But I know that you'll rise to the occasion. You always do."

"He's not even with Kieran anymore." The words are out of my mouth before I really think about them. It's like all the resentment and jealousy was in a pot, stewing in my stomach, and the top just bubbled over.

Mom's eyebrows press together, and Dad cocks his head to the side, like he heard me wrong.

"Lenore, what the fuck?" Wally says, his eyes daggers.

"It's the truth. I don't get why you can't be honest with all of us." *Also maybe I want to take you down a peg or two in Mom's and Dad's eyes, show them that their golden boy is human.* But I would never admit that out loud.

"You always have to be so fucking nosy. It's none of your business—"

"Enough." Mom cuts him off. Her voice is soft but powerful. "We are not going to do this right now." There is nothing my parents hate more than a scene—than us giving white folks an opportunity to look at us and have their stereotypes confirmed—so I know she's pissed without even looking at her. But I'll be honest. I actually feel weirdly satisfied that she might be mad at Wally, for once.

To my horror, though, she's not giving her steely, squinty look to Wally. Her eyes are locked on me.

"Lenore, I'm disappointed," she says, her voice barely above a whisper. And Dad doesn't even have to say anything. I can read everything in his dangerously arched eyebrow.

My chest tightens, and I have the strongest urge to run, to flee. But instead I just mumble, "Sorry," and stare at my plate. Who was I kidding, to think this would go any other way? I should have kept my mouth shut and let the Wally praise party continue on unencumbered. I can feel Alex's eyes on me, but I don't look up.

The conversation moves on, awkward at first, but then it finds its natural rhythm again, as dessert and more drinks are brought to the table. Etta tells the table all about the history of pizza in Naples, where we'll be docking tomorrow, and our parents move on to a spirited discussion about the controversial election for governor, coming up in the fall. Wally stays silent, mean-mugging the tiramisu like he wants to fight it. He's probably imagining my face there.

"I'd love to see them," Dr. Lee says at one point, and the whole table is silent, which makes me look up, finally. All eyes are on me, so I guess that was directed my way.

"Sorry. I . . . I missed that, Dr. Lee," I say.

"Oh, it's fine, honey!" She beams, obviously going out of her way to smooth out the tension from earlier. "I was saying that I've so enjoyed watching you take pictures with your camera on this trip so far. That camera is just so unique, and I can tell that you've got a good eye. I'd love to see all of your photos sometime this week."

"Thank you. I've been having fun with it."

"You better do it quick," Dad chuckles. "Before she moves on to her next project! What did your last photography period last? A couple months? If that? It doesn't take our Lenore long to get bored and move on to something else."

My neck flames and something churns in my stomach like acid. What he's saying doesn't sound mean-spirited, and everyone is laughing kindly. But it feels like another torpedo, sent stealthily over to my side. And this one has sunk my battleship.

I paste a fake smile on my face and try to hold in all my feelings and the words of defense that are burning the back of my throat. This meal is almost over, and I just need to power through.

"All of my respect, sir," Alex says next to me, "but I don't think that's a fair way to characterize Lenore. I've only known her for a week, but already I can see how talented she is, in so many different areas. I think it's a sign of her . . . her ingenuity, not her lack of commitment."

I know Alex probably wants me to fall over myself with gratitude, but instead I feel low-key irritated. He's just making it worse with my dad. And this feels like a resurgence of the Alex I met in the beginning—the know-it-all, trying to take control.

"Stop," I whisper, my words venom. "I don't need you to do this."

Confusion passes across his face, quickly replaced by panic.

"I'm—I'm sorry. I was . . . I was just trying to help," he

stutters. His face breaks open and softens, and his cheeks turn red. All of a sudden, the fury that was building within me dissipates and I feel . . . bad. Was it so terrible what he said? Or am I looking for someone to take my anger out on, since I can't be real with my family?

"I'm sorry," he repeats again, and then he turns to my dad. "I'm sorry, Mr. Bennett." Alex stands up. "Excuse me. I'm going to get some air."

I watch him leave the room, winding between all the tables, and then turn to see everyone at the table staring wide-eyed at me, their mouths in identical Os.

I find Alex outside on a pool lounger next to the empty splash pad, his head in his hands.

"I don't need you to go to battle for me," I say, sitting down next to him.

He runs his fingers through his hair and looks up, his curls sticking out in every direction. He bites his lip and nods, his eyes full of anguish. "I know. You made that clear."

"But also . . . thank you." He blinks at me. I smile. "I know that wasn't easy. And I appreciate that you . . . um, even thought to say something."

He sighs and shakes his head. "It's not like I could just sit there and see you hurting, Lenore, and say nothing."

"I wasn't hurt. It's fine." It comes out without even any thought, a reflex.

"That's not true. We both know it." He reaches forward

and places his hand on mine. His palm is warm, and that feeling spreads to my whole body. "And you don't have to try and convince me that's true. It's okay to be hurt. You're allowed to . . . feel however you feel. You don't have to hide it all with me."

His brown eyes meet mine, melting away all of the tension and hurt feelings that were oppressive in the dining room. And I know—*I know*—that it's only been a short time. I know that it makes no sense. But when he looks at me like that, I feel seen. I feel overwhelmingly accepted. And I'm certain, from the top of my crown all the way down to my baby toes, that I've never been this understood by someone else before.

And *damn*. It's scary.

I flip my hand over anyway, lacing my fingers with his and squeezing tightly.

His eyes widen in surprise and then crinkle in delight. He squeezes back, and then envelops my hands in both of his. This is some G-rated shit. I mean, we're holding hands! I'm pretty sure I skipped right on past this step with Jay, and the other guys I've talked to. But somehow this feels like the most intimate thing I've ever done. Every inch of my skin is on high alert, and my stomach aches in anticipation.

"Was your dad pissed?" he asks, stroking the back of my hand with his thumb.

"Um, yeah. But not as much as I expected." I close my eyes and take a deep breath so I can focus. Which is extremely difficult because I just want to pull Alex in close and inhale him, like I'm in a detergent commercial or something. "I think he was actually a little embarrassed," I continue, staring at an abandoned sparkly pink flip-flop by the splash pad. Instead of staring at our intertwined fingers. Or his smooth brown skin. Or his perfect full lips. "He started trying to smooth it over with, 'You know what I meant, Lenore. Go tell him what I meant.'"

Alex grins. "That was a pretty good Edward Bennett impersonation."

"Thank you. I've had a lot of practice, you know, calling to excuse my absences."

"You did not call your school making that voice." He throws his head back with a laugh. "I mean, you're not *that* good."

"Well, no. But I think I could have passed!"

A cloud passes over his face. "Is your dad going to hate me now? Are the meals and outings going to be super awkward? Have I ruined everything?"

"Yeah, you might as well jump ship now. Before he comes to find you tonight." Alex's whole body tenses. "I'm kidding! I'm kidding! He's totally going to wait until we dock in Naples tomorrow to make you disappear."

I laugh and bump him with my shoulder, making sure to keep our hands linked.

"I'm sorry again that I made things weird and didn't let you speak for yourself. I know you can. I just . . . I can't take them talking about you like you're some sort of work in progress. Like you don't measure up to *Wally* because you're doing things differently than him. Or, you know, different than me." He turns to me, pressing our knees together. "You're willing to take risks and explore new things. And that's all a strength, not a weakness. I don't think there's anything about you that needs to be fixed, Lenore. You're perfect just the way you are."

I search his face for the joke, for signs that this is the first jab in our sarcastic dance that's become so familiar.

But he's completely sincere.

He reaches up to touch my chin, lifting it slightly. He leans in and our noses touch, our breath mingles. And even though I'm sitting down, my knees go wobbly and weak like a girl in one of Tessa's stories. In fact, my whole body feels like it's vibrating, full of wanting, of *needing*.

I close the space between us.

Our lips find each other's, easily, urgently. Like this is what they were always meant to do. My heart pounds in my chest, and the beat is my rhythm for every motion, every kiss. His fingers drift to the back of my neck, threading through my hair and to my scalp. His other hand curves around my waist, pulling me close.

"Oh, Lenore," he breathes against my lips, and it's the sweetest sound.

Is this a dream?

No, it can't be. Because dreams feel real when you're in them. It's only when you wake up that you start to question why no one's wearing pants or you're conversing with an animated cheeseburger. So, if it feels like a dream, then . . . it's not a dream. This is real.

I am kissing a boy who sees me, *really sees me*, and still wants me. I am kissing a boy who thinks I'm perfect the way I am. I am kissing a boy who doesn't want to hide how he feels about me. I am kissing Alex. My Alex.

We pull away from each other, finally, reluctantly, because I *guess* we need oxygen, too. Alex's lips are swollen, and his eyes are bright. He is clutching me so tightly, like he never wants to let go. I don't think I've ever been held like this before. Everything feels brand-new with him.

"We will see each other again," he whispers. "After this cruise is over. You were saying earlier today, in the business center, that we might not. But . . . we will. I know it."

I smile at him and swat his leg. "Awwww man, don't get all corny on me now."

"I am going to do my very best to contain it, Lenore, but no promises." He kisses my cheek, my nose. "Something tells me you're going to inspire maximum corniness." He kisses my neck and then my lips again. "An embarrassing amount of corniness."

We don't do much talking after that.

CHAPTER FOURTEEN

If Future Lenore had come back to tell Prom Night Lenore that I would be sitting in the bright sun outside of the Duomo in Naples, eating gelato with a cute boy's arm tight around my shoulders, I would have 1) questioned her judgment because you could time travel and this what you chose to do? Really, girl? Go stop an assassination or something. And 2) called that chick a liar because there was just no way my life could ever be that perfect, that picturesque.

But that's what's happening. I've pinched myself, I've looked down to see if I'm suddenly naked, I've double- and triple-checked—I'm not dreaming. This is actually happening.

"God, you're so beautiful," he murmurs, his breath warm against my ear.

"Are you talking to your gelato?" I snort.

"No, you," he says. "*You* are so beautiful."

I laugh and slap my knee.

"Oh, is that what my heartfelt compliments inspire? Derisive laughter?" He nuzzles me with his nose, and I can feel the smile on his face. "I take it back!"

"No, no, it's nice," I say, and he makes a face. "Really! I'm just not used to it . . . this, I mean, being authentic? It's, like, a reflex or a defense mechanism or something. I've evolved this way after years of guys telling me this fluffy shit, but not really meaning any of it. It's gonna take a while to adjust."

"Well, you're going to have to get used to it because I don't know if I'll be able to stop telling you how beautiful you are." He pulls his arm from my shoulders and strokes my cheek with his thumb.

I search for all of the warning signs. Marcus would never quite meet my eye. Jay would expect something physical in return.

But Alex doesn't look away. And he treats our kisses like they're something special and important, and not just the lead-up to something more.

I keep looking for cracks in the facade, because surely I don't get this from the universe, this love story—or *excuse me*, this really-really-like story. I'm not delusional. If someone up there made a mistake, though, I'm going to grab on and enjoy it while I can.

I wrap my arm around his neck and pull him close to me, pressing our lips together. I can taste his hazelnut gelato. He wraps his free arm around my lower back, fingers drifting under the lace of my top. It lights up my chest and makes my stomach ache.

I pull away, raising up my camera to my eye and pressing the shutter button before he has a chance to smooth out his face.

"Hey!" he laughs.

"It's gonna be a good one," I assure him. And it is. The clear blue sky and the gleaming white church is behind him, and his eyes are half closed, with his thick lashes shading them. His lips are pink and full. I love it. The picture. I mean the picture, of course.

"Okay, take one of us now?" he asks. He gestures at my camera. "Does that ancient thing do selfies?"

"What, to remember you by?" I smile, leaning into that space between his neck and his shoulder that feels like it was meant for me.

"Sure, but I keep telling you, I'm going to be here after this cruise. You're not going to get rid of me now that easily." He scratches his head and twists his lips to the side. "But I mean that in a totally romantic way. I don't know why it came out all . . . murder-y boyfriend about to be tackled by Mariska Hargitay on *Law & Order*."

"Yeah, yeah, yeah," I say, waving that away. I turn the camera around, hoping we're in the frame. He kisses my cheek right as the camera flashes.

We sit in silence, cuddled close, as we wait for the picture to develop. And I can feel the anticipation between us, almost like we're waiting for this photo to tell us what this is, if we look as good together as we feel.

It delivers. The peaceful look on his face as his lips meet my cheek. His glossy curls mingling with my locs. My eyes all squinty in pure delight. It's everything.

"Oh, that's a good one. I think I might have to keep it for myself."

"Um, yeah right, man. We've already established that it's all mine. Plus, I'm not trying to give you more pictures for your creepy murder-y boyfriend board."

His head falls back in laughter. I want to snap a picture of that too, but I resist. I only have so much film left, and if I try to capture everything that I like about him, I'll run out before the end of the day.

"Am I that then . . . your boyfriend?" His face still has that mischievous smile, like he's joking, but I can see the kernel of seriousness there.

And to be honest, it makes me a little nervous. Because I've never had a guy try to be all boo'd up with me this quick. This is the polar opposite of Jay, who strung me along for months, throwing out scraps of commitment. For the millionth time, I wonder, *How can this guy be real?*

"Okay, I can tell that freaked you out big-time, so I'm going to formally retract that question," he says. He makes a weird noise with his mouth.

"What was that?"

"Rewind. *Clearly.*" He laughs. "Now we are currently

in the time before I asked you that embarrassing, insecurity-revealing question—"

"It wasn't that bad."

He takes a lick of his gelato and then waves me away with his cone. "And I'm going to ask you a totally normal question instead. Can I look at your pictures from today?"

I laugh, grateful to let it go. "Sure."

The ship docked earlier this morning, and we took a thirty-minute train ride out to Pompeii. Well, most of us did. Wally stayed on the ship, and my parents, infuriatingly, didn't say a thing about it. I could tell they were mad, but of course they kept it cool and collected in front of the Lees.

I was honestly a little skeeved out about going to these ruins where so many people were killed by a volcano erupting, but Etta insisted. And it *was* very sad, seeing these freaky body casts where they legit poured plaster into the spaces left by bodies that disintegrated. But I'll admit that parts of it were cool, too—walking through this ancient town that was preserved due to its tragedy. I ended up taking lots of pictures.

I fan them out now in front of Alex. My mom staring up in awe at massive columns. Etta studying her massive guidebook with glee in the Foro while a sea of tourists maneuver around her. Dr. Lee laughing at a dirty picture she saw on the wall in the Lupanare, Pompeii's brothel—it's the same head-falling-back laugh that I love from Alex.

"These are really cool," Alex says, thumbing through them. "I mean, obviously I'm just a passionless pod person here, so take my opinion with a grain of salt—"

"Oh, he's got jokes!"

"—but I like seeing the way *you* see the world. It's very specific, you know, so clearly a product of your mind. I feel like you can tell how . . . curious you are through your pictures. If that makes any sense. It makes me want to see the rest of your art because I'm sure it's all the same way."

There he goes being all unreal and dreamy again. I lean forward to kiss him, soft and tender. We melt into each other as the rest of our gelato melts in our hands.

"Is this what we're doing for the next hour, until we have to meet up with everyone?" I say, breaking away finally. "Because I would be okay with that."

"Actually, there's somewhere I wanted to take you." He steals one more kiss. "Etta let me read one of her travel guides."

"Oh, no? Are we going to some tomb? Or to a museum with one of those audio guides? I don't trust those things! You don't know what kind of ear dirt the people that used them before had."

"You know, that was the first option, but I, too, was concerned about the widespread ear dirt problem." He stands up, pulling me with him with our interlaced hands. "Come on. I think you're going to like it."

He checks something on his phone, and then leads me up a street away from the church, past souvenir shops selling Italian flag bandanas and sparkly pizza Christmas ornaments. We reach a corner store, and I think we're surely going to duck in for the carbonara-flavored chips Alex mentioned being on the lookout for, but instead we turn down a dark alleyway. There's no one here, and I think I know where this is heading, so I stop against one of the graffiti-covered walls, pulling his close to me.

"Oh, plot twist, it was a fake-out, and we *are* going to make out until we have to meet up with them," I say, kissing his neck. "I love it."

He kisses me back, and a little moan escapes from his throat as he stops, the tips of our noses touching. "No, it's real, and as much as it pains me to admit, it's right here."

He gestures to a little shop nearby, with bright-colored tapestries hanging in the big windows, and I realize with embarrassment that anyone inside could totally see me and Alex making out.

"And what's *it* exactly?" I ask.

"Well, this woman is known for doing these huge embroidered self-portraits. They're really beautiful. You're gonna love them," he says. "But there are a whole bunch of these artisan studios, tucked away kinda secret like this, all throughout Naples. I read about them in Etta's book and mapped out a few. I was thinking you might like to explore a few of them."

For a second I'm a little stunned because there is honestly nothing I'd like to do more (except make out with Alex, of course). How did he plan something so . . . me? How does he know what's so me in such a short time?

"Oh, I would love that," I say, and he beams, all proud. I want to pinch his cheeks, he's so cute.

We spend the next hour walking down windy streets and ducking into tiny shops and studios. There's one place that has a whole wall covered in golden masks, and another woman who makes statement earrings and headpieces out of coral. We're in a ceramic shop, admiring a display of hanging, shiny balloons in a pastel rainbow of colors, when Alex squeezes my hand and rests his chin on my shoulder.

"Maybe this could be you someday," he whispers. "With a shop like this, a workplace in the back."

I shrug. "They're different than me."

He looks confused. "They're artists. You're an artist."

"Yeah, I know I am. I've always been. It's not like I need someone to validate that for me."

He nods. "You're right. I'm sorry."

"But they're artists in a different way," I continue. "Like . . . established. They have a specialty. They have . . . I don't know, *a long-term lease*, probably. Their whole lives are committed to this one thing, and as my parents have made so glaringly clear, I'm lacking in the commitment area."

"You've been making art since you were a kid. That seems pretty committed to me. You'll get here," he says, gesturing around the whimsical store. "And even if it's not just one thing, maybe that's *your* thing, you know? And that's a completely valid way of being, too, no matter what your parents say."

And there he goes again, saying just the right thing and making my heart grow three sizes, like I'm the Grinch of love or something.

I pat his back, cup his face and move it from side to side, examining his neck.

"What are you doing?" he asks, looking alarmed.

"Just checking for the power button, maybe some screws in your neck, like my guy Frankenstein."

"And why are you doing that? Also, I'm pretty sure it was the doctor who was called Frankenstein."

"See, too perfect. You gotta be a robot." He laughs, pulling me into him, and we kiss until the woman at the register clears her throat.

We make our way back over to the pizza restaurant where we're meeting everyone for a late lunch, but at the corner, he squeezes my hand.

"I'm not actually perfect, you know," he says, his voice small. "But I'll try to be, for you. I really don't want to mess this up."

I lean in and stroke his cheek with my thumb. His brown eyes look so earnest, so vulnerable.

"You don't have to be perfect," I whisper back. "Just be real with me. That's all I want."

"I will," he says. "You too?"

I wonder if he can see beyond the front I put on. But I guess I've lowered it more for him than anyone else in a long time.

I pull him close and press my lips to his as my answer.

We walk the last few steps to the restaurant, but then drop hands when we get there.

"One more," he says, leaning in for a quick peck. We

haven't explicitly discussed keeping this all on the DL with our parents, but I think we both know that it's in our best interest not to be carrying on in front of them.

"What are you doing?" Etta's unmistakable voice asks, and we spring apart to see her standing there. "The average kiss transfers approximately eighty million germs," she says, sighing heavily. "Just so you know."

Our parents walk up a few seconds later, giggling and talking loudly about something with the tour guide.

"Oh, hello, you two!" Mom shouts, a wide smile on her face.

"Are we all excited to try some of this famous pizza?" Mr. Lee says, leading the way into the restaurant.

"Do you think they saw?" Alex whispers to me as we follow.

I reach up and wipe off a smudge of my pink lipstick on the side of his mouth. "Well, even if they didn't, they definitely saw *that*."

CHAPTER FIFTEEN

They saw. They totally saw.

And by the time we get back to the ship, there are a whole new set of rules, the real killer being that we can't be alone in Alex's room.

Which is real inconvenient because now that we've finally acknowledged how we feel, we can't keep our hands off each other. And I was looking forward to doing that without anyone interrupting us in Alex's ocean-view, Wally-less room.

But our parents escort us to our rooms after dinner, and when I'm about to sneak out around midnight, the phone in my room begins to ring. Wally grunts and pulls his pillow over his head.

"Hello?" I whisper, pulling it up my ear tentatively.

"Oh, hey, Lenore, you're still up?" Mom asks, and I can hear the smile in her voice.

"What freaky parent magic is this?"

"I have no idea what you mean," she says. "But what I do know is you better get that behind back in bed, and keep it there until morning."

"I—uh—" I rack my brain, searching for an excuse and also maybe some protests about where this all was when Wally's been wandering the boat at all hours. But she's having none of it.

"I love you. Good night, baby," she coos.

"I love you too," I mutter begrudgingly.

So, I don't see Alex until the next morning when we're docked in Sardinia, and our parents insist that we accompany them on their tour of Il Castello, instead of letting us go off on our own, like they were totally okay with before.

"Isn't it crazy," Alex says, when we manage to slip away around a quiet corner in the Museo Archeologico Nazionale, "that we're on the other side of the world and we found each other here. When at home, you know, we were just five minutes down the 605 from each other."

"Um, what traffic-less utopia are you living in?" I laugh, snaking my arms around his waist.

"Okay, maybe twenty-five minutes. But still. It's . . . fate." He gives me that perfect, soft smile that melts everything inside of me.

I slap his chest. "Boy, you are so cheesy."

"I agree," Dad chimes in, appearing out of nowhere. I promptly remove my hands from Alex.

"Yeah, son, haven't I taught you better game?" Mr. Lee

says, right behind him. And then suddenly, Mom, Dr. Lee, and Etta are there too. Wally, thankfully, is nowhere in sight.

"Leave them alone! It's cute," Dr. Lee insists.

"I certainly kissed some boys for much less at that age," Mom says, and then I immediately fall into a crack that opens up in the ground to the burning center of the earth and perish. Dead.

That night is the big formal, a fancy dinner and dance that the cruise's brochure hyped as the "jewel of the journey." And yeah, it's way corny, but it's not like we have anything better to do. And I relish that I don't have to do some big will-he-won't-he song and dance with Alex about whether we're going to go together. When we return to the ship, he kisses my cheek, all bold in front of my parents, and tells me he'll pick me up from my room at seven.

Wally gets back in bed and declares he's not going, even after a long, stern talk with Mom. I'm irritated by him, but I'm also grateful that it gives me the run of the tiny room to get myself ready, without knocking into him or fighting over the shower. I twist my locs into a massive bun on top of my head, adorning them with sparkling gold cuffs. I line my eyes in bright teal and put nude gloss on my lips. And then I put on the baby-blue poofy tulle dress that I made a couple years ago, and luckily talked myself into packing at the last minute, finishing the look off with gold beaded sandals and a black clutch.

I look like Cinderella. Not like the cartoon one or the million carbon-copy remakes. No, like, Brandy from the good one that my aunt Stacy has stuck in the DVD player in her Honda Odyssey. I look fucking amazing.

Alex knocks, right on time. I open the door and my chest flutters when I see him standing there in his black tux with shiny lapels and a bow tie. A bow tie! I didn't realize bow ties were my thing, but apparently they are totally my thing.

"You really out here just having tuxes on standby?"

He shrugs, cheeks pink. "It's leftover from prom. I bought instead of renting."

Right. The prom that he was supposed to go to with Natalia. That he would have gone to with her if *she* didn't end things with him. My stomach feels tight thinking about it.

But he's here with me now, I remind myself. And he's staring at me all wide-eyed and dreamy right now, like I'm the most special person in the world. Has anyone ever looked at me this way before?

I need to let go of all the baggage holding me back. I need to just let myself be in this, fully.

Alex shakes his head like he's coming out of a trance. "Oh, I brought something for you." He holds up a clear container that I didn't notice before because I was so distracted by the bow tie. Inside is a white anemone in a cluster of baby's breath, attached to a thin gold band.

"Is that . . . ?"

"A corsage. Which, yes, I know is cheesy"—he laughs and holds his other hand up—"but we've firmly established cheesy is my brand."

I'm so surprised, so touched, that I can't get any words out, which he must interpret as a bad thing because he rushes to explain. "I thought—because of what you said about your prom—that maybe this could be a redo. Because you're just . . . you're so great, Lenore, and you deserve it all, the perfect prom night. And I can't do the limo and the fancy dinner reservation, obviously, but I could at least do this. If you don't like the flowers, we can stop at the florist again on the third deck, Barbara could totally remake it with something—"

I stop his babbling with a kiss. "I love it. Thank you."

He beams at me. "Oh, well. Good."

His hands have the slightest tremble as he slides the corsage onto my wrist. I toss the empty container back into our room.

"Hey, Wally!" I call. "Can you get up for a second and take our picture?"

He groans in protest but reluctantly pushes the covers off and walks over to the doorway, hands on his hips. I pass him my clunky camera and my phone. "On both of these, please. Thank you!"

Alex stands behind me, his hands around my waist. The flash is bright in our eyes, making this all feel like a dream again. And wasn't this my dream, just a few weeks ago? When I was taking prom pictures with my friends, the odd one out?

We walk to the formal, hand in hand, and I can't help but compare how I'm feeling now to how I felt on prom night. I was so stressed and anxious then, hoping for maybe a couple dances and some secret making out with a guy who wouldn't even claim me as his date. But there's only calm with Alex now. And it's not just because he's made me feel so certain of his feelings. It's also that I'm not gearing up and getting ready to perform, like I feel like I have to so often at home, with my friends and everyone at Chrysalis. I've been with Alex constantly for days, but I don't feel depleted with him, like I do with everyone else. I can just be. Without doing too much thinking about how I'm being.

I don't think I ever anticipated finding this peace with someone. And it makes me dare to imagine some wild stuff. Like, that maybe I've found my person. My one true . . . well, whatever.

The Crown Room, where we've eaten all of our breakfasts and dinners, is totally transformed. The lights are low, except for bright pink spotlights that cast the room in a rosy glow. The tables, adorned with massive centerpieces of pink and red roses, are pushed closer to the walls, making room for a white, sparkling dance floor. And it's already crowded with people shaking their groove things with varying amounts of skill.

I spot Mr. Lee doing something that resembles Carlton's moves from that old show *The Fresh Prince of Bel-Air*, while Dr. Lee looks on in glee, and I point him out to Alex.

"I guess it's better that you see it now. That's the future you have to look forward to," he says with a smile, totally unaware how those words make me feel some type of way.

I kiss his cheek and cuddle in close. "Oh, do I?"

The night feels like magic. We eat course after course

served by waiters in white tuxedos. We dance with our parents to the Cupid Shuffle, which I'm pretty sure they requested from the DJ.

We don't, thankfully, see Natalia or her family all night. I'm sure that Alex likes me, wants to be with me—but that doesn't mean it wouldn't be awkward.

And when we're all sweaty and giddy and buzzing from the sugary crepes that they served for dessert, the DJ finally plays the first slow song of the night.

It's a Leon Bridges song I've heard before, peak sappy Mom Jamz, but as Alex takes my hand and leads me to the center of the floor, looking at me intently, adoringly, like there's no one else in the room, it starts to feel like it's a song written just for us.

He wraps his hands around my hips and presses our foreheads together, rocking me to the music. He begins to mouth the lyrics to the song, his brown eyes locked on mine.

My heart is racing. I know he can feel it with us this close. And words appear in my mind, echoing the beat: *What if? What if? What if?*

What if my life can turn out totally different than I planned? What if things I thought were not possible for me . . . are?

I didn't think I would find anything like . . . *whatever* this is, with Alex. I didn't think this was meant for me.

And if this is possible, what if everything else—everything I haven't even dared to consider—is too? What if I could have freedom to figure my future out? To take my time, to really throw myself into something. To not worry about being the best, not worry about messing up, because I can just try again.

Because my parents have been right. I don't know what I want. I don't know what my path should be.

But I *do* know that I want that to be okay. For now.

"Lenore, what's up?" Alex asks. I must look confused because he clarifies, "I could tell from your face that you went somewhere else. No pressure, but if you want to talk . . . I'm here."

And I feel this overwhelming urge to tell him everything. Because I know he'll listen. I know he'll assume the very best of me. He has so far.

The DJ has switched back to some fast Motown song. I look around for our parents and see that they've already organized two lines of dancers, and they're whooping and hollering as couples shimmy down the middle. They're distracted and probably will be for a while.

"Yeah, let's talk. Maybe . . . in your room?"

He threads his fingers through mine and leads the way.

The lights are off in Alex's room, but the reflection of the moon is bright against the water, shining in from his open curtains. He takes off his jacket, draping it across the miniature sofa, and flicks on the lamp next to his bed. We sit down, still holding hands, and I remember the last time we were here, barely tolerating each other. It all changed so fast, but it doesn't feel too fast. Everything with Alex feels just right.

He brushes his lips against my temple, and I think that

maybe we're going to throw this whole conversation out and do more entertaining things, which I would be totally fine with. But he pulls away and searches my eyes. "So, what's going on? You've got this, like, Disney princess face, you know? I can read every feeling on it."

"Well, first of all, the only Black Disney princess is a frog for most of the movie, so—"

He cuts me off. "Be real. Just tell me."

And so I do. I tell him all about how I'm considering blowing up my whole life the summer before my freshman year. How I think the solution to my parents' push for focus is no focus at all.

"I want to keep pursuing my art," I say as he nods encouragingly. "Maybe photography, maybe fashion, maybe something else completely different I haven't even discovered yet. But I think . . . *I know* I want to do it just for myself. And maybe . . . without that pressure to be perfect, to be the best, I won't keep psyching myself out and jumping ship before I even have a chance to fully explore what I can do. I don't know. I DON'T KNOW. Does any of that make sense?"

His arm that's around my waist pulls me in closer.

"It makes sense to me," he says. "But are you going to be doing this all at NYU? I know you laughed at the gap year suggestion before, but I think you should seriously consider it. You shouldn't go all the way to New York if you don't want to . . . and, like, correct me if I'm wrong, but I don't think you do, Lenore."

Do I want to go to NYU? The place I felt like I was supposed to go? In the city I felt like I was supposed to love?

No. Not at all.

I want to stay in Long Beach, the place I know I love already.

"I don't want to move to New York," I say. It's such a relief to be honest. "I don't want to move at all. I . . . I *know* I don't want to go to college this fall. Not yet. I want to stay in Long Beach and . . . make art. On my terms."

My eyes go wide when I say the words, and I can't help but look around the room, as if my parents are going to jump out of the shadows and revoke my Black Excellence card.

"Well, okay then," Alex says. "That's what you're going to do."

"But wait," I say, side-eyeing him. "Are you just encouraging all of this so I'll stay in California and be close to you?"

"I mean . . . I'm not *not* suggesting it because of that," he laughs, eyes twinkling. "Long Beach and Brentwood are pretty close!"

"See, there you go with your weirdo traffic-less estimations. Long Beach and Brentwood are gonna be, like, two hours apart on a Friday afternoon after classes are over for the week. Have you even *been* on the 405?"

"You'll just have to come up Thursday night then."

"Oh, so in this scenario, *I'm* driving to *you*?" I bump his shoulder with mine, and I can feel the cheesiest of all cheese faces on my cheeks.

"But no, for real," he says, the smile on his face smoothing out into something more serious. He traces the lines on my palm as he continues. "I just want you to do what makes you happy, Lenore. You deserve to be happy. And you have a better idea of what will do that than anyone—better than me, better than your friends, better than your family. You are this, this . . . brilliant, dynamic, beautiful girl. And if the path you take is different, well, it doesn't make it wrong."

"You really believe that?" I say. "Mr. Future Doctor? Mr. Twenty-Year Plan?"

"Of course I do. I believe in you."

The words strike me like an arrow in the chest, and I feel my breath catch. Has anyone ever said that to me before? It's usually me saying that to my friends, hyping them up. And my parents? Maybe. But if so, it was probably quickly followed up with a suggestion on how I could improve, a critique of the ways I didn't get things quite right.

"Thank you," I say, my voice small. I let my head fall into his chest, so he won't see all the feelings passing across my apparently Disney princess face.

"God, am I kidding myself, though?" I sigh. "Telling you is easy. Telling my parents is going to be a whole 'nother story. Like, how am I going to explain to them that I'm throwing away college, something that they fought so hard for, this opportunity they're basically handing to me on a silver platter?"

"You're not throwing it away. You're just pressing pause, so you don't waste the opportunity—"

"And what about the money? They might be able to get the

tuition back, but are they going to lose money on the housing deposit? That shit wasn't cheap. Man, I'm going to have to get a job. Like, immediately. Because there's no way my parents are letting me stay at home without a job. But do I even want to stay home? I don't think I could afford my own apartment, though, and I'm not trying to get some crusty roommates—"

Alex squeezes me tight. "I'm not trying to be one of those irritating guys who tells a woman to chill, but . . . Lenore, you need to chill." He presses his forehead to mine, and I can feel my speeding heartbeat thumping against his chest.

"We'll make a plan. Together," he whispers. "As you know, that's sorta my jam."

"Mr. Twenty-Year Plan."

He frames his face with one of his hands. "That's my name. Don't wear it out."

I take a deep breath. "Yeah, okay."

There are a lot of uncertainties ahead of me, but comfort is starting to bloom inside of me too. Because I won't have to go it alone, I won't have to put on a front for someone. And that makes all of these life-changing decisions feel a little more manageable. Or at least, that's what I'm telling myself as I let all of the other worries fall away, for now, until it's just me and Alex, *right now*.

"I believe in you, too," I tell him. "For the record."

"Thank you."

We're so close I can feel his breath against my cheek. We're in his room, on his bed. Alone.

No one knows where we are, which means no distractions, no interruptions.

He must have the same realization because he reaches up to cradle my face, kissing me slowly, deeply, in a way he hasn't before. I wrap my arms around his neck and tug him closer, down to the bed, feeling his warmth on top of me. He hitches up my hips, lips never leaving mine, and pulls me to the top of the bed, so my head rests on his pillow. It feels like every inch of my body is touching every inch of his. It feels right.

"Hey," I say, in between kisses. "I have an answer to your question. From earlier. From yesterday."

He pulls away, his lips swollen, his eyebrows pressed together in confusion.

"I'm sorry, but I'm having trouble remembering anything before two seconds ago."

I laugh, fingering his bow tie. I tug on one end until it unravels and pull it from his collar. "You asked if you could be my boyfriend."

He bites his bottom lip and nods. "I did."

"And I've decided that, yeah—" I shrug. "I guess you can be my boyfriend."

"Oh yeah?" His eyes light up, and I begin to unbutton his shirt.

"Yeah."

CHAPTER SIXTEEN

I leave Alex's room sometime after midnight. He wants to walk me back to my room, but I feel like that's just asking for trouble. Who knows where our partying parents are lurking, and it's better if we're apart, with plausible deniability. So, instead he puts his jacket around my shoulders and kisses my cheeks, watching me walk away with sleepy eyes.

I open my door quietly and tiptoe across the dark room so I won't wake Wally up. But then I notice his perfectly made, *empty* bed. So, I guess he's out wandering and reading his English lit textbook for fun again. I should be worried, but he's made it pretty damn clear it's none of my business. So, I put on my pajamas and pass out, letting Wally do whatever it is that Wally does.

When I wake up the next morning, the shower is running and steam is pouring out from under the door, so good, I guess. He didn't fall overboard.

I get dressed quickly in a royal-blue high-waisted bikini with a green striped dress, and then head out the door before I have to struggle through an interaction with Wally. We're docked in La Spezia today, and Alex and I have big plans to jump into the sea at Cinque Terre. I've seen so many pictures of the rainbow buildings perched precariously on the edges of cliffs, and I can't wait to see it in person. And also cuddle up with Alex on the sand. But there's something I want to do first.

When I get to the business center, it's not empty like it was last time. There's an older white man wearing a Jimmy Buffett uniform typing furiously, probably doing *actual* business, and another guy closer to my age who is definitely just cruising Reddit. I take a seat as far away from both of them as possible and use the internet card Alex loaned me to log on to my email account.

There's one message from Theo:

Tessa has informed me that she's spoken with you, and I am offended. I trust you will recall that I was your friend first. The least you can do is send me photographs as you explore Bel Paese.

Sincerely,

Theodore

PS Tessa also tells me you've found a suitor. Please ensure that you examine his passport and that he is who he claims to be. Lavon has been making me binge-watch *Unsolved Mysteries* with him on

Netflix, and you are just the type to be kidnapped internationally.

PPS I guess I miss you, but if you tell anyone, I'll deny it.

I roll my eyes and snort-laugh, earning a dirty look from Margaritaville Man. I send him one right back.

The rest of my emails are from Tessa, begging for updates on Alex, and I feel almost giddy as I connect my phone to the computer with a USB cord and send her the pictures from last night.

I jump when the video chat request comes through approximately two seconds later.

What the hell? It must be—I check the clock—past midnight there. Did she set up an alert or something? Knowing Tessa, she probably set up three.

I try to accept the video chat, but it fails each time. So, I open up a chat.

Lenore: Sorry, I'm not the only one using the computers today. I don't think it'll go through.

Tessa: TELL ME THE MEANING OF THESE ADORABLE IMAGES IMMEDIATELY.

Lenore: They had this formal night on board last night, so we went together

Lenore: Also, I guess he's my boyfriend now

Tessa: AHHHHHHHHHHHHHHHHHHHHHHHH

Tessa: !!!!!!!!!!!!!!!!!!!!!!!!!!!!!!!!!!!!!

Tessa: 🕺🎉🙌😍

I laugh again. I knew she would react this way, and I kind of love it.

Lenore: So are you excited then? I can't tell

Tessa: All of my dreams are coming true!

Lenore: Girl, you gotta get bigger dreams

Tessa: I knew this would happen! It's what you need after that douchebag Jay!!

Tessa: A little summer fling before college. YOU DESERVE!

That word makes me bristle a little—"fling." I really think what Alex and I have is . . . more than that. And Tessa's always talking about true love, it's what all of her stories are about. Why is this big news I'm telling her automatically downgraded to a fling?

Lenore: The thing is, it's not just a fling

The three dots appear, telling me that she's typing. And they're there for a long time, so I'm expecting a novel. But finally, all that appears is:

Tessa: Of course!! I'm sorry!

Lenore: It's fine!

Tessa: Where is he going to school? New York?

Lenore: No, UCLA

It doesn't feel right to tell her all the things I decided on last night. Not yet.

Tessa: Oh well, long distance relationships can totally work out!

Tessa: I can't believe all of this has happened in like a week! Wow!

And I know that tone gets lost in messages, when I can't see her face or hear her voice. Plus, she doesn't even have all of the information. Alex and I *won't* have a long-distance relationship if everything goes according to plan. But still, her words hit me as . . . patronizing. They make me feel silly and small. Which is stupid, because isn't she the one always trying to push these ridiculous love stories on me? Not that what me and Alex have is love . . . but still.

Lenore: Well, I need to run! We're going to Cinque Terre today 😎

Tessa: OMG YOUR LIFE

Tessa: Take pictures! I love you!

I push down the weird feelings about Tessa's comments and head out to the main deck to find Alex. We planned to meet up twenty minutes before our families, so we could strategize a way to sneak away to one of Cinque Terre's villages on our own, without their prying eyes. The deck is crowded though, so it takes me a while to spot him. And when I finally do, my brain rushes to catch up, to process what I'm seeing.

There's Alex, wearing seersucker swim trunks and a crisp white shirt that makes his brown skin glow. He looks tired and his curls are all messy, like he just rolled out of bed, but it only makes him even more gorgeous.

Except he's not alone. There's a girl standing next to him,

standing close, and I realize I recognize that shiny black hair and super thin figure. It's Natalia.

Natalia has her hand on his. Natalia is saying something that makes him throw his head back and laugh, just once, like I love. Natalia is the one now leaning in for a hug, tight, her head resting on his shoulder. Natalia is murmuring something in his ear.

I should walk away. I should cut my losses. It's so obvious what this is.

But something reckless inside of me makes me Nancy Drew it and creep closer, even though I know I'm not going to like anything I find. I need to know for sure.

It's really loud out here, with families calling to each other and *Mediterranean Majesty* employees trying to wrangle their tour groups, so it's hard to make out what they're saying. But when I'm just a few feet away, hidden behind a couple with matching neon fanny packs, I hear Alex's voice, loud and clear. "Lenore."

He hasn't seen me though. He's still talking to Natalia. And then, a few seconds later: "—just until we get home."

I squeeze my eyes shut and look down. I don't need to hear anything else to understand what's going on.

My throat is tight and thick. I feel my face burn.

I'm surprised, but do I have a right to be? This has happened to me enough that I shouldn't even be able to claim shock anymore. I've always just been the waiting room some guy is hanging out in until he finds his real love. I mean, if every time I put my trust in a guy, he chooses someone else . . . well, only a fool would keep jumping in for more. Only a fool expects different outcomes.

And I'm a fucking fool.

Hot rage is boiling and bubbling in my stomach. I want to scream. I want to charge into them like a bowling ball into pins and knock them overboard. I want to flip a table like that Real Housewife who went to jail.

But most of all I want to cry.

I will not cry.

Before I've even made the conscious decision to do so, I tug off my Sea-Bands and chuck them at Alex. One sails past him into the water, but the other one hits him right on his left cheek. They're not hugging anymore, so I don't get two-for-one. But still, not bad for a girl who wasn't allowed to do organized sports.

Alex looks up, and he has the nerve to smile at me. Like I didn't just see what I saw. Like everything is perfectly fine.

My scrunched-up face must make it clear that that's not going to fly, though, because first his eyes narrow like he's not seeing me clearly, and then they go wide. He holds up his hands.

"Lenore." Just my name. No explanation, because there isn't one.

Natalia turns now and cocks her head to the side, examining me. Is she feeling sorry? Smug?

I take a deep breath, feeling the edges of my eyes begin to prickle.

I will not cry. I will not cry.

Instead I run.

The traitor tears at least stay where they're supposed to until I make it into my room, out of Alex's sight, but then everything goes to shit.

I throw open the door and collapse onto my bed, letting out a sob. A fucking sob. Like an idiot in a soap opera. And once I've let one tear escape, the rest flood out of me, uncontrollable and unrelenting. My face and chest burn with the effort

"What's wrong?" Wally's voice makes me look up from my pillow, and I see him standing there, frozen, eyes full of concern. "What happened, Lenore?"

I should feel touched that he even cares enough to ask, but it's such a one-eighty from how he's been acting that it just makes me mad.

"Don't act like you all of a sudden care about me now," I say, my words daggers, and he visibly shrinks back.

"I always care, it's just—"

I hold my hand up, cutting him off. I don't have it in me to listen to excuses right now. "Tell Mom and Dad I'm sick. That I'm staying on the ship."

I leave the next part, "like I've done for you this week," unspoken, but I can see from the guilty expression twisting its way across his face that he got that part loud and clear.

"Okay," he says, nodding resignedly. "I, um—I hope you feel better."

With that, he's out the door and I'm alone. Well, not quite alone because I have my thoughts screaming and hollering in my head. They're so loud and terrible that my temples throb and it feels like the room is spinning.

All this time, did he like me just because I was there? The proximity made me a convenient choice, so he could check another item off his ten-year plan.

Natalia was on his time frame, his high school sweetheart, all set to go to the same university as him. He thought he had that one-true-love, happily-ever-after bullshit on lock, but then that got messed up, so he had to fill in her spot quick. And I was the first girl he saw. Like he literally scanned the room and found me. He didn't even try to hide that! I knew from the beginning!

So, what the hell was I thinking, dreaming this could be real? How did I let myself get swept away, *again*, when it's been so clear all along that I was only a placeholder? Someone to have around "just until we get home."

I'm sad, but mostly I'm furious at myself for being so stupid.

And all of the stuff we talked about last night, too!

Did I really convince myself that I could just *not* go to NYU in the fall? That I could take a gap year and make art and—stupidly, vaguely—figure out my path instead?

God, I'm such an idiot. My parents would disown me. They would *murder* me. I would become the subject of one of those eight-part Netflix documentary series, and my parents would be all well lit in our kitchen, talking 'bout ". . . and we never saw Lenore again."

Thank the lord I haven't told them yet. I was living in a fucking dream world, and it hurts, but I woke up just in time.

There's a knock at the door, and I sit up in my bed. Wally could open it with his key, so maybe it's my parents coming to make me get up—which, for the record, they never did with Wally. Or it could be—no, he wouldn't dare.

"Lenore." Alex's voice is muffled through the door. "Can we talk?"

So, apparently, he would dare.

"Fuck you, Alex!" I yell. It occurs to me that if he can hear me through the door, my neighbors on either side can probably hear me too, but I don't care. "Leave me alone!"

"Lenore, please. I don't know what you thought you saw . . . well, no, I *do* know what you thought you saw, but you need to let me explain."

It's the "need" that gets me, that makes me feel like steam is shooting out of my ears and through my nose. My stomach sloshes as I run over to the door, throw on the chain, and glare out at him, all "here's Johnny."

He looks terrible. His eyes are sunken and his hair is even more of a mess. But I'm not going to let that sway me. He *should* feel like shit.

"I don't *need* to let you do anything," I say to him, spitting out each word. "I saw you two, the happy couple, with my own

256

eyes, and there's no way you can explain that away."

"Lenore, it wasn't like that," he says, shaking his head. "I promise. We were—"

"So that's what it's like, huh?" I cut him off. "It doesn't even matter to you who it is? You just need someone to fit into the partner slot on your dumbass twenty-year plan. Might as well upgrade to a future lawyer if Natalia will take you back, huh?"

"Lenore, come on. Don't do this." His voice cracks. "You know me."

I can feel my face harden, my armor against the way that voice—the same one that made me feel seen and special—is trying to get through to my heart. "I don't know you, Alex. It's been ten days. Ten. Days." He winces, like the words flew from my mouth and pierced his chest. "And you sure as hell don't know me if you think I'm going to fall for any of this ever again."

A wave of nausea hits me, and something toxic and hot bubbles up in the back of my throat.

"Go away. We're done."

I slam the door in his face.

CHAPTER SEVENTEEN

I spend the rest of the afternoon crying. I cry curled up into a ball, my chest aching with the effort. I cry so loud, apparently, that my neighbor bangs on the wall, and I bang it right back. I cry until my tear ducts sputter out and are all like, "Girl, are you really out here trying to get dehydrated over a man?"

And then I get up.

The nausea is back.

At first I thought I was feeling sick because of Alex's betrayal. But, no, it's just like the first few days of this cruise. I can feel every sway of the ship, even as we're docked. My stomach rocks and my skin is all clammy and I have to take deep breaths to swallow down the impending vomit.

Why did I throw my Sea-Bands at him? I could have thrown anything, my purse, my chunky-heeled clogs—those suckers would have hurt. I should have gone for the plastic chairs on the pool deck, really made a statement. But instead I threw the one thing that was magically keeping me from emptying the contents of my stomach, allowing Alex to ruin everything in yet another way.

I don't know how many hours pass before Wally returns to the room—the alarm clock fell behind the tiny dresser when I threw my pillow, at one point, in anger, and our windowless box of a room pretty much erases the concept of time. But I must be in bad shape because he opens the door and then quickly makes his way over to my bed and hugs me.

Hugs me!

I can't remember the last time this happened—definitely not at my graduation, or any recent birthdays and Christmases. Wally and I are just not huggers. But he pulls me close, leaning his head on top of mine, and whispers, "I'm sorry."

"It's not your fault," I say between sniffles, because apparently I'm crying again.

"Still, I'm sorry. Whatever happened. I'm assuming it was . . . with him."

I nod, wiping my eyes with the back of my hand.

"Did . . . did he hurt you?"

I shake my head. "No, no. Just my heart."

"Well, I sort of want to kill him for that, too."

I let out a laugh, surprised because Wally has never pulled the protective big brother card, not any time recently. And then he starts laughing too, and soon we're giggling together on my bed, like we're little kids again.

Maybe it's because he feels like the Wally I used to know,

that the words slip out of my mouth. "What about Kieran? Do I need to do some killing for you?"

Almost immediately, Wally's whole face shutters.

"That's different. I don't want to . . . I *can't* talk about it now."

I study his face. His jaw is tight and I can see that his breathing has gotten shallower. The easiness from a few seconds ago is gone, and stiff, closed-off Wally is back.

"Fine."

"You should go take a shower," he says, standing up, looking everywhere but at me. "And then we can walk to dinner together."

"Okay, yeah."

I have no appetite, but I know that food will help with the nausea. And all we have to eat in the room is a bag of pesto-flavored chips that I took from Alex's stash. Those make me feel even more sick, just looking at them. Plus, if I skip dinner, Mom and Dad will be on my case big-time, which is something I can't handle right now, on top of everything.

So, I get myself cleaned up, run cold water over my eyes so they look less puffy, and put on a bright yellow tiered maxi dress. If I'm going to see the guy who broke my heart, at least I'm going to look good doing it.

I stay close to the walls as we make our way to the dining room because that seems to make everything spin less. I know I need to get new Sea-Bands or some meds soon, but I need to make it through this dinner first.

Alex won't try anything, not in front of my parents, I assure myself. Hopefully he doesn't even have the nerve to show up. There's only three days left of the cruise—Marseille tomorrow, another sea day, and then we dock in Barcelona. Maybe we can just avoid each other for these last couple of stops, and then we'll never have to see each other again. I can erase him from my heart, like I've done with every other guy who's treated me like a stepping-stone to a real relationship. I try to push down what I know for sure already—that doing so with Alex is going to be much harder.

Wally squeezes my shoulder when we reach the dining room entrance.

"He's not here," he whispers, and I stretch my neck and squint to confirm that it's true.

I let out a deep sigh. I can do this.

We make our way over to the table, maneuvering around a stage that's been set up in the center of the room because it's karaoke night, apparently. A skinny white man in a Hawaiian shirt is belting out a Lizzo song with little regard to the actual lyrics but an aggressive amount of enthusiasm. I'm already making plans for a quick exit.

When we sit down at the table, I search everyone's faces for signs that they know anything, but they all look normal—if anything, a little *too* cheery. But maybe that's just my bad mood clouding my vision.

"Isn't this fun?" Mom beams at me, gesturing to the stage. I try to match her smile. "I need to get up there," she says.

"Please don't," Etta mutters. But Mom ignores her and turns to Dr. Lee. "Ronni, do you know 'Survivor'? Why am I even asking—of course you know 'Survivor'!"

Yeah, I definitely need to dip out of here soon if my mom is about to attempt a Beyoncé impersonation in front of all these people. And I realize, with a sudden pang in my chest, that Alex and I would be cracking up over our moms' performance, if everything hadn't fallen apart. If he hadn't ruined it all.

"Baby, are you okay?" Mom whispers, leaning in to me. "Your face just got so sad. You can tell me . . . if something's bothering you."

The way she says it, I almost believe her, but I know very clearly now that that sentiment only really applies when what's bothering me doesn't interfere with the image my parents expect me to uphold, who they prefer me to be. My mom doesn't want to hear all of the thoughts and stupid plans that have been running through my brain the past few days.

"I'm fine."

"Okay," she says, eyebrows pressed together. But just as quickly, her face shifts into a strange smile. "Well, whatever it is, I think something might be about to happen that will cheer you right up."

"What does that mean?"

Before she can answer me, the first notes of a Leon Bridges song start to play over the speaker. *That* Leon Bridges song, the one Alex and I danced to last night.

"Please welcome our next performer to the stage!" the announcer booms.

No, no, no. NO.

He wouldn't dare. After what just happened . . . he *must* know I don't want this.

The big smiling faces of our parents and the horrified look on Wally's face confirm the terrible truth.

"This is for you, Lenore. I'm so sorry."

I look to the stage and see Alex standing there, eyes locked on me. Along with hundreds more eyes because now everyone, at every table, is staring at me too.

"Awwwwww!" I hear some woman at the table next to us coo. "Isn't that the sweetest thing? I love this song!

Alex puts the microphone up to his lips and begins to sing.

"Don't wanna get ahead of myself
Feeling things I've never felt."

Fuck this. I don't have to sit around for this show that's surely not for me.

I push my chair out with a screech, causing my mom to gasp and jump next to me. I throw off her hand on my shoulder and take off, keeping my gaze down on the ground so I can avoid all of the questioning eyes.

There's a roar in my ears, making me feel like I'm underwater, but I vaguely hear his singing stop, the microphone drop.

There are footsteps coming after me, but I don't turn to see if it's him or my mom. I don't want to talk to either of them.

I make it down the fancy stairs into the main lobby and out onto the deck before I have to stop. My head is spinning and my stomach is sloshing. I grab hold of the railing and close my eyes, trying to keep the vomit bubbling up in my throat down by sheer force of will.

I hear someone walk up next to me. "Lenore, I was trying—"

I open my eyes and glare at Alex. "Were you even doing that because you thought it was what I wanted? Or just what *a girl* should want? Did you forget that you told me all about your empty grand gestures?" He jumps back with the force of my words. "You don't even care who you end up with, as long as it's someone who fits your time frame. You're using the same kind of shit on me that you used with Natalia. Where is she, anyway?"

"This was for you," he says, his voice small. "You said—I thought . . . I wanted to show you how I felt, how important you are to me."

"*That* wasn't for me. It's part of your stupid, soulless plan." I shake my head. "What happened with Natalia, huh? Did she change her mind again, and now you have to go back to your backup? I heard what you said, about this"—I gesture between us—"just being until we got home."

He reels back, shocked, but then has the nerve to smile.

"That's what you heard? Oh, Lenore, oh my god. That sounds so bad, but it wasn't like that. I *promise* it wasn't like that." He presses his hands together. "It was closure. I was telling her all about *you*, and she was joking about how I sounded more excited, more passionate than I ever did with her. And it's true. I've never felt this way about anyone before." His smile falls, and he runs his hands through his curls, his eyes wet and wild. "Because . . . I love you, Lenore."

Those three words hit me in the chest like a cannon. Did he really just say that? Those words I've always wanted to hear?

"That's what I was talking to Natalia about," he continues, shaking his head. "That's what you overheard. I was trying to decide if I should tell you now or wait until we get home. Because I know it's only been a little while and I shouldn't be feeling like this. I didn't want to freak you out by telling you too soon and coming on too strong like I have in the past, but . . . *fuck*. I'm so stupid. I went and did that anyway."

This is the perfect explanation. It would be so easy to accept it and move on. This was all just a misunderstanding.

But it can't be true. I can't let myself believe that it's true and be devastated all over again. This is all too scary. Too much of a risk.

I force myself to look at him in the eyes and say, "This isn't what you thought it was." Each word feels like an effort. "This was . . . a stupid fling, Alex, and you need to move on. You're being delusional."

I know I'm being mean. Dishonest. But I know how this goes, how this always ends. And I'm determined to say whatever I need to put my walls back up. To protect myself from him hurting me anymore than he already has.

"Don't do this, Lenore." he asks, his face breaking apart. My heart breaks again with it. "Talk to me! Be real. We promised we'd be real with each other."

I swallow furiously. My throat is burning and everything is spinning. I can feel sweat pouring down my back, even though the night air is cool.

"I—"

But I don't get to finish, because something other than the words I know I need to say comes rushing out of my mouth.

I throw up all over his bright white sneakers.

And then, before he's even had a chance to process what's just happened, I turn and run in the opposite direction.

CHAPTER EIGHTEEN

Not long after, my whole family is crowded into my tiny room. Mom helps me wash my hair in the shower, scrubbing my scalp like she did when I was little, and spraying my hair afterward with my leave-in conditioner that smells like eucalyptus. Dad picks up Dramamine from the gift shop, and Etta tries to help in her own way, informing me of all the side effects I can expect—drowsiness, blurred vision, constipation—until I firmly tell her to shut up. Still, I know I'd gladly take all of that compared to how I'm feeling now.

We sit in silence and watch a stupid rom-com that's been playing on the movie channel this whole cruise, one of two movies they've been cycling through. No one asks any direct questions about what happened, exactly, with Alex, though I can feel them, heavy and thick, in the air. Mom does whisper at one point that they're sad and disappointed with how things worked out. Disappointed my heart was broken? Or disappointed that I couldn't make it work with this boy who's living the kind of life they wish I was? I don't ask her to clarify. And I fall asleep right as the movie's couple is breaking up, which is just as well because that's where these silly fantasy movies should end.

When I wake up the next morning, I'm alone. I rack my brain trying to remember where we're docked today. Marseille. That's right. The cute French town that looked like Belle's hood from *Beauty and the Beast* in all the brochures. Alex and I planned to . . .

Well, that doesn't matter anymore.

I check the clock. It's somehow noon? So they must have all gone on without me. I wonder if they're seeing the island alone, or if they kept their tour plans with the Lees. Is Alex with them right now? All of them playing happy family and pretending like nothing's wrong . . .

No, I can't go down that mental path either.

I look around the dark, windowless room. I'm definitely not stepping foot in Marseille and risking seeing Alex with my family, but I sure as hell can't stay here all day. I pop another Dramamine—Etta told me I could take up to eight a day—and lie there, making a plan, as I wait for it to go into effect.

An hour later, I am freshly showered, wearing a wide-brimmed straw boater hat that mostly hides my face, and heading out of my room. I'm going to get an overpriced cold-pressed juice, something tropical and delicious, and then I'm going to lay out in the sun by the pool for the rest of the day and have the kind of summer that I deserve. I refuse to let the rest of this trip be ruined. No one deserves that kind of power over me.

I take the elevator up to Deck 5 and check the huge map there for the juice bar I know I've seen before. I scan the thing with my finger, finally figuring out its coordinates, but when I turn to leave, I bump right into someone.

"I'm sorry!" I shout, but then my eyes go wide when I see who it is I just apologized to.

Natalia is standing there, fresh-faced in expensive-looking leggings, holding a jumbo-sized green juice.

"Oh, hi! Lenore, right?" she says, beaming at me. "Alex told me all about you!"

I narrow my eyes at her, trying to determine what angle she's going for, and her bright smile falters.

"I know yesterday, things looked a little . . . cozy, but it wasn't like that at all. Alex and I have just been friends for so long." I continue to stare at her, which makes her voice speed up and get higher. "I hope you two were able to work things out last night. That performance at dinner . . . well, I get why you ran out. All the attention. But that's Alex! He loves his big romantic moments, doesn't he?"

The big romantic moments that he used to do for you, I think, but I don't say out loud. Instead I continue to stare, my muteness probably veering from intimidating to just awkward. My eyes catch on something tucked under her arm. A yoga mat.

"You going to a class?" I say finally, gesturing to it.

She looks down at the mat and then gives me her huge toothpaste-commercial smile again, probably grateful for the conversation bone I threw her. "Oh yes! I've been practicing yoga for years! I think I want to do my teacher training on weekends this fall. I found a great place near UCLA. Do you practice?"

"No," I say, but meanwhile my mind is whirring. She's been doing yoga *for years*. Is that why Alex was there that first sea day? Was he hoping to run into her, and instead he got me?

"Listen," Natalia continues, leaning in close to me like we're old friends. I take a step back. "I really hope you and Alex are able to work things out, whatever happened. He was so happy when he was talking about you yesterday, and he's just so wonderful."

All I can think about is how much better she knows him. How she was and will probably always be Alex's first choice. How she's trying to push her castoffs onto me.

But no, I need to stop. I can't do the petty thing where I search for things wrong with a girl just because she's been involved with the same guy as me. Natalia is probably great. And I'm sure I'd be able to appreciate that under different circumstances.

I just need to go.

"Thank you, but I don't think so," I say, and then wave at her. "Have fun at yoga!"

I turn and walk away. I can feel the confusion wafting off her, but I've given all I have right now. I head outside, abandoning my plans to get juice. Juice is stupid. I want coffee instead. Or maybe the swirled soft-serve ice cream that they have on every level of this ship. I could survive on soft-serve for the next two days, and avoid the dining room until we dock in Barcelona.

There are a lot of people on the main deck. I wind around groups playing shuffleboard and taking selfies. Kids splash in the pools while their parents sip on drinks with giant umbrellas and read paperbacks. All the loungers and chairs by the pool are filled with people. I probably won't get one after all. Why are all these people hanging out on this stupid ship when there's a French city with fancy churches and museums *right there*? It's not like they've got an awkward situation with an almost-boyfriend to avoid.

I realize, suddenly, that I recognize one of those people. On a lounger in the shade, pulled far away from everyone else, is Wally. He's holding his phone and a giant textbook on his lap, probably the English lit one I caught him trying to hide in our room.

I stride over to him. "Hey, nerd!" I call, cupping my hand to the side of my mouth.

His head pops up, and his eyes are saucers. Caught.

"I can't believe you're out here reading that," I say. "But, actually, I guess I can believe it. It's totally on brand for—" As I get closer, I see that he's not looking at me. His eyes are unfocused, strange. He's breathing fast and heavy, I can hear it from where I'm standing.

"Wally?" His hand reaches up to clutch his chest. "Wally! Stop playing!"

"Lenore, I—" He falls forward before he can finish whatever he was going to say, his forehead hitting the ground. I rush to his side.

"Help! I need help!"

The ship's medics act fact, popping out of seemingly nowhere and clearing the deck, like they were lying in wait for this to happen. It turns out they have a whole mini-hospital on board, at the very bottom of the boat. And not just a janky cruise ship one. No, it's equipped to perform the blood tests they need to do on Wally. Even a chest X-ray, to hopefully explain that terrifying way he was clutching his chest.

All the while, I sit in the waiting room, praying more than I have since I was a little kid. I *feel* like a little kid, here alone with no idea what's going on. I wish my parents were here to take over, to make everything okay, but there's no way to get in contact with them until they're back on the ship. And technically, I'm an adult now. I should be able to handle this. But I've never felt more small, more insignificant, than I did seeing them take Wally away on a stretcher, knowing there was absolutely nothing I could do.

I don't know how much time actually passes, though it feels like months, when a doctor finally walks out. He's a tall man with dark brown skin and an accent that I can't place. And he starts talking fast, giving me all the information I've been desperate for, but my brain can't catch up.

Finally, he pauses and smiles. "He's fine. He's asleep."

My whole body, which was clenched tight, releases, and I let out a deep sigh of relief. *He's fine.* But the worry picks back up quickly. "What *was* that? He looked like . . . like he was having a heart attack. Do we need to take him ashore? To the hospital there? Not that I don't trust you, Dr.—" I check his name tag. "Dr. Ademola, but, like . . . is this place even legit?"

Dr. Ademola lets out a loud laugh that feels out of place in this sad space, and then he smiles. "Yes, Ms. Bennett, I assure you this place is legit. And you are welcome to seek out additional care in Marseille, but I think it would be best for your brother to rest now. That's usually the best course of action after a panic attack."

"Wh-What?" I ask, my mouth falling open in surprise. "That's it?"

"Yes, your brother suffered a panic attack. And while, yes, it's not as severe as what it appeared to be on the surface—panic attacks can often mimic something more life-threatening—it was certainly a physically taxing experience for your brother. He will need some time to recover. We've given him something to help with that."

A panic attack? Wally had a panic attack? I'm struggling to fit this all together, to make it make sense. Because this just doesn't fit with my idea of my strong, confident, kinda pompous older brother.

"Does your brother have a history with anxiety?" Dr. Ademola asks.

"I don't know." Why don't I know that? I should know that!

Dr. Ademola furrows his eyebrows. "Well, we'll wait to talk to him more when he wakes up, but he should talk to his doctors about this at home, especially if it's happening regularly. It's possible that he has a panic disorder, which may require he consults with a psychiatrist for medication and begin therapy if he hasn't already."

I just stare at him, blinking. None of this makes any sense.

"You can go be with your brother now," Dr. Ademola says, gesturing to the door they brought Wally in forever ago. "I'll check back in a little while." And with that he's gone.

I walk into the room, and my breath catches in my throat. Lying there in that bed with an IV in his arm, my big brother looks so small. Growing up, I used to see him as invincible. I guess I still do. Nothing seemed to be able to shake the great, golden Wally. But if what Dr. Ademola says is true, that he could have a panic disorder, then a lot's been shaking Wally. He's just been hiding it from all of us.

I reach up to rub my face and feel the tears there. I don't remember starting to cry.

They must have given him some good meds because he sleeps for another two hours, which gives me a lot of time to scan my memory, searching for signs of Wally's supposed anxiety. But I find nothing. I'm ashamed that I find nothing.

My head is in my hands when I hear his voice, scratchy and quiet. "Etta told me this was down here. They have a full functioning morgue, too." I look up and see that his eyes are finally open. He's turned his head toward me, and there's a small smile on his lips. "I'm glad we're seeing this and not that. But I guess if you're there, you don't have much of an opinion about it—"

"Wally, you collapsed." I cut him off. "I thought you were having a heart attack. What is going on?"

He closes his eyes and takes a long, deep breath. When he looks at me again, his face is full of resolve.

"I was in the campus store, buying a blue book for an exam, when the first one happened. I couldn't breathe. My chest was tight. I felt like . . . like I was dying. I barely made it to the student health center before I collapsed. Right there in the waiting room. When they told me later that it was just—just a panic attack, I felt embarrassed, like I had freaked out over nothing. Like I had wasted their time."

"When was this, Wally?"

He rubs his forehead, feels the cut there and winces. "Toward the beginning of fall quarter."

"That long ago! Why didn't you tell us?"

He shrugs, looking away from me. "I thought it was a one-time thing. And when it happened again, I thought I could . . . handle it on my own. But then I started having them—the panic attacks—more and more. By winter quarter, it was happening once a week. I don't even know what the triggers were exactly. One minute I would be totally fine, and then the next, I was just . . . lost. I failed a midterm that should have been easy for me, just totally bombed it, because my heart started beating fast, and I knew I had to get out of there before I made a scene."

"Wally, I'm so sorry. I should have noticed."

"There's no way you could have. I made sure of it. The only person who I talked to about it, outside of the campus doctors, was Kieran, and then I went ahead and ruined that." Wally takes two more deep breaths, pressing his lips tight. "He kept pushing me to go to therapy, said he wanted to talk to Mom and Dad and tell them I needed to slow down. But . . . I didn't want to hear it. I was—*am* so close to everything I've always planned for myself, everything Dad has wanted for me, and I . . . I thought I just needed to work harder. I wasn't working hard enough."

He touches the cut on his forehead again, and I reach out to grab his hand, squeeze it tight.

"I thought I could handle it all on my own, but it's only getting worse this summer. I can't sleep. I can't . . . think straight. Especially with this big secret . . ."

"Well, the breakup with Kieran isn't a secret anymore. I made sure of that. God, I'm sorry for being such an asshole."

"It's not that." Wally shakes his head. Inhales, exhales, like he's gearing up to sprint away. I wonder if I should slow him down, tell him that's enough for now, because I don't want to trigger another attack. But he continues on. "Lenore, I didn't actually graduate." I can feel my eyes go wide, and I try to get my face under control. "That midterm I failed . . . it was for a gen-ed literature class that I stupidly put off until senior year. I don't even know how they let me do that, honestly. But I thought it would make the semester easy, especially with the internship, the LSAT, everything . . . But then I didn't turn in any of the papers. I couldn't get myself to start. And I missed the final too, just slept right on through it because I was up all night with anxiety." He puts his head in his hands. "So, the school let me walk, but I don't technically have my degree. I've been trying to fix it all this summer, retaking the class online, so I can start law school in the fall and Mom and Dad don't have to know. I only have two papers left and a final to take. I've been writing the essays in the Notes app on my phone, and then going into the business center at night to submit them and post in the class discussion board. I used some of my grad money to pay for that stupid expensive Wi-Fi." He sighs deeply and closes his eyes. "And then it will all be worked out. I can fix my dumb mistakes, if I can just get myself together, get my messed-up brain under control."

I'm reeling from this reveal. I never in a million years would have expected this. In the past, I would have felt smug, even a little satisfied that the great Wally had fallen. Now I just want to give him a hug. I want to protect him from the way he's beating himself up.

"Wally," I start slowly. "Maybe that's not the best path."

"It's the only path," he says, his eyebrows pressed tightly together. "You know how Mom and Dad are. Can you imagine Dad's face if he found out I might not go to law school in September?"

I can picture that face clearly. It's the same one he gave me when they sat me down for a talk after the grad party, lecturing me about how I should be more like Wally.

"But, look at you," I say, throwing my hands out at him. "You're in a freaking hospital bed during our European vacation! What will it be like for you in the fall, if you keep going like this? I'm pretty sure law school is one of the most stressful environments ever."

"Um, I think people in literal war zones would beg to differ," he says with a smirk. I'm relieved to see a spark of the Wally I know.

"Whatever. You know what I mean. Is this how you want to live your life? Are you even happy?"

He considers it for a second before shaking his head resignedly. "No. No, I'm not happy."

I squeeze his hand again, leaning closer onto the bed. "You deserve to be happy, Wally. And maybe you will be happy being a lawyer, eventually. But not right now. Not like this. You need to take care of yourself first, so you can keep going. You need to do what's best for you, outside of Mom and Dad's expectations."

I realize as the words come out that this is advice for him, yeah, but it also applies to me, too. Why can I be so sure that it's right for him to do what makes him happy, but scared to take that leap myself?

Almost as if he can read my mind, he asks, "And what about what you want?"

"What do you mean what I want?" I say, shrugging my shoulders. "I'm going to NYU. I'm going to study art history."

He shakes his head. "That's not what you want."

"How do you know that?" I know I sound like a belligerent little kid, but it's almost a relief to fall into that role with my big brother.

"Because you make that stank face every time you say it!" I can't help but laugh. This face must be real bad, to have everyone notice it like this. "And art history? I can't see you being happy doing that for four years, let alone forever! You need to create! You've always needed to create, Lenore."

"I know."

As much as I've been trying to convince myself differently since everything fell apart with Alex yesterday, Wally's words make it clear that I still want what me and Alex talked about: a gap year, space to figure things out. Even if the way I came to that conclusion is forever tainted, the conclusion is still right, authentic.

So, I tell Wally all about what I'm considering. And when I'm done, he laughs. But it's not judgmental. Instead, it makes me feel connected to him, because he understands the reality of what I'm proposing, like no one else can.

"God, Mom and Dad would hate that."

"You don't gotta tell me."

"But like *you* just told *me*, we deserve to be happy." His face clouds over. "But I know it's not that easy. That's why I'm . . . here. It's scary, to disappoint them. Because of where they started, and how much they've accomplished and sacrificed for us, so we could do the same. Anything but putting our heads down and working as hard as we possibly can . . . it feels indulgent."

"It really does. I feel like such an ungrateful, privileged asshole, not wanting to go to NYU, with my tuition paid in full with my parents' savings." I shake my head. "But maybe caring for ourselves is the ultimate celebration of how they've raised us. Having options, you know? Not just surviving in this world . . . but living." I feel like I'm convincing myself as I say it.

Wally considers me, the skepticism plain in his arched eyebrow. "Lenore, you're dangerously close to sounding like some white girl influencer's caption on a picture of her at, like, brunch."

"Shit! I do. I really do!" I laugh. "But see, we deserve that freedom. That white girl at brunch freedom! And no matter how corny it sounds, you know I'm right!"

He laughs too. "You are. You really are."

"Hey, say that again. I could get used to this version of Wally."

"I don't know what they've got me on," he says, rolling his eyes. "It might be impairing my judgment."

I roll mine right back, making him laugh even more.

"So what's next?" I ask. I may be helping him right now, but he's still my big brother. And I know that whatever's going to happen, I can't do it without him.

"I think," he starts slowly, "we need to talk to Mom and

Dad. Be brave. And open with them. Finally."

Right at that moment I hear Dad's booming voice in the lobby, Mom's commanding tone that she uses in donor meetings, demanding to know where Wallace Bennett is located.

"Looks like we're up," I say, trying to sound more confident than I actually am.

CHAPTER NINETEEN

The *what* questions come fast.

> *What happened to you, Wally?*
> *What tests have they done?*
> *What have they given you?*
> *What's the diagnosis?*

But after those are all posed and answered, we're forced to face the *why* and the *how*, and my parents are not about to address all that—family business—in front of prying eyes. So those questions are put on pause until Wally's released with instructions to rest, and we all make our way to my parents' room, marching down the hallway in a silent, straight line.

Wally lies down on the pull-out sofa that doubles as Etta's bed, Mom and Dad sit on their bed, and Etta leans against the sliding glass door to their balcony. I can see her fingers itching to grab a book from her stack on the coffee table. But either she can read the room and see that it's clearly not the time, or she just doesn't want to miss the scene that's for sure about to go down. I ease myself into the tiny armchair, studying my parents' faces.

Finally, Mom exhales and looks around at each of us. "Should we eat first? I feel like no good is going to come from talking about all this on empty stomachs."

"Mom," Wally says from the couch. I can see the frustration on his face. "I really don't think I can go to the Crown Room right now."

"Oh, I know, baby." She walks over to him and sits in the little curve of sofa by his stomach, stroking his hair. He softens, leaning into it.

"Room service," Dad says, clapping his hands together. "I think this calls for room service."

He walks over to the nightstand and pulls out a leather menu. "What do you think? Burgers? Chicken Caesar salad? That's always a good room service bet."

"Wait, wait, wait. Hold up," I say. "We could have been out here doing room service this whole time? And y'all didn't think to mention that when I was dying of seasickness in my room?

Dad arches an eyebrow. "Correction, *we*—as in your mother and I—could have been out here doing room service. *You* were gratefully eating the gourmet food in that there fancy dining room that we already paid for."

He cracks a smile, and my face curves into a matching one.

"Uh-huh, well, in that case, order me a cheese pizza. And some crème brûlée."

"You got crème brûlée money?" he chuckles, flipping through the menu. I shake my head and laugh too.

We all pick out what we want, and Dad places a massive order over the phone, cracking jokes with the operator about getting a discount. But once that is handled, we're met with the reality of what happened again. And it's clear that my parents—usually so straight to the point, tackling challenges head-on—aren't going to bring it up. Are they scared? I saw Mom's hand rise to her mouth, my dad's pained expression when Dr. Ademola said the words "panic attack" to them. Should I start the conversation, to take the burden off Wally?

But he sits up on the couch, leaning forward onto his knees, and glances between them. He looks tired, but sure. "Mom, Dad . . . I have something to tell you."

As Wally explains what's actually been going on the past semester, Mom gasps and starts to cry. Dad's face hardens as he takes in the news, and when Wally's done, he leans forward with his head in his hands.

Finally, after the longest minute there ever was, Dad gets up and sits next to Wally, putting his arm around him.

"I'm sorry I didn't notice, son," he says, voice barely above a whisper. "I'm sorry we weren't here for you."

There's talk of therapy, of seeing a doctor about the right medication. Dad, to my surprise, brings up deferring law school until next semester, maybe even until the following year.

"I love you, Wally," Etta says, leaping off the floor to hug him. And I join in for the tight family hug too, marveling at how little this happens, that we're all together, this close.

It all goes much better than I expected. We've cleared this hurdle together, as a family. And I'm fine leaving it at that. My issues can wait for another time, once we're back home. But Wally taps my foot with his and nods in my direction. I shake my head, and he nods even more aggressively.

"Lenore," he says urgently, and then everyone's eyes are on me.

I guess I can do this.

"I . . . I kind of have something to tell you, too."

Mom's eyebrows press together. "Baby, maybe now's not the time. We need to focus on Wally right now."

I get a flash of irritation, and I roll my eyes before I can stop myself. Should I have expected anything different?

"Now, I saw that, and you will not disrespect your mother like that," Dad says. "What's gotten into you? Is this because of what happened with the Lee boy?"

"This has nothing to do with Alex," I spit out, holding in another eye roll.

Except that's not true.

Would I have gotten to this conclusion without him? I don't think I would have let myself wish for this, even considered it as a possibility for me. But I know that without him, it's still what I want. My . . . *thing* with him—that may have been a silly, unrealistic dream, but this isn't.

And I need to tell them now. Right now, before I lose my nerve. Even if they don't think it's the right time.

"I know that Wally needs you right now, but I need you too," I say, my voice getting stronger with each word. Wally reaches out and squeezes my hand in encouragement. "Before this trip, you two sat me down and told me I needed to figure out my path and get focused. And I think . . . I *know* what that is now. I've decided that I want to take a gap year. I want to defer my enrollment to NYU, and maybe . . . not even go at all."

Mom's eyes go wide, and Dad's jaw is tight. I continue on.

"It's not what you want for me. I know that. But I'm sure it's what I want—what's right—for me."

"Lenore . . ." Dad starts. I can feel the anger, the worry, pulsing off him.

"Lenore, this is unacceptable," Mom finishes for him. "Taking a whole year off—it's not an option."

"Mom, I—"

"No," she cuts me off. "I don't want to hear any more of this ridiculousness right now. Really, with everything that's happening with your brother, you thought *this* was the time."

"Mom, please don't use me as an excuse to not listen to what Lenore is trying to tell you," Wally says, and Mom startles next to him on the couch, like someone else just appeared there. "If anything, what's going on with me . . . it should give you even more of a reason to listen to Lenore. Before it's too late."

The mood in the room changes as Wally's words set in. The pot that was about to boil over is now simmering, slowed. Mom's forehead is creased in concentration, and Dad stares at his clutched hands.

"Whatever worst-case scenarios you're dreaming up in your head, you gotta let them go," Wally continues. "First of all, she's way too fashionable not to find a career that supports her clothes habit." I feel a smile creep onto my face. "But also because she's smart and capable and driven. You *know* this because you raised her that way. If this is what Lenore wants, I think y'all should at least hear her out."

He grins at me, and I'm overwhelmed with gratitude for my big brother.

"What I'm proposing isn't forever. Just for a year," I say, meeting both of their eyes. "You both accused me of bouncing around, of not being focused, and you're right. That *is* what I've been doing, for . . . a long time. But I think the reason for that is I've been scared to really commit, to give myself completely to something, only to realize I'm not the best at it. I've felt a lot of pressure to be the best, especially in our family. So much so that I've given up on a lot before I even had a chance to really begin. And I want to see what happens—what I choose for myself—if I let go of that pressure, those expectations, you know? I want to see what I'm really passionate about, passionate enough to make a life doing."

Dad exhales loudly, shaking his head. "If you have a degree, Lenore, no one can deny you."

"It's not like I'm not going to get a degree!" I say. I feel anger rise in my chest. Is he even listening at all? But I take a deep breath and try again. I'm not going to sway them like that. And I need to be respectful of where they're coming from, all of the battles they've fought to get to where they are—so I can even be considering this as a possibility in the first place. "I know you want what's best for me. I know you both have done things a certain way, and your lives—*our lives*—are wonderful because of that. I admire you, Mom and Dad. So much." I swallow down my fear, the desire to just end this conversation right here. "But at some point, you need to trust how you raised us . . . and let us figure things out."

"It's not you I don't trust, baby," Mom says quietly. "It's the world."

"You gotta be ten steps ahead or you're behind," Dad says sternly, pointing his finger. "This world wasn't built for us. This world doesn't want us to succeed, and we can't forget that. We can't be complacent."

"I know that. You're right. You're both right." I rub my face. I feel tears, more traitor tears, that I didn't even know were there. "But maybe . . . living how we want to in the face of that is the biggest act of resistance."

We're all silent. Mom is looking out the window and Dad's face is frozen in a grimace. And that might just be the end of the conversation for now. I have to be okay with that. I shouldn't have expected to change their opinions all in one shot. At least I got everything off my chest, and they know how I'm feeling. There's relief in that.

"Statistics show that students who take gap years tend to outperform their peers when they return to school," Etta says quietly, finally breaking the silence. "And it's becoming more and more common. In the past five years, it's varied between fifteen to twenty percent of incoming freshmen."

A loud laugh escapes from my lips. "How do you just know that off the top of your head?"

Etta shrugs. "I researched it. One of the students in my online sociology class at Long Beach City College mentioned taking a gap year, and I didn't know what that meant."

"See!" I say, turning back to Mom and Dad. "If your Black Excellence prototype says it, will you listen?"

I'm joking . . . but not really. The bite in my voice is clear.

"Oh, Lenore," Mom says, reaching out for both of my hands. "You *are* excellence. Whatever you choose to do. You are so brilliant, so creative. I'm always amazed at the way your mind works. How could you ever think we would see you differently?"

"I know we've always pushed you to excel. To be the best," Dad says. His words come out slow, halting, like he's processing them as he goes. "We just wanted . . . the whole world for you. But we are proud of you, always. Your best is the best."

I sigh. "Well, that isn't always loud and clear."

Mom and Dad look at each other, something unspoken passing between them. When they turn back to me, both of their faces soften.

"I'm so sorry for that, baby," Mom says, pulling me into a hug. I can feel Dad join in too.

"We'll talk. We'll *listen*," he says. "We'll figure this out together."

We stay like that awhile, until a knock on the door interrupts. "Room service," a muffled voice calls from the other side.

The guy wheels in two carts full of food, and we all crowd together, around the tiny table, eating and laughing and talking. It feels a lot like the night before, when we were all together in my and Wally's room. But this time there isn't silence. There aren't big unspoken feelings. I'm not trying to fill in the gaps with the worst possible things they could be thinking. This time feels right.

"Lenore, I think you're brave," Etta says, between mouthfuls of the butter pasta she ordered. "For making your own path, I mean. Mae Jemison was a dancer at first, and then she double-majored in chemical engineering and African American studies. And *then* she went to medical school and joined the Peace Corps, all before she was accepted into the astronaut program in her thirties. People don't always follow a straight line."

"Well, let's not get crazy here," I laugh. "Don't get Mom and Dad's hopes up. I'm not going to be Mae Jemison."

"I think you could be anything," she says, beaming at me with wide, dancing eyes.

The tears come again, and I let them.

Later that night, Wally is asleep in his bed, and I'm so grateful that his chain-saw snoring only annoys me a little bit.

I hardly hear the soft knock at the door because he's so loud. I look through the peephole, see who's there, and silently debate whether or not I should open it. Curiosity wins out.

"Hi."

"Hey," Alex says, a small, hopeful smile on his lips. He's wearing a black-and-white-striped button-up and jeans. His curls perfectly fall in his eyes. He looks good. Too good. I immediately doubt my decision to open the door.

"I know you don't want to see me. I just . . . wanted to make sure everything was okay. I heard what happened."

I try to keep my face and my tone cold, impassive. "He's fine."

He nods. "But what about you?"

That throws me off. Why in the world does he still care about me? I thought I had very thoroughly ended all of that.

"I'm fine," I say. My voice cracks and I hate it.

He looks at me in that searching way, as if his brown eyes can see right into me. And I'm hit with this overwhelming desire to fill him in on the conversation I just had with my parents, the plans I'm already starting to make for how this next year might go.

I know he would be excited. More than anyone.

But wait. I stop myself.

I don't want to open doors that should remain closed. I want to keep my heart, my happiness, protected.

"Tomorrow's the last full day on the ship, you know," he continues, taking the opening. My feelings must be all over my face. He can read it so well.

"I know."

"We got assigned the first disembarkation time, I'm pretty sure, in Barcelona. So we'll be off the ship early, but we're not flying back home until the next day. I think we're going to Park Güell. What time are you—"

"Safe travels, Alex." I cut him off. I know what I have to do. I know this needs to end here. I can't risk my heart anymore.

His face falls, and it makes my chest feel tight, my throat hurt. I feel even more sure about my decision because I can't be with someone who affects me like this. One sad look, and I'm falling apart inside. That's too dangerous.

"I hate that you're doing this to us," he whispers. "Stopping us before we even get a chance to really be—"

"Good night." I step back so I can shut the door.

His eyes search mine, and he must find what he's looking for because he nods just once and then gives me a small wave.

"Good night, Lenore." He shoves his hands in his pockets as he walks away.

CHAPTER TWENTY

The last day is a sea day, as the ship makes its way to our final stop, Barcelona. I order room service for breakfast with my parents' consent because, as I argue, Wally needs to rest. And after eating fluffy French toast piled with berries, Wally and I meet up with them on the pool deck and spend the afternoon screaming and sliding down the twisty waterslides and floating in the lazy river. Etta acts like a typical ten-year-old without being instructed to, skipping around the splash pad and eating too much soft-serve—and actually seems to like it. It sort of feels like we're having a whole different vacation. And it feels so good to be light, to have no secrets between us anymore.

Later, after Dad requests a lie-down for his old-man knees and the rest of them hit up bingo, I head over to the business center, one last time. I still have Alex's unlimited internet card—it's not like I'm going to go find him to give it back. And I need to talk to Tessa, right now. Maybe this isn't the best way;

maybe I should wait until I get home. But I feel like I have to keep this trend of honesty and openness going. I'm worried if I put it off, I'll just fall into old patterns with her because it's easier.

If I'm doing the math right, it should be six a.m. back at home, but somehow I just know Tessa will be there. And sure enough, she answers my video chat request right away. She has a pink satin bonnet on, and she rubs something crusty out of her eyes. It's clear I woke her up. But still, she smiles when she sees my face.

"Hey, girl, what's up?"

And with those words, I fall apart.

I don't know if I've ever cried in front of Tessa before. I take that back. I *know* I haven't. I've always been the one comforting her, being the moral support.

And I'm not just sorta crying. I'm *crying* crying. The kind of crying you only do alone in your room. Boogers streaming from my nose, gulping and gasping for air, loud sobs that surely shake the walls. It's like all the tears I've been holding in for years saw the coast was clear and decided to explode out of my face and have a big ol' tear party.

I feel self-conscious. I feel naked. But when I look up at Tessa, she doesn't look horrified. She doesn't start making up an excuse to log off and escape. No. Instead, her eyebrows are knit together in concern. Her hand is reaching toward the screen as if she could reach through and touch me.

"Oh no, Lenore," she says, her voice soft and soothing.

"What's wrong? Tell me what's going on."

So I do. I tell her everything. And not just from this trip, but from the very beginning. I tell her all about Marcus and Jay—not the cool, calm, and collected stories I told her at the time, but the real feelings, the ones I swept under the rug. I tell her how I've felt sidelined in our relationship at times, the support but rarely the supported. Partly because I've kept it that way, but also because she's never tried to change it. I tell her how I'm not going to NYU, how I'm going to take a gap year and take my time to figure out what makes me happy. How this was probably what I needed to do all along but I didn't want to feel like a failure in my parents', or anyone's, eyes. And I tell her all about Alex, how I let him in, how he broke my heart. And how I've accepted that maybe it all really *was* just a misunderstanding, but I'm sure as hell not going to let him in and risk being shattered like that again.

The Jimmy Buffett guy walks in at one point, takes one look at my face, and then walks right back out.

And when I'm done, Tessa is crying too.

"I'm sorry. I'm so sorry. For missing all of this. For letting you weather all these storms alone."

"It's okay," I tell her, sniffling. "It's okay. I didn't want you to see."

"I should have anyway. I—I haven't been a good friend to you. And I thought I knew better now. I should have been a better friend."

"You haven't been a *bad* one."

"Well, that's not enough. I'm gonna be better. I'm gonna ask you how you're feeling every day—"

I hold my hands up and laugh. "Whoa, girl, let's roll it back a little bit. I don't need all that—"

"Starting right now." Her eyes twinkle and she pulls off her bonnet. "I want to delve into what happened with this Alex guy some more."

"Oh lord! I take it back! I take it back! I have no feelings. Zero feelings."

"I know you say it's all over, but I think I may know what happened there."

"They're closing the internet down on the ship! I'm losing you!"

Tessa lowers her chin and narrows her eyes at me. "Be real. Let me in, Lenore."

I roll my eyes. I sigh. I wish I could give her a big hug. "Okay."

She squeals and claps her hands, but then seeing me start to huff, she tempers the giddiness and gets real serious. "I think you really like him. And from the sounds of it, he really likes you too. I know he hurt you, and if he's really with that girl—which I think we both know he isn't—I'll be the first to hunt him down and make him pay." Her face gets all murder-y, and it's so out of character that it makes me laugh some more. "I'm worried, though, that you're using this as an excuse to put your same walls back up. You're pushing him away and then feeling vindicated when he leaves . . . a sort of self-fulfilling prophecy? I don't know the guy, I'll admit, but Alex isn't Jay. He's not Marcus. And the least you can do is give him a chance to explain himself, especially if he's doing dreamy things like serenading you to try and do so."

"I don't like that kind of stuff. All that attention," I mutter. "He shouldn't have done it in the first place."

"Another thing you can talk about . . . when you talk," she says. "And is that all you're going to take away from all that wisdom I just dropped?"

She glares at me and leans closer to the screen. And then closer. Until her nose is touching the screen.

I laugh. "Okay, fine! You're right. You're right! Stop showing me your nose hairs and shit." She sits back and starts laughing too. "I know what you're saying is true," I continue. "It's just . . . this time really hurt, Tessa. More than I've ever been hurt before. I don't know if I can take being hurt like this again."

"Oh, I know, girl, I know." She presses her lips together, her eyes welling up. "But I think this is all part of it. Putting yourself out there, risking this heartbreak, getting hurt and then trying again, even when it feels like the stupidest thing in the world. I think it's all part of falling in love."

That word—*the* word—makes my whole body feel like it's frozen. "No one said anything about love."

She arches an eyebrow at me and leans back on her bed with her arms crossed.

"Well, then yes, you better just give up now. Because you're right. If he isn't something special, if you weren't falling in love, then it's not worth giving him a second chance. Get out while you're ahead."

I cross my arms too. I sputter. I look everywhere but at her.

"I think we both know that's not the case, though. Right, Lenore?"

I finally meet her eye, and she's beaming at me. Probably doing a little dance in her brain because she's got me right where she wants me, right where she predicted that day when we were getting ready for prom in her room.

"Love is worth the risk. So I guess what you have to ask yourself is . . . is it love?"

Her words echo in my brain all night, waking me up more than Wally's snores. And they're still there in the morning, when I'm taking a shower, brushing my teeth, and starting to fill my suitcase.

I shouldn't have left all of the packing until this morning because there's just so much to do, and we have to have the suitcases sitting in the hallway for the porter by nine. Wally, of course, has already finished and is out eating breakfast with my parents and Etta. But instead of trying to wrangle all of my stuff, I lay in bed thinking about Tessa's words and trying to decide my answer to the question.

Is it love?

How would I even know? What do I have to compare it to?

I fold all my clothes, get my toiletries out of the bathroom, try to hunt down all the jewelry I've left lying around. And an hour later, I'm almost done. All that's left is my camera. I need to put it back in the case and into my backpack, so I can use it around Barcelona today.

I pick it up off my desk, running my finger along the scratch across the bottom, the chip of paint missing from the right corner. I remember being devastated when the scratch happened at Disneyland, stomping around and blaming Wally because he threw his hands up on the Dumbo ride and knocked it out of my hands. But I don't remember what caused the other mark. Could that have happened when I tossed it in frustration at my grandparents' house, like Grandma Lenore told me about? I gave up on photography altogether that day, just because the shot wasn't perfect. God, I was trying to protect myself from failure and the related hurt, even then.

My eyes catch on the stack of photos sitting next to my camera. I didn't have a place to put them. I'd planned to get an album, maybe display them once I got home. Now I spread them out. All these moments I captured in film over the past two weeks, to memorize. But I know already that they'll be with me forever, regardless, every detail crystal clear.

I put them in order. That first day in Rome at the Trevi Fountain, where I spotted Alex in the crowd. The produce in a rainbow of bright colors in Sicily, where Alex and I argued, assuming the worst of each other. A donkey from the steps in Santorini, and a shot of that beautiful view. Alex embarrassing himself at *DDR* in the arcade. A close-up from that day in the business center, with every detail of his face that I memorized. A selfie of us in Naples, him kissing my cheek. And then the final picture of us, all dressed up for the ship's formal. I look so happy, and he's looking at me.

Laid out like that, they tell a story. Not just any story, but a love story.

Our love story.

The kind I thought I would never get.

I had a boy who treasured me, a happily ever after on the horizon . . . but then I blew it all up at the first chance because I was scared of failure. Because I was scared of getting hurt.

I gather all of the pictures, put them safely in my backpack, and then take off out of my room, hoping there's still time to change our ending.

CHAPTER TWENTY-ONE

I race to the elevator, but there's a long line of families, maneuvering overflowing luggage carts and tote bags full of souvenirs. So instead, I sprint up the stairs to his deck, taking the steps two at a time, stopping to grab my knees and huff halfway through because I remember I'm out of shape.

I run down the hallway to his room and bang on the door. "Alex! Alex, it's me!"

Then, because I'm trying to make him want to be with me again and not scare him away, I smooth my hair down and try to stop breathing so heavily. And I knock again three more times for good measure.

I hear footsteps, and when the door finally opens, my racing heart stops. But . . . it's not him. It's a gray-haired woman in a *Mediterranean Majesty* polo shirt holding a mop and looking pretty irritated.

"Can I help you?"

"Um, the boy. The one whose room this is. Is he . . . is he here?"

She cocks her head to the side, looking at me like I'm not making any sense, probably because I'm not.

"It's not his room anymore, sweetie. This block of rooms disembarked at six a.m."

"Six a.m.?" I yell, too loud, and she startles. Her face shifts from just irritated to pissed.

"That's what I said," she says, pasting on a plastic smile. "Now if you'll excuse me—"

"I mean, he did say they were leaving early, but I didn't realize that early meant *this* early, like before ten a.m. early," I say, still talking for some reason. "Where does disembarkation happen? Do you think there's a chance he may still be on the ship? Like, if there was a delay maybe? That happens, right? Delays?" She blinks at me. "Because . . . I really need to find him. Today. Right now. Because, you see . . . I've finally realized our love story's not over, it's just beginning. And I'm scared if I don't find him and tell him that I'll lose my chance with him. I'll lose my chance at real love."

Now the gray-haired woman just looks concerned. She leans her mop against the doorframe and then takes two tentative steps toward me. "Sweetie, have you been watching that rom-com on the movie channel? The one they've played on repeat this whole trip?" She gently pats my shoulder. "Let me guess . . . you have an interior room? No windows? Real tiny?"

"No! Well, yes. But no! It's not like that."

"Mmm-hmmm, sure it's not," she says, eyes wide and nodding. "May I suggest you get some fresh air? There's farewell piña coladas out on the pool deck."

"I don't need piña coladas! I need Alex!" I am mostly aware that I sound unhinged, but I'm past the point of caring.

"Well, this Alex boy is long gone, so I suggest you settle for the drink," she says with a nod. She walks back over to the mop, her patience depleted. "Have a majestic day!" she says, gently but firmly, shutting the door in my face.

Okay. That's okay. That's only one obstacle. Things aren't completely hopeless yet.

I head back to the stairs now, a little slower this time because I'm not trying to get sweaty, and walk to the Crown Room. My family is there, eating breakfast, and maybe Alex's family is with them for one last meal. But when I get there, it's just Mom, Dad, Wally, and Etta. I feel my chest deflate.

"What's your problem?" Etta asks, making everyone turn to look at me.

"Lenore?" Dad asks. "Are you okay?"

"Have you seen the Lees? I went to Alex's room, but he's not there. I really—" My throat catches, the emotions overwhelming me. I take a deep breath and try again. "I really need to talk to him."

"Oh, they already left, baby," Mom says, rising to stand next to me, rub my back. "Ronni and David came to say goodbye to us last night. They had the earliest disembarkation time."

I let out of grunt of frustration, falling down into a chair.

I waited too long. I sabotaged myself. The moment has passed.

"I don't understand. They live right by us at home. She can see the boy then," I hear Dad saying through the pounding in my ears.

"Oh, hush!" Mom says back. "You remember how this felt."

"I'm sorry, Lenore," Wally whispers next to me.

While Mom rubs her hand in circles on the small of my back, I try to let the feelings go. Maybe this is all for the best. Maybe there was no chance there after all, and I was just going to embarrass myself. I replay our last conversation at my door, searching for signs that he was already done. That this would have been a futile mission.

But no.

I'm not going to let myself go down that path again. He came to check on me, to see how I was feeling, even though he didn't have to. He wasn't coming to say goodbye. That was all me. In fact, he was even telling me where he and his family were headed today in Barcelona—

"I need to go to Park Güell!" I shout, shooting up out of my seat.

"Say what now?" Dad asks.

"Park Güell. I think that's what it's called? I don't know. I can look it up on the way. But that's where the Lees are going. Alex told me. I need to go right now!" I turn to leave, but Mom grabs my wrist.

"Lenore Mae Bennett, you better slow your butt down right now," Mom says, fixing me with a stern glare. "There's no way you're running off this cruise ship alone."

"You bet you're not!" Dad chimes in.

"That's right," Mom continues. "You're going to take Wally with you."

"She is?" Dad says.

"I am?" I say at the same time.

Wally shrugs. "Sounds good to me."

"Marla, should we talk about this?" Dad asks, turning to Mom, but she fixes him with the same look she gave me. "Our kids aren't kids anymore. They're adults. And they're smart. Capable. We've *raised* them that way. Now we've gotta trust that we did our job."

They look at each other for a long time, a whole conversation happening in head movements and raised eyebrows and pursed lips. Finally, my dad turns to me and says, "Okay."

"Can I go too?" Etta asks.

"No," they both reply at the same time.

Mom squeezes my hand. "Now go. We'll handle checkout. Take your passport with you. And if you don't meet us at the hotel by two o'clock this afternoon, I will forget all of this 'capable adult' business and put you on lockdown for the rest of your life, you hear me?"

"Yes, Mom. Thank you, Mom." I kiss her on the cheek and hug her tight. Wally stands up, getting ready to leave.

"Lenore?" Dad says, and I'm worried he's going to lay down the law and make me stay. Chasing after a boy in Barcelona is definitely not on his list of approved activities. But instead he's smiling. "Your mother and I were talking about it last night, and we're starting to come around to your plan for this year. This 'gap year' business." He holds up quotation marks, as if it's some brand-new phrase that I made up myself.

"Oh yeah?" I say, my hesitant words not matching the huge smile I can feel taking over my whole face.

"Yeah." He nods resignedly, and I let out a squeal despite myself, running over to give him a hug.

"But you know you're going to get a job," he says, patting my arm.

"Of course I'm going to get a job!"

"And pay rent."

I reel back. "Whoa, whoa, whoa, that might be taking it—"

He narrows his eyes at me.

"And pay rent! Happily! Gratefully!"

"All right," he says, nodding once. "Now you and Wally get on with this before I come to my senses."

I run out of that dining room and don't look back.

"Do you have his number?" Wally asks, twisting his neck around, surveying the scene.

"No, we didn't use our phones on the ship."

Wally nods. "All right, all right. Did he tell you exactly where he was going to be?"

"No, just Park Güell."

"Okay, cause this place is pretty—"

"Big. I know."

Park Güell looks like something out of a fairy tale. It has big stone structures with bright white curved roofs and intricate mosaics on every surface, sparkling in the afternoon sun. We're standing in front of a grand white staircase, framed by a checkerboard pattern of rainbow tiles on either side, lush greenery sprouting up all over. And it all leads up to a building with tall white columns, looming at the top like a castle. In any other circumstance, I would be pulling out my camera, excited to document each unique detail.

But.

"I'm not trying to kill your dreams or whatever," Wally continues. "But . . . it's crowded."

Like, really, really crowded. Like, we can barely move crowded. There are tons of tour groups moving in mass around the grounds, families tugging along bored kids with headphones, girls in dresses posing for the gram, lots of people cheesing for selfie sticks.

"I'm not saying he won't be here," Wally says, squeezing my arm. "This just might be more difficult than we initially expected."

"I know," I sigh. I close my eyes.

I knew it was a long shot that he'd even be here. They could still be at their hotel, checking in. They could have changed their plans altogether and gone somewhere else in Barcelona. There was no guarantee.

But this felt right. Maybe I'm totally losing my mind, crazy from cabin fever after being stuck in a windowless room for two weeks, like that gray-haired woman thought. But I was so sure I would come here and find him. That I could pick him out of a crowd, just like I did that first day at the Trevi Fountain.

Because it was meant to be. Because I deserve a ridiculous, romantic, completely far-fetched love story like this.

I turn around in a circle, eyes bouncing everywhere. I examine every face, searching for the one I need to see.

"We can always go to the hotel and regroup," Wally says. "Maybe we can try to find him on social and message him that way? And I know it's not as exciting, but, like, he does live really close at home. Also . . . I kind of have to make a phone call."

I spin to look at him. "A phone call?"

He bites his lip. "Yeah, a phone call. To Kieran. I—I finally emailed him back last night. Things aren't better yet, but he wants to talk." He shrugs and smiles nervously. "It's late there, but I wanted to see if I could catch him before he went to bed—"

"Wally!" I cut him off. "Why didn't you tell me? I wouldn't have asked you to do this if I knew that. Oh my god! Okay, you are telling me everything later. Let's go!" I grab his hand, pulling him toward the curb where the taxis are lined up.

I spot his hair first. Tousled black curls falling into his face. Then I recognize those arms that wrapped around my waist and made me feel so safe and treasured. His smooth brown skin that's gotten darker, golden, as we've spent our days in the sun.

He's talking to his mom, and she must have said something

funny because his head falls back in laughter, one single "Ha!"

It's him. I know it's him. I've never felt more sure.

"Alex!" I call, and Wally jumps next to me.

"Lenore, are you—"

"Alex!" I yell louder, waving my arms. "Alex! Over here!"

He stops talking and twists his neck around, searching for whoever is calling his name. I start to run to him.

"Alex!"

Our eyes lock, and for a moment I'm terrified that he's going to roll his eyes or laugh because I took this too far, because I'm being weird and couldn't let it go like a reasonable person. But his lips stretch into a smile that takes over his whole face, his brown eyes dance with excitement, and before I know it, he's running to me, too.

We meet in the middle, attracting stares from all the tourists nearby. Out of the corner of my eye, I see phones rise, cameras cover faces, but I don't even care. He is all I see, all I want.

He opens his mouth to speak, but I cut him off. "I'm sorry. I'm so sorry. I was scared you were going to change your mind. Scared that I'm too much and also not enough at the same time. I was scared you were going to break my heart."

He closes the space between us, tenderly cupping my face in his hands. "Lenore, I'm never going to break your heart."

I smile, leaning into his touch. "You can't promise that. We don't know. There's no way for us to know for sure. But I guess what I'm trying to say is, I want to risk it with you. Even if I'm not perfect at it, I want to be in love with you."

His eyes crinkle as he smiles at me. My whole body warms up, and those goddamn butterflies are having a party.

"Well, that's good."

"It is?"

"Yeah, because I'm already madly in love with you."

He pulls me into a kiss as cheers erupt around us. And I have no idea what the future will bring. I don't know what my life is going to look like in five years, let alone next month. But I do know that in this moment I'm happy—authentically, blissfully happy—and that's all I need right now.

ACKNOWLEDGMENTS

I wrote the first draft of this novel during the spring and summer of 2020, so first I need to thank noise-canceling headphones, every Postmates driver and Shipt shopper, romance novels, and Taylor Swift.

Alessandra Balzer, this book was so much easier to write because of all that I have learned from you. Thank you for holding my hand and cheering me on. I don't know what it's like to put a book out into the world with anyone else, but I kind of don't ever want to find out. You make it so magical.

Everyone at HarperCollins has been so good to me, and I'm grateful to have such brilliant people championing my books. Thank you especially to Caitlin Johnson, Donna Bray, Suzanne Murphy, Andrea Pappenheimer, Kerry Moynagh, Kathy Faber, Nellie Kurtzman, Aubrey Churchward, Audrey Diestelkamp, Shannon Cox, Patty Rosati, Mimi Rankin, Katie Dutton, Ann Dye, Megan Carr, Raven Andrus, Kadeen Griffiths, Sonia

Sells, Alexandra Rakaczki, Marinda Valenti, Alison Donalty, and Jessie Gang. And Michelle D'Urbano—you plucked Tessa and Lenore right out of my head and portrayed them both beautifully. Thank you for treating my girls with such love and care.

Taylor Haggerty, you make me believe in myself, and I feel so lucky to have you by my side. Thank you for all the work you do that makes it possible for me to live this dream. Also, many thanks to everyone at Root Literary (especially Jasmine Brown and Melanie Castillo) for all that you do, and to Heather Baror-Shapiro for bringing my stories to readers all over the world.

Danielle Parker, you read this book with a sharp eye and gentle heart, and it's much better because of it. I'm so grateful for your friendship and I can't wait to watch you shine.

Releasing my debut novel, *Happily Ever Afters*, in a pandemic was really lonely at times, but so many incredibly kind authors reached out and supported me in both big and small ways. Christina Hammonds Reed, I don't think it's possible to thank you enough. Your friendship has been such a gift in my life. Brandy Colbert, you are my author role model, and I'm so happy I get to be your friend now, too. So much gratitude also to: Susan Lee, Tracy Deonn, Kelly McWilliams, Becky Albertalli, Jamie Pacton, Liara Tamani, Namina Forna, Karen Strong, Leah Johnson, Kristina Forest, Julian Winters, Camryn Garrett, Ronni Davis, Sarah Enni, Jordan Ifueko, Sarah Henning, Jason June, Marissa Meyer, Ashley Woodfolk, Debbi

Michiko Florence, Julie Murphy, Angie Thomas, Ibi Zoboi, Graci Kim, Tiffany D. Jackson, Morgan Rogers, Lane Clarke, J. Elle, Charity Alyse, Farrah Penn, Aminah Mae Safi, and Emily Henry.

Nicola Yoon, thank you for making space in this industry for books like mine and welcoming me in with open arms.

I love my city, Long Beach, and I'm so grateful for the love my city has shown me. Thank you especially to Jhoanna Belfer at Bel Canto Books, Mike Guardabascio and the Long Beach Post, the Long Beach Library Foundation, vanilla honey oat lattes from The Merchant, and every person who's stopped me around town to talk about *Happily Ever Afters* and made my kids think I'm famous.

Thank you to all the people in our community who made it possible for me to write over the past year, especially Bernadette Nicholas, Amber Norman, Jahmeilah and Brandon Roberson, Dr. Mireya Hernandez, Shannon Kennedy, and Sonia Ramirez.

Shavonne, thank you for just . . . everything. I can't even put into words the good you've brought into my life.

Rachal and Bryan, I'm so lucky I get to go through life with you by my side. Thank you for the endless inspiration and the unconditional love. I love writing siblings because I love you two so much. And welcome to the team, Eddie!

Mom, you've always believed I could have the whole world, and your faith in me has allowed me to dream the biggest dreams. And Dad, I'm forever in awe of your sacrifice and